Rogue Touch

Rogue Touch

CHRISTINE WOODWARD

NEW YORK

marvel.com

TM & © 2013 Marvel and Subs.

Library of Congress Cataloging-in-Publication Data

Woodward, Christine.
Rogue Touch / Christine Woodward. — First edition.
pages cm
ISBN 978-1-4013-1102-5
1. Young women—Fiction.   2. Outcasts—Fiction.
3. Identity (Psychology)—Fiction.   I. Title.
PS3557.R24R64 2013
813'.54—dc23
2012047321

Book design by Judith Stagnitto Abbate / Abbate Design

FIRST EDITION

10   9   8   7   6   5   4   3   2   1

THIS LABEL APPLIES TO TEXT STOCK

We try to produce the most beautiful books possible, and we are also extremely concerned about the impact of our manufacturing process on the forests of the world and the environment as a whole. Accordingly, we've made sure that all of the paper we use has been certified as coming from forests that are managed, to ensure the protection of the people and wildlife dependent upon them.

To Hadley Gessner

AN OLD MAN SPOKE TO HIS GRANDSON. "MY CHILD," he said. "Inside everyone there is a battle between two wolves. One is Evil. It is anger, jealousy, greed, inferiority, lies, and ego. The other is Good. It is joy, peace, love, hope, humility, kindness, empathy, and truth."

The boy thought for a moment. Then he asked, "Which wolf wins?"

A moment of silence passed before the old man replied. And then he said, "The one you feed."

• —NATIVE AMERICAN FOLK TALE •

Rogue Touch

I WAS WALKING TO WORK, MINDING MY OWN BUSINESS, WHEN I saw James lurking in the shadows.

Of course at the time I didn't know it was James. I thought it was just some tall, creepy guy who didn't know better than to scare young girls after dark. Either that or he really *did* plan on leaping out and grabbing me. Of course that could be a lot more dangerous for him than me. Whatever the case, the main thing I felt when I saw him leaning in the doorway of Maybelline's Collectibles was irritated. He didn't smoke, or look at the ratty-ass beaded purses Maybelline had hung in the window, or do much of anything except watch me walk down the street. A tiny little part of me kind of enjoyed being watched this way. It's a sad state of affairs when an eighteen-year-old girl never gets to have her legs admired.

But still. Couldn't he be polite and cross the street to prove he wasn't some kind of rapist? Hadn't his mama taught him this little piece of late night manners? One of the reasons I liked my job at the Sunshine Bakery was that I hardly ever saw a soul on my way to work. Jackson, Mississippi, isn't exactly New York City — people pretty much tuck themselves into bed by midnight. So in the dusky wee hours, I felt pretty safe without my leather. Every night I left my government-subsidized apartment wearing shorts and a T-shirt. It had been a long, hot summer, and walking to work was the only time I ever felt even the barest prickle of a breeze on my skin.

Now for the first time since I started this job three months ago, I had to think on how to avoid walking near someone with my skin exposed. The closer I got to the stairs that led down to the bakery kitchen, the clearer it got that El Creepo had no plans to move out of my way. That's what I decided to call him, El Creepo, even though by now I'd got close enough to see that he looked like a pretty sexy guy. I guessed he was only a few years older than me, with long, dark hair. It looked like he hadn't shaved in a couple days. It was too dark out to tell for sure, but I had this feeling he had blue eyes — piercing blue. Not only that, he wore this long, black leather coat.

Now, why in the world would anyone except me wear leather in the middle of a Mississippi August?

But never mind that. Even if El Creepo wasn't a rapist, or a mugger, and even if he looked devilishly handsome, the entrance to the bakery stood exactly next door to Maybelline's. I couldn't risk him reaching out to touch my arm, or tripping as I passed by and trying to grab hold of me for balance. So I crossed the street myself, walked down about twenty feet on the other side, then crossed again. I had to walk a little ways in the opposite direction to get to the bakery. El Creepo had turned around now, apparently so he could keep watching me, and I stared straight back at him in a way that hopefully told him I'd just done what he should have — crossed the street, that is. It took every ounce of willpower I had not to give him the finger, because not only did his presence mean that from now on I wouldn't be risking the shorts and T-shirt even at this late hour, it also meant that I couldn't stand at the top of the stairs, looking at the knickknacks in

Maybelline's window, the way I usually did before heading down to work.

I didn't have money to buy anything from Maybelline's anyhow. I never used to be the sort of person who wasted time daydreaming about what I couldn't have. That habit's one I got from Cody. So truthfully it was just as well for me to go without window-shopping. But sometimes I got awful tired, of all the things it was better to go without.

DOWNSTAIRS AT THE SUNSHINE BAKERY I PUT ON MY HAIRNET and iPod and set straight to work. This late night shift — fixing all the muffins and donuts and scones that would go on sale first thing when the store opened — was the third job I'd had since coming to Jackson from Caldecott, and the first one I really liked. If I couldn't touch people, at least I could feed them. The owner, Wendy Lee Beauchamp, kept all her recipes in a big manila folder, and all I had to do to make sure everything turned out right was follow them precisely.

Once I'd got all the baked goods into the ovens, I went into the tiny little bathroom. On the day she hired me, Wendy Lee told me I'd have to keep the bathroom clean. By this I figured she meant I had to keep it tidy, and not leave my personal effects lying around. Because, why would you want the same person who baked your pastries cleaning the bathroom? Lately, though, I'd noticed rings around the sink and toilet, and started to suspect I was meant to do the scrubbing. Deciding there was no time like the present, I fished out a dented container of Comet.

When that was done, I changed into my leather jeans and black turtleneck, then pulled on my gloves. Since it had got so hot, I'd switched from leather gloves to white cotton, the sort you'd wear to a fancy tea party. My sleeves covered my arms well enough, but since my arms were the most likely place for someone to try and touch me, I wore a leather jacket, too. As for the black, it didn't make a difference what color I wore in terms of protection, except for making me look scary enough that no one ever *wanted* to touch me. Same for the white streaks in my long, brown hair, the ones that showed up after what happened to Cody.

Before Wendy Lee arrived, I still had ten minutes to bring everything I'd baked to the front of the store, so I put my iPod back on, cranked up "Jesus, Take the Wheel," and mopped the little bathroom.

"ANNA MARIE. ANNA MARIE!"

By the time I heard Wendy Lee screaming my name, I guess she'd been calling me for a while, because she marched toward me with her arm outstretched, like she planned to tap me on the shoulder. I jumped aside so fast I hit the little shelf with all the paper towels and toilet paper on it. Everything came raining down on my head, and all over the floor, so you couldn't even see how nice and clean I'd got it.

As I pulled out my earbuds, I could see that the oven with all the scones was smoking like a chimney stack. "Dang," I said. Even in my agitated state, I remembered to watch my language around Wendy Lee, who considered herself a God-fearing woman. Instead of heading toward the scone oven — those were already a lost cause — I went for the muffins. They looked a teensy bit brown on top, but in a nice, crunchy, golden way.

The scones, on the other hand, were all burned up. Wendy Lee pulled them out of the oven herself. She was one of those women who got herself up all fancy — hair bleached and poofed, eyebrows plucked, nails done, makeup thick as a mask — so even one hair out of place could make her look completely disheveled. At that moment, at least three hairs had moved out of place, plus she had a little smear of black on her cheek from the charred scones.

"God damn it, Anna Marie," Wendy Lee said. Now on top of burning the scones I'd made her take the Lord's name in vain. "What the hell am I supposed to sell this morning?" She took a deep breath to calm herself down, and I could tell that I wouldn't like what she had to say next. And I was right. I stood there, listening to her rattle off a list of reasons why I was not working out at the Sunshine Bakery.

"I don't want to hurt your feelings, Anna Marie, but the way you dress is very peculiar."

"But nobody ever sees me! I work downstairs in the middle of the night."

"People see you coming out in the morning, Sugar. They wonder why the person baking their muffins is dudded up in black leather in the summertime."

She said that someone had seen me hanging out in front of Maybelline's and worried I was casing the place, which I couldn't believe. Who the hell saw me window-shopping at one o'clock in the morning? I immediately suspected El Creepo. Could be last night was the first time I saw him but not the other way around.

She went on. "Now, I don't like to point fingers. But three times since you started working here the change drawer has come up short."

"I never even go upstairs. I swear it, Wendy Lee."

Obviously that was the real reason I was getting fired. Wendy Lee thought that I was stealing from her. But she didn't want to dwell on that, probably because she couldn't prove it. When she said I never cleaned the bathroom, I ran over and opened up the door, then started putting all the paper towels and toilet paper that I'd knocked down back on the shelf. "Look," I said. "I just cleaned it this morning. Look, Wendy Lee, I mopped and everything."

I could feel my face all shiny with sweat, and my crazy white hair coming out of my hairnet. If Wendy Lee had looked mad, I might have stood a chance. But she just looked sorry for me. So I ripped off my hairnet and threw it at her feet.

"Fine," I said. "You can have your dang job." I still didn't have the heart to cuss in front of her. I also didn't have the dignity to leave before she cut me my last check, and I just stood there sweating and tapping my feet while she wrote it out for me. I didn't know Wendy Lee's age — she gussied herself up so plastic, she could've been anywhere between twenty-five and fifty. What kind of memories would Wendy Lee have? I thought that I almost *would* kill to ice a cake as pretty as she did.

OUT ON THE SIDEWALK THE AIR ALREADY FELT HOT AND MUGGY, and I felt powerfully down and blue. Not only had I lost a job I actually liked, I hadn't even worked there long enough to get unemployment. The measly check in my pocket would not last long. My heavy-soled boots stuck to the pavement, making a little suctiony noise as I walked. Delivery trucks rattled down the street. I stopped for a moment to collect myself in front of the Jackson Diner.

A young couple about my age sat at the table just behind the window. They were so involved in talking that they didn't notice me — the weird Goth girl with the crazy white shock of hair, all frizzy and smoke-filled from the bakery. The girl at the table was very sad and very pretty, with freckles and a face that could have belonged to a fairy from one of the old books my mama used to collect. Even though she was crying, her eyes didn't look red at all.

Maybe the boy was breaking up with her. I looked at him — they still hadn't noticed me — and saw his brow kind of crinkle up, and he had tears in his eyes, like he felt awful sorry for her but didn't know what to do. As the girl talked, she fiddled with the plastic salt and pepper shakers. All of a sudden, the boy reached out his hands to stop her fidgeting. He closed his fingers around hers, and they just sat there for a moment, staring into each other's eyes and holding hands. It seemed to calm her down, that touch. It seemed to comfort her.

There's only so much a person can bear. I stepped back, away from the window, and headed toward home.

I WALKED UP THE DARK STAIRWAY OF MY RUNDOWN, SECTION 8 apartment building. It was the only place I qualified for where I could have a whole apartment to myself. Technically I don't even think you could call it an apartment, because it was just one room if you didn't count the bathroom. I locked all four deadbolts and skinned out of my leather pants, then turned on the three rickety fans I'd bought at Goodwill and crawled between my sheets. Nothing left to do but sleep, even though I knew I'd have what I called The Dream. I had it almost every time I slept, and it never started out the same way, unless you count the fact that it always started out happy. Happy like fireworks. Happy like you can't even stand it but you don't ever want it to stop. Maybe if the damn dream didn't start out so happy, by now I'd have figured out how to wake myself up before it got too late. But I never could stand to leave the beginning. The beginning made it almost worth it.

So I very nearly welcomed it. I didn't know how it would start out exactly — what I'd be doing, who I'd see. I only knew I'd be happy until it all went wrong. Terribly, awfully wrong.

SURE ENOUGH THE DREAM STARTED OUT WITH THE HAPPIEST thing in the world: Me and Cody, the way it used to be, walking up the hill on his mama and daddy's farm. In the dream it must have been springtime, because everything around us was blooming like crazy and it didn't feel so horribly hot. Birds were chirping and I could feel a nice breeze. When I say I could feel it, it's because I wasn't decked out in head-to-toe black leather. Instead I had on a thin, flowery dress, the sort I used to wear back in my old life, when touching people didn't mean sucking out all their memories, all their abilities, all their life force. I can't say how the dress looked, but it felt just beautiful. Soft cotton fluttered against my legs. My hair blew back in the wind, and I knew there were no stupid white streaks, it was just brown. Not mousy brown, but rich and dark, like the bark on the old chestnut tree in Cody's front yard. One time in real life Cody and I stood under that tree and he told me there was nothing prettier in all the world than a brown-eyed, brown-haired girl.

Here in my dream Cody looked just like he used to, like the sweet boy-next-door of every girl's dreams, with sandy brown hair that flopped over his forehead, and freckles, and hazel eyes. He used to love to play baseball, so his arms were sinewy and muscled. At seventeen he could fix any problem in any car. He loved to drive his daddy's old tractor, and there it was right now, parked beside us on the hill. Cody climbed on and I followed him. I wrapped my arms around his waist and let my chin rest on his shoulder as he turned the key and started the motor.

We rode past the neat rows of cotton. I could hear and smell the Mississippi River, and an old loblolly pine rose up in the distance. Cody's hair wisped against my face, it smelled of straw and cottonseed and Ivory soap. I moved my hands up from his waist and pressed them against his heart. I could feel it beating beneath my fingers: *thump, thump, thump,* just about the most cheerful sound you could ever imagine. A crow flew overhead, so low I thought its talons might brush the tops of our heads, and I couldn't help pressing my lips against the back of Cody's neck, his skin, the spot between his hair and his collar.

That was it: all it ever took. Me touching him. It never happened in the dreams exactly the way it did in real life. But it always ended up with Cody on the ground, everything inside that used to make him *him* just gone.

I woke up sitting bolt upright, a scream strangled in my throat and the sheets down around my ankles, my whole body covered in sweat despite all those noisy, rattling fans.

THE STATE OF MISSISSIPPI CHANGED THE NAME OF ITS FOOD stamp program to SNAP, which is supposed to stand for Supplemental Nutrition Assistance Program. If you ask me, the name sounds a mite too perky. I may have grown up a far cry from rich, but that didn't mean I liked admitting I needed handouts.

But admit it or not, it was time for me to head on over to SNAP. That last check from the Sunshine Bakery didn't go very far (thinking on how Wendy Lee didn't give me any severance, let alone notice, made me wish I'd used every cuss word I knew). So far I'd had no luck getting a new job. You wouldn't think touching people would be so important when it comes to menial employment, but it's damn near impossible to get through an interview when you can't shake hands. The only reason I'd gotten around it with Wendy Lee was she interviewed me while she iced a cake for the Devereaux wedding and didn't have a free hand to offer. Anyway, you can't exactly wear gloves to an interview in Mississippi summertime, and as I said before, the old skin condition excuse doesn't go over very well if you want to get into the food service industry. Or any other industry, come to think of it.

So until I could make a new plan for myself, it looked like I had a date with SNAP. Have I mentioned that back at school in Caldecott County I got straight A's starting from first grade? Even Aunt Carrie felt sure I was headed to Ole Miss on scholarship. At the age of eighteen, I should've been living in a dorm and eating school cafeteria food. Not living in Section 8 housing and applying for what were still damn well food stamps.

That pretty much occupied my mind on the bus ride over to North State Street. I didn't worry about the old lady who stared at me like I might open up my mouth and eat her, even though I'd stood up to offer her my seat. I just thought on how humiliating it would be, heading to the Department of Human Services with all the other freaks and losers, my hand held out in front of me. But just as I was working myself into a good, sorry-for-myself snit, the bus rumbled past the Old Capitol Museum.

Looking at that stately old building — the most historic in the state of Mississippi — I felt flooded with this memory of walking into the grand front entrance hall, holding a mama's hand. I say *a* mama instead of *my* mama because it wasn't my mama. It wasn't even my memory. What I remember of Mama I remember fondly, but she was too busy growing her own food and sewing her hippy skirts to worry about taking me to Jackson, let alone to a museum. And honestly I don't remember her ever holding my hand.

The person in this memory was Mrs. Robbins. Cody's mama. I looked around at the high ceilings, and the various artifacts under glass, but what I mostly just felt was loved, and taken care of, and happy to have this smiling lady all to myself.

With a wheeze, the bus crossed over from South to North State Street. I got off at my stop, feeling a little better about things. Even though the love didn't belong to me any more than the memory did, it lifted me up inside, and gave me the strength to walk through those depressing glass doors.

IT TURNED OUT CODY'S MEMORY ALSO GAVE ME THE STRENGTH to yell at James, when I saw him waiting in line along with all the other wretches. At least I suspect that's what did it. I can't think how I would have got up the nerve otherwise.

"Hey," I yelled, the second I recognized him. "El Creepo!"

The two of us stood in different lines, but he caught my eye immediately because other than me, he was the only one dressed for a cold winter day. What I mainly noticed was that long, black leather coat. When I called out his name — or my name for him, anyway — he turned around and looked at me right away. But then, so did everyone else in the welfare office.

By now he was standing about five feet away, and just as I'd thought, his eyes were piercing, stunning, electric blue. But all I could think was how he'd ratted me out. I got out of line to march over to him and demand why he'd thought to tell Wendy Lee I'd been casing Maybelline's store. When he realized I was coming toward him, he looked around, maybe hoping to identify someone else who could be my target.

"No way, mister," I said. "I'm talking to *you!*"

He turned and ran. For a second I felt bad about him losing his place in line. Then I remembered I'd lost mine, too. I ran after him.

As James ran, his long coat fluttered behind him, and a bunch of papers fell to the ground. I stopped chasing him long enough to stoop and pick up what he'd dropped. It was an envelope stuffed with different driver's licenses and pay stubs and canceled rent checks. In other words, it was everything you'd need to scam your way into getting food stamps.

By now a guard had decided to make us his business. He walked over to me, and when he saw what I was holding, he yelled out for someone to stop James. Another guard, who was standing by the door, grabbed his arm just before he left the building. I could tell my guard was about to grab me, too. I dropped all the phony paperwork so he'd have to stoop to pick it up instead. By the time he righted himself, and I hadn't run, he figured I'd stay where I was without being touched.

Two guards dragged James over to where I stood. He looked out at me from under long, straggly, yet kind of sexy hair — those blue, blue eyes staring right at me. I saw that his cheeks were sunken in. He looked hungry. Seriously hungry.

Still I couldn't help but ask him. "Why?" I said. "Why'd you tell Wendy Lee I wanted to rob Maybelline?"

He just stared back, not saying a word.

"Do you know this man?" my guard asked me.

I shook my head. The guards yanked him away. I felt a powerful rush of shame, that somebody would keep on going hungry because of me. Then I did the only thing I could think of, which was get back in line to get my own damn food stamps.

THAT NIGHT FELT LIKE OLD TIMES, EXCEPT FOR THE FACT THAT I decked myself out in all the necessary protection. I knew they wouldn't have brought El Creepo to jail, because he hadn't got so far as putting those documents to work. They would've just shown him the door and told him not to bother coming back. Don't ask me how, but I felt very certain that he'd be right where I last saw him: lurking in the doorway of Maybelline's Collectibles.

I walked down the dark, empty streets, wishing I was heading to my old job baking breakfast pastries. And while I was at it — wishing, that is — I wished that Cody was not only up and around, but walking beside me. Tomorrow I'd have to go by the library and use the computer — see if I could find any news of him in the Caldecott County paper. For all I knew, maybe he *had* woken up.

But really, I knew it in my heart. Cody hadn't woken up from his coma. Most likely he never would.

A few minutes later I stood in the doorway of Maybelline's. Could she possibly have sold all those silly little purses? In their place was a display of hand-painted mirrors in different sizes. One was a wide, square mirror, with a pretty aquamarine frame. It looked like it went over a bathroom sink, but Maybelline had it leaning low down enough that I could pretty much see my entire freakish self. I didn't have time to feel the usual dismay over this sight, though, because within seconds I also saw the reflection of El Creepo. He stood behind me, his long hair and long coat flowing behind him, his face pale and hungry, his eyes blue as an arctic wolf's.

Well, I thought, staring at that reflection. *At least I know he's not a vampire.*

He reached out to touch my shoulder, and I ducked out from under his hand. Even with a turtleneck and leather jacket, I didn't want to take any chances.

"I wasn't going to hurt you," he said. Little did he know.

He sounded like he came from far away, definitely not anywhere south, maybe not even anywhere in the U.S., plus his voice was husky and out of breath, like he'd run here. Not only that, but he looked at me like pretty much nobody had ever looked at me before. Which is to say he looked at me in a way that made me feel stark naked.

I took another step back, reached into my pocket, and pulled out a bunch of food stamps. I held them out to him without saying anything. To be perfectly honest, my throat had gone kind of dry. He just blinked, staring down at my white-gloved hand like he couldn't imagine what exactly I was offering him.

"What's that?" he asked. "Your currency?"

"Currency?" I said, finally finding my voice. I wondered if that trace of otherness I heard when he spoke meant he came from a different country. "It's not *currency*. It's food stamps. SNAP? What you almost got arrested trying to scam?"

"Ah," he said, still looking down at my hand. "This is what I use to get food?"

"Yeah," I said slowly. "You go into a grocery store and you use it to buy food. Not all food. I mean, there are rules. Like, you can't buy prepared food." I realized I was rambling. "Look," I said. "How come you were all ready to risk fraud charges if you don't even know what these things are?"

He didn't answer my question, just reached out so he could take the food stamps. I could feel the tips of his fingers skim the fabric of my gloves. What marked him as different — one of the things, anyway, they certainly did seem to be mounting — was the fact that he didn't ask me about being so bundled up. He didn't even look at me like he thought it was strange. But then, he was dressed like winter was coming, too.

He stuffed the food stamps into the pocket of his coat. "Do you know," he asked, "if there are any food stores open at this hour?"

"Well," I said, wishing I'd at least thought to bring him a banana or something. It was getting a little clearer to me why he'd been loitering outside a bakery. Despite being so unusual, and apparently starving to death, there was something kind of elegant about James. I hated to think of him Dumpster diving. "It's a pretty sleepy town," I told him. "But there's a Kroger that I think stays open. It's over on I-55 near Northside . . ."

Before I could even finish talking, he had turned and started walking up the street. "Hey!" I said. "Can you let a lady finish talking?" He turned around and looked at me. His face had gone a little softer, and I didn't feel quite so naked. Plus, I felt glad I'd decided on helping him, though why exactly I couldn't say.

He waited for me to speak, and I realized I didn't know what to do. Ask him how he planned to get out to I-55 without a car? Or why he was so damn hungry? Instead I said, "What's your name?"

"James," he said. He had a quiet, almost gentlemanly voice. This guy might've been strange, but suddenly I saw nothing creepy about him.

"James," I said. "I'm Anna Marie."

"I know," he said.

Well! That kept me quiet a minute. I stood there, gathering back my breath, ready to ask him how the hell he knew my name, when he said, "I didn't tell her I saw you. I never spoke to this Wendy Lee. But I'm sorry you got fired."

And then he turned and walked away, leaving me gaping after him, that crazy coat billowing like something from the nineteenth century, from a time where mystery and mist were every bit as common as Mississippi sunshine.

AFTER JAMES WALKED AWAY, I LURKED AWHILE IN MAYBEL-line's doorway myself. At this point it didn't matter if they thought I meant to rob the place, so I figured I could wait and see my replacement at the bakery. To my surprise Wendy Lee had hired a huge, bald man whose tattoos I could see even in the dim streetlights. If you ask me he looked as much like a criminal as I did, but there wasn't much I could do about that except go home and sleep. But I couldn't sleep. I had this feeling, this weird excited feeling. Like something was about to happen.

After a while I got out of bed, pulled out a plain, lined piece of paper from my old school notebook, and sat down at my folding card table. *Dear Mr. and Mrs. Robbins*, I wrote.

I stayed up working on that letter for more than an hour. Then I stuffed it into an envelope, stamped it, and wrote out the address I knew by heart. Tomorrow I would do what I'd done about four times since I'd run away to Jackson. I'd take the bus. Each time I took the bus to a different town, and I decided that tomorrow I'd go all the way out to Vicksburg. Then in the Vicksburg bus station I'd sneak onto another bus, bound for someplace far away, like New York City or Gainesville, Florida. Back when I was a regular girl in Caldecott County, Mississippi, I used to dream of going to those places myself. I had maps tacked to my bedroom wall and an old out-of-date atlas I'd bought at the used bookstore in Dodson.

So far I hadn't been able to bring myself to leave my home state, and tomorrow wouldn't be any different. I wouldn't stay on the bus; I'd just leave my letter on one of those seats, hoping a traveler would find it and mail it once she got to her final destination.

Not that I'd signed the letter. But the Robbinses were sure to know who had written it. Who else would know so many of Cody's memories, not to mention how much he'd loved his mama and daddy? I couldn't risk a letter postmarked Jackson. Because the main thing I knew, other than that I had to write these letters, was that I sure couldn't run the risk of anybody finding me.

· 2 ·

AUNT CARRIE ALWAYS SAID I HAD IT IN ME TO BE EVIL. I DIDN'T used to believe it. But now I couldn't be sure. Actually, it's not true that she *always* said I was evil. My earliest memories of her get all mixed up with what I have of Mama. The two of them used to be like two peas in a pod, with flowers in their hair, giggling in the tall grass down by the banks of the Bayou Pelage. They'd take me walking by the bayou, and I'd stand on the banks while they waded in the thick black water looking for nun's orchids, neither of them a bit scared of the gators or water moccasins. Back then Aunt Carrie was a hippy, bless her heart, just like Mama. She and Mama even looked alike, with blond hair and blue eyes and bright, sunshiney smiles. Nothing like me, all dark and glowery. I must favor my daddy, though I can't say I remember much about him, and I never did see a picture. The only thing I know for certain is that his name was Conrad. I looked up that name on the Internet one time and found out it means "brave," so that's always how I think of him. Brave.

After we lost Mama, Aunt Carrie changed. She left the commune and took me back to the family farm. It wasn't easy for her. By the time I ran away, she was teetering on the brink of foreclosure with the rest of the state of Mississippi. When I'm feeling charitable, I think she was just scared I'd turn out like Mama — freethinking and wild, and then one day gone. So she always kept a close, strict eye on me, and never was shy about using the belt when she thought it was needed. "Anna Marie," she would say. "You go fetch that belt. I'm gonna beat the evil clean out of you."

I guess she didn't beat me hard enough.

THE MORNING AFTER I GAVE JAMES THE FOOD STAMPS, I WOKE up with a funny kind of Christmas feeling. But it only took three steps across the room and a glance in my mini-refrigerator to get me worrying again. When I opened the door, all I saw was what I didn't have. No coffee, or eggs, or anything besides a skinny pint container of milk with one little swirl of sour liquid. I slammed the door shut and sat down on the rickety wicker chair I'd found out by somebody's Dumpster. My window was pushed all the way open, but nothing even slightly like a cool breeze came through it, just hot air so thick I could have caught it in a jar and grown mushrooms.

Down on the street, all kinds of people walked along wearing summer clothes. Young mamas held on to their children's hands. Middle-aged women walked in high heels and crinkly skirts, like they had someone to meet. I imagined them arriving at a restaurant and giving their friend a hug before they sat down to order their fancy eggs. Cody's mom used to make eggs over easy with vinegar sauce.

Mrs. Robbins liked me. In fact she was the last person on Earth to kiss my cheek. I walked through the door of her kitchen, and she kissed me and said, "Did you have any breakfast, Anna Marie?" She knew I'd say no even if I already had, I loved those vinegar eggs she made so much. The best part was the toast, soaked through with the egg yolk and vinegar and butter. I always closed my eyes when I went in for that first bite.

Still standing by the window, I felt my stomach turn over hungrily. I had food stamps of my own stuffed into my wallet, not many on account of the ones I'd given James, but enough to get me through the week if I just got pasta, maybe a carton of eggs.

On the other hand, maybe I could just stay here in my apartment. Stop eating altogether. I wondered how many days it took for a person to starve to death. One thing I knew for sure, nobody would come knocking on my door till the rent came due. That was two weeks from now, and I hadn't any idea how I'd make it. So what if I just gave up? Hopefully the danger I posed to others, to everyone, would die along with me.

A little gasp formed in my throat and burst out of my lips. I shook my head and moved out of the window so nobody would see me. I needed food. I needed money. I'd have to go to the library and look on craigslist to see about a job. So I started pulling on the hot, hateful clothes that kept the world safe from me.

What is it that drives a person to survive, even when she has nothing to live for?

AT THE EUDORA WELTY LIBRARY I FELT PLEASED TO SEE IT WAS a slow day, with several computers available. On craigslist I found some openings at Jaco's Tacos and the Mermaid Café, but all during daytime shifts. Back in Caldecott I'd worked summers and after school waiting tables at Bette's Diner, and I remembered how often people would reach out to tap me, or even grab my wrist. Obviously that wouldn't work now.

I clicked over to the *Caldecott County Record* website and typed "Cody Robbins" in their search line. Three old articles came up. I'd already read all of them. Surely the newspaper would've reported it if he'd woken up; there wasn't exactly a lot of big news in that sleepy bayou town. In fact probably the biggest news that had ever happened was when Cody Robbins — the star pitcher of the high school base-ball team — fell down beside the banks of the Mississippi River and never got up again.

That fateful day, after I ate the eggs his mama made me, Cody and I went for a walk. It wasn't far from his house to the Mississippi River; he and I had taken that walk plenty of times before. Not that he was my boyfriend. Not exactly, anyway, even though he'd given me a ring with my birthstone — a tiny little amethyst — the Christmas be-fore. The two of us had been running around together since we were itty bitty. Everyone — Aunt Carrie, Mr. and Mrs. Robbins, even Cody and me — thought of the two of us just as pals. Which didn't mean I hadn't been a little bit in love with him for quite some time.

Cody and I walked down toward the river, way out of sight from his house and everyone in it. Out of sight of everyone in Caldecott County. Just Cody and me, on a perfect autumn day, the sun high in the sky, the tiniest nip of chilly in the air. We talked about silly things, like baseball, and the kittens that Aunt Carrie's barn cat had the day before, and Shelby Zimmerman's new haircut. After a while we found ourselves underneath a tupelo tree, its bright red leaves swinging above us and hanging around us, so that someone looking our way might only see two pairs of legs, one wearing jeans and one bare un-der a short, frilly skirt.

Cody was so lanky that even a tall girl like me had to stand on her tiptoes to reach his lips. I put my hands on his shoulders and gave him a big old kiss. He didn't seem surprised at all, and he sure didn't com-plain. He just put his hands on my hips and kissed me back, and for a full minute, maybe more, the whole world was perfect.

And then, suddenly, the world was as imperfect as it would ever get, and far as I could see, it wasn't ever turning back.

• • •

ALL THE WAY TO THE HOSPITAL I STARED AT MY REFLECTION with the new, white streaks in my hair. "It must be from the shock," Mrs. Robbins said, in the one second she took to notice. I didn't care a bit about my hair, I just prayed this wasn't my fault. That it was a crazy coincidence that he started convulsing right when we were kissing. But even while I prayed, a part of me knew. I'd felt a kind of convulsion, too, felt Cody's whole self rushing out of him and into me. In that moment before he hit the ground, I hardly even realized he'd fallen because the sensation was so intense. For a second I had sucked it all in, like a wolf sucking the marrow out of a deer's bone. Greedy. When I came to my senses and ran back to the house for help, I covered the distance not with my own speed, but Cody's. I could remember a thousand bases beneath my feet, and the thud of my cleats sliding into home plate.

"Did anything unusual happen," the doctor asked me, when we got to the hospital, "right before he fell?"

I couldn't speak, but I shook my head. I shook it hard. They took me at my word. Why wouldn't they? I'd always been a good girl. The doctor rushed after Cody as they wheeled him into the hallway. I wasn't allowed to follow, but his mama was. I sank down into a seat in the waiting room and remembered coming to this same hospital when I was seven to get my tonsils out, and all the pistachio ice cream they'd let me eat. Except I hated pistachio ice cream and I still had my tonsils. What the hell was happening?

Evil. Just like Aunt Carrie always said. I was evil.

There was only one way to find out for sure if it was me who'd done this to Cody. So I snuck out of the hospital and took the bus to downtown, then ran the four miles back to our farm in my flip-flops. By the time I got home, the sun had started to set. I could see the lights on in the kitchen and Aunt Carrie moving around getting supper ready. I went around to the barn, then climbed up into the loft where Stormy the one-eyed calico lay purring and nursing her newborn kittens.

Kneeling in the straw, I peered down at them. Eleven little babies. Maybe a less experienced mama would have been in danger of losing a few, but Stormy's children and grandchildren and great-great-grandchildren roamed all over Caldecott County. I had no doubt she could handle nursing every last one of these kittens. Still, I chose the teensiest one. I picked it up by the scruff of its neck, out of the pile of its brothers and sisters and the warmth of its mama. The kitten was black. It squirmed in my grip, but nothing happened to it, nothing at all. It just opened its little mouth and mewled.

For a second I felt a rush of joy. It wasn't me! I hadn't hurt Cody. It was just a coincidence that he fell after we kissed. Then I realized that the kitten's fur protected it from skin-to-skin contact. We weren't touching, not really. So I took a deep breath and brought the kitten to my face. Its little eyes were squinched up tight, and I knew it couldn't hear anything either. Still, I whispered, "I'm sorry, little kitty. I sure hope I'm wrong." And I pressed my nose against its wet little black kitten nose.

It didn't take near as long as it did with Cody. The kitten was so tiny. A few seconds passed and the squirming turned into convulsing. I set it down on the straw. But it was too late. The kitten lay there, still and tiny and stone-cold dead.

I felt a shudder go through me, then tried to blink, but my eyes were sealed shut. I was blind as a bat, or a newborn kitten. Oh, it was the very least punishment my wicked, wicked self deserved. Sorrow and exhaustion took over. I covered up the kitten with straw then crawled into the corner of the loft and curled up under the slanted eaves.

When I woke up, it was morning and my eyes opened just fine. Light poured in through the cracks in the barn. Maybe if I'd woken up in my own bed I could've pretended for a minute that it had all been a dream. Not now, though, with hay in my hair and Stormy marching all around in a fury, pawing at her poor little dead kitten. I picked my way around the two of them and climbed down the ladder. Aunt Carrie's car wasn't there — likely she'd gone looking for me. Hopefully I'd have enough time to gather what I could.

I put on jeans and a turtleneck and a pair of woolen mittens. I packed all the clothes that would fit into my old green duffel bag, and pulled the map off my wall. I took every penny of the waitressing money I'd stashed beneath the loose board under my bed. Then I went into the bathroom to collect my toothbrush.

Now, a kitten that's not lived two full days doesn't have a whole lot of memories to absorb, and it pretty much has no abilities. But when I looked up from the sink into the mirror, I could hardly believe what I saw. My eyes had turned from their lifelong brown to bright green. Layers of jade, brilliant and sparkling, not like any eyes I'd ever seen in a human head. They glared back at me in a way that would've looked like an accusation, if they hadn't been so damn scared.

IN THE EUDORA WELTY LIBRARY, I STARED AT THE COMPUTER screen with those same green eyes. I wondered if Cody dreamed about me while he lay there in that coma, and if I looked like my old self in those dreams or like the new one. I wondered if his dreams started off happy and ended with fear and misery. At the top right corner of my craigslist page sat the Google search bar. I typed in "Do coma patients dream?" and sat there awhile reading articles, different fancy ways of saying *Nobody knows*.

I logged off and pushed back my chair. As I stood, who should I see but the mystery man formerly known as El Creepo — James, sitting at the end of the row of computers, staring at the screen like he'd never seen anything more interesting in all his life. For a second all I wanted to do was call out his name. *James! It's me, Anna Marie. Remember me?* Instead I ducked around the chairs where people waited and crept into the stacks. I could watch James unseen by peering through the top of a row of audio books.

Had it seriously been just last night that I'd handed him those food stamps? I could hardly figure how he'd managed to change so much in just over twelve hours. He must have found some very nutritious bargains over at Kroger because he looked like he'd just had a couple weeks at a spa. His complexion had gone from super-pale to a nice rosy color. He looked like he'd put on a good ten pounds — all muscle. Of course I could only see his profile. I tried not to wish he'd look my way, so I could see if there'd been any change at all to those bright blue eyes. My heart melted a little just imagining that, and I pulled my jacket sleeve up the tiniest bit so I could give myself a good, hard pinch. The way I found myself feeling about James, as I peered over those fat CD cases? It was just as good as wishing him dead.

James was bundled up like it was November in Nova Scotia. He'd left his long leather coat at home but had on blue jeans and a big white wool fisherman's sweater. I could see the collar of a red-and-black checked flannel shirt poking out. Sure the library was air-conditioned. Even I felt nearly comfortable in my crazy getup. But if I had a choice? You bet I'd be wearing a filmy summer dress or shorts.

Once I wrote a paper on the subject of hope for my favorite high school English teacher, Miss Eloise Fitzsimmons. I wrote on how even though my parents had disappeared when I was so little, and I could hardly remember Mama and Daddy one whit, some days I still expected the two of them to come waltzing right into my bedroom and carry me away with them. Miss Eloise particularly appreciated my quoting Mr. Alexander Pope to underscore my point: "Hope springs eternal in the human breast."

To show you hope sprang eternal in me, here's what I thought about James: Maybe he has the same affliction as me. Maybe that's why he's all covered up head to toe. If it could happen to me, it could happen to someone else. Right?

As soon as this idea quit forming in my head, James turned toward me, just like I'd wished he would, and just like I'd been terrified of. I ducked down a little lower, but not quite so low that I couldn't see what I longed to, those blue blue blue blue eyes, staring my way. He had his hair pulled back in a ponytail. And although he couldn't possibly have seen me, something inside me fluttered when his mouth tugged into a small, perplexed kind of smile.

Even though he was looking straight at me, I felt confident that he couldn't see more than the top of my head, if that much. So I took a moment to squash hope way down deep where it wouldn't be tempted to rise up again. On top of everything else I felt disloyal to Cody, whose little ring I still wore, the boy who slept forever on account of kissing me. So I stayed bent over and slunk out of the stacks, out into the bright, hot daylight of North State Street.

EVEN THOUGH I HAD TO MAKE WHAT MONEY AND FOOD STAMPS I had stretch a piece, I sorely needed some kind of treat, so I bought a pint of ice cream on the way home. Before I ate it, I peeled off my clothing — sticky with sweat — and stood under a cool shower. When I got out, I could hardly bear to put on a single stitch. If I'd had more than that flimsy curtain in the window I would have stayed stark naked, but I settled for a pair of panties and a tank top. I put my biggest fan, the square one, into the window, and then sat down right in front of it with the ice cream. For the first time all day I felt clean and cool. I took a second and looked at the map of the U.S. that I'd taped on the wall above my bed, the same one I'd had in my room back in Caldecott County. Maybe if I got another job, one day soon I'd have enough money to buy a ticket on one of those long-distance buses.

I dug my spoon into the ice cream then looked out through the window. And just who do you think I saw standing there on the sidewalk, hands in his pockets, staring straight up at my building? James.

What in hell? That's what I should have thought. And I should have felt creeped out, or angry. But instead? Christmas morning! Happiness and excitement exploded in my chest. For a split second I felt like a girl my age ought to feel, giddy and weak in the knees at the sight of a handsome man.

I put my ice cream on the card table. My hair fell crazy and loose around my shoulders. I wasn't wearing gloves, or leather, or long sleeves — hell, I wasn't even wearing a bra. And more than anything in the world, I wanted James to see me like this. A regular girl in skimpy clothes. So I knocked on the window.

He looked straight up at me, through the glass. Even from this distance I could see something like appreciation rearranging his features. He smiled. And not only did I smile, too, but I waved, like a goddamn teenager without a care in the world, or a thought in her head.

"YOU CHANGED," JAMES SAID, AS HE WALKED IN MY DOOR.

He looked as disappointed as he sounded. While he was on his way up, I'd thrown on my full regalia, including two pairs of tea gloves. At the Jackson stores, they were already displaying clothing for the fall, and the other day in a window I'd seen a sweater that had fingerless gloves attached to the sleeves. That would take care of that dangerous space between my wrist and forearm, but when I went in the store, the price tag said eighty-five dollars, and I didn't even have half of that to my name.

Luckily James didn't try to shake my hand, or touch me at all. He walked right by me and plopped himself down on my bed. It seemed awful personal for someone I'd just met on the street. I sat myself down in the wicker chair and tried to look like this happened every day, a handsome and somewhat peculiar stranger showing up on my doorstep and sitting down on my bed. Thank goodness I'd made it up this morning.

James clasped his hands in his lap and looked around the room. It had only been a matter of hours since I spied on him at the library, but he looked even better — kind of rosy and robust, with a fair bit of stubble across his jaw. I was struck by a powerful wish to be back in my previous and very skimpy outfit. I pictured myself getting up from the wicker chair and crossing the room to sit in his lap. My mind flooded with the notion of all the skin-on-skin this would entail, and though my mouth was still open, I found myself unable to speak.

James didn't say anything, but he shivered a little, which made me think that maybe he could read my mind. After all, he'd known my name without me telling him, hadn't he? Surprisingly, this didn't embarrass me a bit. I kind of hoped he *could* read my mind, because then the two of us would be doing together in my head what we could never do in real life.

James said, "Do you mind turning off that machine?"

I looked around the room, trying to think what machine he could mean. Other than the toaster and microwave and coffeemaker, I didn't have a whole lot of electronics.

"That," James said, pointing to my window fan. "It's a little cold in here."

"Cold!" I said. "Cold like a blast furnace. Are you crazy?"

Soon as the words were out of my mouth, I realized they were the first things I'd said to him since he'd come in. I might not have had the fanciest upbringing you ever heard of, but I was not so without manners that I couldn't feel like a bad hostess. So I reached over and switched off the big fan. James looked over at the other two, the little oscillating fans, and I stood up and turned those off, too, wondering where on Planet Earth he came from that he didn't know to call them "fans."

James nodded like it was better now. "Sorry," he said. "It's a lot warmer where I come from."

Warmer than Mississippi in August? I tried to imagine where that might be. I knew there were places in the world that were plenty hot — like Southeast Asia, and Africa. But on my way home from the library the temperature clock at First Bank of Jackson had read ninety-six degrees. Even in, say, Ho Chi Minh City, I didn't think ninety-six degrees would be considered *cold*.

"Huh" was all I could think to say.

James smiled and said, "I just wanted to come by and say thanks. I hadn't eaten in a few days, and I really couldn't think straight. But with those certificates you gave me, I was able to recharge, and that helped me start figuring things out." He reached into his pocket and pulled out a great big wad of cash. I near about fell off my chair.

"Here," James said. He peeled the wad in half and held a fistful of twenties out to me. "I thought you could use this. Money, right? Better than what you gave me?"

All I could do was sit there and stare at the money. I couldn't even worry about his hand, hovering so close to me. "What did you do?" I said. "Rob a bank?"

James pulled the money back toward himself. He looked a little confused, and almost like he'd got his feelings hurt. But the last thing I needed was some fugitive bank robber in my apartment.

He said, "But, you need this. Don't you?"

This was about all I could take. I stood up and put my hands on my hips. "Need it?" I said. "Why the hell would I be working the late shift at a bakery if I didn't need it? Why would I be at the goddamn welfare office? Oh no, I don't need it. That's why I'm living here in the lap of luxury, in this lovely *over-cooled* high-rise apartment!"

"Oh," James said. He put the bills back in the original wad and shoved it all into his pocket. "I'm sorry, Anna Marie," he said. "I guess things aren't as clear to me as I thought."

James stood up. Like I said before, I am a tall girl — five-foot-eight in my bare feet. But James was a whole lot taller, taller even than Cody. I felt very confused, and a tiny bit frightened, and at the same time I couldn't help imagining how far on my tiptoes I'd have to stand to reach his lips, which looked very soft and full. And kind. Loud as my instincts might be yammering various contradictions at me, that was the word that came through the loudest, even louder than sexy or handsome or crazy. *Kind.*

It had been a good long while since any kindness had come my way.

James took a step toward me. I came to my senses and stepped back, nearly falling over my chair. I kicked it out of the way and moved around it, which brought my back right up against the wall.

"Look," I said. "I'm not sure what's going on here. I don't know why you're cold when it's closing in on a hundred degrees. I don't know why you've suddenly got more money than Donald Trump when just last night you were grateful for a few food stamps. And I don't know why you're here. But you have to leave. Right now."

"But Anna Marie," he said. His voice cracked a little, like this was the saddest thing anyone had ever said to him. "I thought you'd be happy to see me. I'm very happy to see you."

He took another step toward me. I held up my hand, hoping that whatever hot place he came from, this was still the universal symbol for *halt.*

"You just have to go," I said. "That's all."

James sighed. "OK. If that's really what you want."

He paused for a little minute, like he was waiting for me to admit I didn't want that at all. Then he turned and let himself out. His back leaving my apartment was about the most pitiful thing I ever saw, and for the next hour or so it was almost like I had touched him, I felt so flooded with a sadness that shouldn't have belonged to me.

THAT NIGHT, MY APARTMENT HAD NEVER SEEMED DINGIER OR more lonesome. Maybe it was because James had been there. But for the first time since I'd run away, I found myself longing for my room back home. Sure Aunt Carrie could be awful mean, and she never was shy about telling me everything I did wrong. But she provided a roof over my head. I had my memories of her younger, softer days. And she always kept the refrigerator full, with eggs from the hen-house, and milk from her own cows — thick, unpasteurized milk, the store-bought stuff never would taste right to me. It wasn't much to be nostalgic for, but right at this moment — with thirty dollars and a few food stamps to my name — it sure did seem like something to remember fondly.

Just then my eyes fell on the ring of keys I'd thrown on the card table. I could see the two keys I'd been too sentimental to throw out, the one to Aunt Carrie's old blue pickup truck, and the one to the front door of her farmhouse. But what I also saw was the biggest key on the chain, the key to the Sunshine Bakery, which in all our various other dealings, Wendy Lee had forgotten to take back. I squinted across the room at the microwave. It was 8:30. The bakery had been closed for more than three hours. It would be more than four hours before Mr. Clean showed up to start in on the morning baking.

In other words, plenty of time for me to mosey on over there and fix myself a snack.

I WALKED PAST THE STORE WITH THE SWEATER IN THE WINDOW, but there was no time for window-shopping. As if to prove my point, I tripped a little over an apple-sized rock someone must have kicked into the middle of the sidewalk.

At the bakery my key turned easily. Good thing for me Wendy Lee hadn't changed the locks. Now I just had to hope she hadn't changed the alarm code, but when I pushed the door open, the panel sat there dark and silent. Despite this seeming like good luck, it was a bit unsettling, since Wendy Lee usually was a tiger about setting that alarm. I guess today she'd had other things on her mind.

No time to reminisce. I unfolded my bag and went straight to collecting what I needed. First stop was the big walk-in refrigerator. I took a bunch of eggs and a couple blocks of butter. Then I heaped in all different kinds of berries. Funny that here in the city berries seemed like such a luxury. This time of year at home, we lived on berries because there were so many growing wild to be had for free. By now the strawberries would be gone, but pretty much every hill would be covered in the blueberries that cost nothing but stains on your fingers.

Pretty quick I realized that I should've brought two bags. This one was nearly full, and I still had to get to the pantry to stock up on flour and chocolate and whatnot. Then I remembered Wendy Lee must keep her bags for the store somewhere down here. I tried to think where they might be as I headed out of the walk-in.

And there, right in the middle of the kitchen, pointing a big ole .22 right at me, was Wendy Lee herself. Dang.

I put my hands up in the air but didn't drop my bag, just let it dangle from the crook of my elbow. When Wendy Lee saw it was me, she lowered her rifle a little bit. The she reconsidered and aimed it right back at me.

"Anna Marie," she snarled. Unlike the last time I'd seen her, she was in all her perfectly turned out glory, with her fake blond hair poofed up and her makeup painted on thick and just so. "Just what in the wide world do you think you're doing?"

As soon as I started to bring my hands down, she cocked the rifle like she wanted me to know she meant it. Instead of scaring me, this made me downright furious. First she lands me in this sorry situation, then she plans on shooting me for stealing dairy products?

"I'm hungry," I said. "On account of you putting me out on the street with no fair warning, for no good reason."

"No good reason! I thought you were a no-good thief. Turns out I was right."

"I never was a thief until right this minute. You didn't fire a thief, Wendy Lee, you created one!" Soon as the words were out of my mouth, I knew they were true. It made me so mad that I put my hands down and marched past her into the dry goods cupboard. Just as I suspected, she didn't shoot me. "Wendy Lee," I called to her. "You want to tell me where you keep your extra bags? 'Cause I don't think I can fit everything I need into the one I brought."

I heard a little clatter, which I figured was Wendy Lee putting the rifle on the counter. "Anna Marie," she yelled at the top of her voice. "You take your time and get everything you need. I'll just be calling the police."

My hand froze on the bar of dark chocolate. The police. I'd forgotten all about *them*. There were only two phones in the Sunshine Bakery, one upstairs behind the counter, by the cash register, and the other also upstairs, in Wendy Lee's office. I rushed out of the dry pantry and stood right in front of the door that led to the stairway.

"Anna Marie, you get outa my way."

"No ma'am," I said.

She put her hands on her hips. I noticed that she was even more gussied up than usual, in a flowery skirt and a sequined top and heels that brought her up to my chin. Probably she had an after-dinner date with some fat old bible salesman. Any minute he might come walking through the door to collect her, and then I'd have two indignant Southerners to deal with. I'd seen the men Wendy Lee dated. None of them looked like they'd be shy as she was about shooting me.

So I figured the best thing to do was just give up. I said, "Just forget it, Wendy Lee. You go ahead and call them."

I started to walk away from the door, figuring she'd take the chance to scurry right through it and run on up the stairs. But that's not what she did. Instead she reached out and grabbed my arm, just above the cuff of my sleeve. Her plump little hand closed tight, and I froze where I stood. Wendy Lee's grip felt firm and almost motherly.

I panicked, and at the same time I kind of relished it, another person, holding me, even if it was in anger. Also I felt a powerful rush of relief, and gratitude for the layers of clothing separating my skin and hers. That moment didn't last long. Because Wendy Lee's thumb slid down my cuff. Just the barest brush, the startling feeling, the sparkly charms on her bracelet jangling against my arm, and her one-of-a-kind thumbprint nestled against the white sliver of skin between my glove and sleeve.

I held my breath. The thing about an affliction like mine, one that had come on so sudden, is that there's no way of knowing if you've still got it. I couldn't go around killing kittens every day of my life. And even though something deep inside me told me that I hadn't got better, a girl couldn't help but hope. *Hope springs eternal in the human breast*, just like I'd written in my paper for Miss Fitzimmons. So in the split second between the touch of skin and any kind of reaction, this wild rush of hope came over me — that it had gone away, and I could peel off all my layers, put on a sundress, and go . . .

But there wouldn't be any hand-holding in my future. Even though I came to my senses and snatched my arm out of Wendy Lee's grasp, something came over her. Her face quivered, then turned into a kind of stone, then started in quivering again like the stone was going to crack and shatter. At the same time something came over me, a rush of something entering me, my fingers and then my whole body tingling. A rush and a whoosh went all the way through my body, including my toenails and the follicles of my hair. Absorbing something I was never meant to have. Wendy Lee. Everything that happened to her over the years of her life, everything that had made her up to begin with. She fell to the floor.

I had to get out of there. Not only that, I had to get out of Jackson, Mississippi. But I also had to get Wendy Lee help. I hadn't touched her near as long as I'd touched Cody, and she was a whole lot bigger than the kitten. I could see she was still breathing. So instead of heading up the kitchen steps to the street, I went on up to the bakery. I stood behind the counter and dialed 911. "There's a lady in the kitchen downstairs at the Sunshine Bakery. She's unconscious. Please send an ambulance right away." Then I hung up, grabbed a stack of chocolate bars from the front counter, and headed out the door.

Wendy Lee was thirty-seven years old. She used coconut oil to make her pie crusts flaky. She married her high school sweetheart when she was seventeen, on account of he'd got her pregnant, but she lost the baby right after the wedding, and he struck out for his family's ranch in Colorado and never did send her a penny. He even took their dog, a Bluetick Coonhound named Radar. I could see her husband's face right in front of my eyes. He had freckles and red hair and a lopsided smile. I hated that face and I loved it, all at the same time.

The night air was hot as a sauna, but I felt cold right down to my bones. As I passed the store with the sweater in the window, I decided to leave Mississippi for good. Who knew where I'd go, or how I'd get there? But I couldn't come back here, not ever.

Off in the distance I heard a siren, hopefully an ambulance headed to assist Wendy Lee. But who was coming to assist me? Not anybody on this whole ball of mud called Planet Earth. I looked down at the ground. There was the rock I'd tripped over on my way to the bakery. So far I wasn't turning out to be a very effective criminal. But what did I have to lose? Surely the police wouldn't be very far behind that ambulance. Well then, let them just try to bring me in. I knelt down and picked up that rock. Threw it right through the plate glass window, which must have been made years ago, because it shattered easily. Didn't even set off an alarm. I didn't bother wrenching the sweater off the mannequin, just stepped on through the window and gathered up an armload of the mediums stacked on the table. Then I stepped back through the broken glass and made my way back to my apartment for what I knew would be the very last time.

• • •

BACK AT MY PLACE I JAMMED THE STOLEN SWEATERS INTO MY duffel bag, along with some other clothes. Then I stood on my bed and untacked my map, folded it neatly, slipped it inside, and zipped the whole thing shut. I locked the door behind me, having left just enough behind so that maybe it would look like I planned on coming back.

Outside I had one decision left to make: which car to steal. It had to be something that the whole world wouldn't notice as I drove by. And it ought to be an American-made car, because that's the kind Cody had the most experience fixing. In a weird way this was just the teensiest bit exciting. All these months I'd known, courtesy of Cody's memories, how to start a car with nothing but a screwdriver.

My heart skipped three beats as a car puttering up the road backfired. I got to the corner of North State and Magnolia and was looking wildly up and down for a likely prospect when the same car honked at me. Just great. The car looked as sorry as it sounded, with dents and rust spots and a convertible top with threads hanging down from it. And as it pulled up beside me, who should I see behind the wheel but James, wearing his long black leather jacket, plus thick black leather gloves that looked like they had sheepskin lining.

"Anna Marie," he said. "Hop in!" His voice sounded bright and cheerful, like he was inviting me to go to the movies or a dance or something. I didn't get into the car just yet, but I poked my head in.

"How far you going?" I asked.

"How far do you want to go?"

If he'd racked his whole brain for a million years, he couldn't have come up with a better answer. The car had a bench seat. I threw my duffel bag in first so it could be a buffer between us. Then I hunkered down in the front seat and set to searching for a decent radio station. It was going to be a long, long ride.

THE CAR WAS HOTTER THAN HELL. NOT ONLY DID JAMES HAVE
the windows rolled up, he had the heat cranked. "You gotta be kidding
me," I said. He glanced over like he had no clue what I was talking
about.

"You think we could use the air-conditioning instead of the heat?"
I said.

"Sure," James said. He sounded so calm, that same kind of elegant,
almost musical voice. "Please do whatever you like. I'm still trying to
figure everything out."

"Yeah," I said, giving him a little leeway. "It's an old car, for sure."
I leaned over and switched the dial from red to blue. The chances that
the air conditioner in this old jalopy worked were slim. Luckily Cody
knew just how to fix the air-conditioning in an old Camaro, so even if
it didn't work now, I could repair it on up the road.

"What does that do?" James asked, as I fiddled with the dial.
"Clean up the oxygen?"

"The oxygen? What're you talking about?"

"You called it an air conditioner. So is the air going to get a little cleaner? Easier to breathe?"

"You don't know what an air conditioner is?"

He paused, like he knew he'd made a mistake. Then — hallelujah — cold air started flowing from the dashboard, and he set into shivering. I rolled my eyes and clicked it off.

"Here," I said. "A compromise. We'll turn off the heat, which makes the car hotter, and also turn off the air conditioner. Which makes the air colder. Not easier to breathe. Do you want to tell me why you're the only person in the world who doesn't know that?"

James nodded at the windshield. Up ahead there was a big highway sign, giving us the choice between 220 South or 55 North.

"Do you want to talk about my knowledge of automotive terms?" he said. "Or do you want to tell me which way we're going?"

"North," I said, feeling a little guilty for wanting to head to cooler climates. "Definitely north." I waited for him to complain, say he wanted to head where it was hotter, but he didn't. He just eased the car onto Interstate 55. I listened for sirens blaring behind us and didn't hear anything. A sign by the road said it was 544 miles to Winona, Tennessee. I asked James, "How do you feel about driving straight through the night?"

"Works for me."

"In that case, we don't have to talk about a doggone thing, if you don't want to."

James smiled to himself, and nodded. He reached out like he planned on patting my hand, and I pulled it back. I had on tea gloves underneath the fingerless gloves of my sweater, but still. Best not to get into the habit. He winced a little, like I'd hurt his feelings again, but he kept his eyes on the road. This gave me the chance to study him for a bit. At first glance, with the long hair and all the leather, he might seem scary. Luckily I'd learned that most people can't afford much more than a first glance. So they wouldn't see the things I did, such as the barest little bump on his nose, like maybe it had been broken a time or two, or the way his big hands gripped the wheel, looking strong, like they could do anything at all in this world.

The light in the car changed in patterns, depending on the streetlights rushing by and the headlights from the opposite side of the highway. I didn't take my eyes off James, and he didn't seem to mind. It had been so long since I'd just sat next to somebody. So long since I'd been along for the ride, and not just purely on my own.

All of a sudden this thought came into my head. Less like a thought, more like a memory. A memory of riding in a car almost exactly like this one, with a bench seat and rickety convertible top. Except in my head, the man driving wasn't James at all, but a balding, potbellied fellow. In my memory, I didn't mind this at all. In fact I kind of liked it, and I leaned over the seat and unzipped this fellow's pants while he was driving. "It ain't safe," he said, but he sounded halfhearted, so I just laughed. Then I took out what he had in there and . . .

Wendy Lee! To think all that time I'd thought she was God-fearing.

I BLUSHED SOMETHING FIERCE ALL THE WAY TO CANTON. LUCK-ily it was dark and James didn't seem to notice. You'd think the two of us would've been talking a blue streak, what with all the questions between us that needed working out. In my head I tried to figure on what I would tell James when he asked why I wanted to leave Jackson in such a hurry. But he didn't ask, just kept his eyes on the road, driving.

"You want me to drive awhile?" I asked, after three quiet hours had passed.

"No," he said. "This is fun for me."

"You mind if I go to sleep then?"

"No," he said. He smiled that little smile he had, the one that made me think of the word "kind." "You go ahead and get some rest."

I wriggled out of my jacket and folded it into a fat square so I could use it as a pillow. Just as I leaned it against the window, I thought of that kind way James had. I could just imagine, once I'd fallen asleep, he'd be the sort of person who'd reach over and stroke my hair, or give my cheek a little pat.

Don't forget I used to be a regular girl. I knew the things that passed between people like they were nothing at all. My girlfriends back in Caldecott County used to touch me all the time with their fluttery fingers. Even Aunt Carrie sometimes tiptoed into my room and kissed me on the forehead when she thought I was sleeping. That was the only time she ever seemed to like me, when I slept.

"Listen. James," I said.

"Yes, Anna Marie?" He talked so proper I had to smile to myself.

"I'm going to say something kinda strange right now," I warned him. He looked away from his driving for just a second and smiled encouragement at me, like I was allowed to say any old strange thing I wanted. I took a deep breath. "You can't touch me," I said. "Not when I'm awake and not when I'm asleep. It's nothing personal against you. And I'm not saying you even want to touch me. But I just need you to promise me that you won't. Touch me, that is."

"OK," he said.

"Promise?"

"I promise," he said. It surprised me that he didn't ask any questions, but then I figured he was just returning the favor about me not interrogating him. I settled my head against the window, with my jacket underneath it, and started to close my eyes. But still it rankled me a little bit, and I never had learned to keep my mouth shut.

"James?" I said.

"Yes, Anna Marie?"

"Don't you want to know why you can't touch me?"

"Well," he said, "I do want to know. But I suspect it's a little bit like me not knowing what an air conditioner is. Isn't it?"

A little rush of fear, mixed together with excitement, rushed into my heart. "Yes," I whispered. "I suppose it is." I leaned my head against the window and closed my eyes. Another of Wendy Lee's memories came over me, this one a damn sight more wholesome, of her leaning against a car window to doze in just this manner. The man driving was different, much younger, her ex-husband before he became an ex. His name was Joe Wheeler. In this memory he reached out real sweetly and stroked her hair as she fell fast asleep. "Thanks, Jo Jo," I muttered, which couldn't have made much sense to James, but I couldn't see his reaction, because I dozed right off.

WHEN I OPENED MY EYES AGAIN, THEY BLINKED INTO THE SUN-light pouring through the windshield. James was pulling off Highway 55, to get gas I supposed. I looked at the exit sign: Grenada. Tennessee! So far it looked a whole lot like Mississippi. Then it struck me: I hadn't dreamed about Cody. I hadn't dreamed at all. I couldn't remember the last time that had happened.

"Good morning," James said. "I'm glad to see you got some rest."

"Thanks," I said, stretching out my arms. I hoped my breath didn't smell too bad. James pulled up in front of a gas pump and I fished in my duffel bag for my toiletries. "I'm just going on into the ladies' room," I said. "I can drive awhile, if you want, so you can get some rest."

"OK," James said. On my way to the bathroom, I turned around and looked at him pumping gas. He looked like a towering and fearsome person. Nobody would ever guess how downright agreeable he could be.

The bathroom sure could have used a cleaning. As I brushed my teeth, I ought to have been thinking on Wendy Lee, worrying about her and hoping she was all right. Of course I did all those things, but I also felt this rush of gladness that I had James for company and protection, especially since he'd taken the news about not touching me so well.

When I came out of the bathroom, James was in the little minimart, stocking up on snacks. "You want anything?" he asked. I remembered the chocolate bars in the pocket of my jacket. Probably I'd smooshed them all to pieces last night. Still, they'd make a fine breakfast. Eventually I'd have to figure out how to pay my own way for gas and food, but since I was going to drive, I guessed it would be all right to let him buy me a cup of coffee.

THAT DANG OLD CAMARO DIDN'T HAVE ANY CUP HOLDERS, SO I had to balance the Styrofoam cup between my knees. James and I divvied up the chocolate bars, and I let him use my jacket as a pillow since he didn't want to take his off.

"James," I said, settling on the one question I just couldn't keep quiet about. "I'm going to ask you a question, and if you don't want to answer it, that's just fine. Just say so. OK?"

"OK," he said, even though he'd already closed his eyes to settle down to sleep.

"When I first met you, you seemed kind of . . . down on your luck. And now you've got plenty of money."

James sat up. He furrowed his brow a little, like he was trying to work out how to answer my question without addressing the larger ones that surrounded it. "Well," he said slowly. "The first time I saw you, I hadn't been in Mississippi very long. I was still trying to figure out how things worked."

"How'd you know to get all that stuff to scam the food stamp system?"

"I was staying in Smith Park. There were other people sleeping there, and one of them noticed I didn't have anything to eat. He gave me a bag of apples, and then that paperwork. Told me where to go to get the food stamps."

"So how'd you get from there to that big stack of cash?"

"One thing about me is, I'm very good with machines. Like those computers you saw me using in the library."

"You saw me in the library?"

He ignored this. "In Kroger, I saw those little cards people use, to pay for things. I watched people take cash out of those windows . . ."

"ATMs?"

"Yes, of course, ATMs." James went on, telling me how on the computer he'd typed in one of the names of the banks he'd seen on an ATM, and set up an account for himself.

"You created a phony bank account? But James, that's just like stealing."

He shrugged. "From what I can see, it's just numbers on the computer. Very odd form of currency. Also very easy to replicate. All I had to do was type in numbers. The bank thinks those numbers are how much money I have. Anything I buy, the person selling it gets paid. Though I guess it is stealing from the bank."

I looked at James, his big blue eyes starting to droop shut, and I thought about all the houses in Caldecott that the banks had foreclosed on in the past couple years, even after they got that bailout money from the government. Aunt Carrie sometimes had to call about late mortgage payments herself, and they never showed her an ounce of mercy. And once I'd overheard Emma Deane Wilford's mama on the phone with them, pleading to lower her credit card payments, but they wouldn't budge even though her husband was out of work. Truth was I did not mind James's little scam at all, not in the slightest. Stealing from crooks to save my skin felt just fine to me.

"You go on and get your beauty rest," I told him. "I got some miles to cover."

THE THING IN THE WORLD CODY LOVED MOST WAS CARS, FIXING them and also driving them. But he never got to do what I was doing, just pressing my foot down on the pedal and heading into the great wide yonder. While James napped, I zoomed from one highway to another, heading north. Places I'd dreamed of visiting all my life just flashed by my window. There went Memphis and all that barbeque people said was so delicious, plus Graceland. Then I veered east, whooshing past Nashville and the Grand Ole Opry, and on up into Kentucky. At least there I could see the pretty grass and sometimes even horses from the road. Mostly the whole world passed me by in a blur of trees and highway signs. Under different circumstances I'd have liked to make the very same trip in days instead of hours, stopping to try food and music and sights along the way.

James woke up somewhere in Kentucky. I was real glad, because my stomach had been growling for hours but I didn't want to wake him.

"Hey, sleepyhead," I said. "You feeling hungry?"

He blinked, groggy, and ran his hand over his head, smoothing his long hair into place. "Sure," he said. "I could eat."

It was pretty rural, and starting to get dark. I expected him to complain about the direction, the fact that we were heading north, but he didn't. He just picked up my jacket and put it over himself like an extra blanket. We didn't find anyplace to eat till we were almost in West Virginia, where I pulled over at a little barbeque place that looked like it had been nailed together out of plywood. It had chickens running around loose out front, and I wondered if they'd end up on tomorrow's plates.

There weren't many people inside, just a table full of what looked like young farmers, and the old man behind the counter. Still it was noticeable how the place went quiet when James and I walked in. Despite the highway, I guess they didn't get a whole lot of visitors who looked like us, all done up in leather, one with a pair of white skunk stripes in her hair. I ordered us two plates of pulled pork and collards and let James pay for it. He reached into his pocket and pulled out that wad of bills while I winced, reminding myself to mention that he shouldn't be waving all that cash around. Old Gramps behind the counter narrowed his eyes, very suspicious, as James handed him some money.

"You got a ten?" Gramps said. "I'm real low on change."

I think he was hoping James would tell him to just keep the extra money, but James didn't catch on. Instead he started shuffling through that big pile of money and said at the top of his voice, "No, I don't have any tens. I have tons of twenties, though."

I grabbed our tray of food and told Gramps to keep the change. Then I jerked my head, real pointed, for James to follow me. The men at the table had started to look more like thugs than farmers. I could see them watching us real close, but I tried to avoid looking their way as I stabbed a little pile of greens with my fork. Not that I felt particularly hungry anymore. Outside the sky had started to darken, and no other cars pulled into the lot. In other words, the perfect scenario for jumping us when we headed back to the car.

"You know," I said to James, real low. He was shoveling food into his mouth without a care in the world, "you might want to be a little more discreet about your cash."

He got this confused sort of look on his face and put his hand into his pocket, like instead of being discreet he planned on pulling it out for another look. I held up my hand. "Just don't," I said. "Keep it in your pocket. We'll talk in the car."

He shrugged and kept on eating. Over at the other table, the farmers were collecting their trays. They didn't look at us as they shuffled back to the counter and said good night to Gramps, and I calmed down enough to take a bite of my barbeque, hoping I was just being paranoid. It tasted real vinegary and kind of dry, and I sure did still regret not being able to try the barbeque in Memphis.

By the time James and I walked out of the restaurant the night had gone completely dark, just the stars and a flickering street lamp lighting our way to the car. I'd pretty much calmed down about the farmers, or whoever they were, having heard a car pull away not long after they left. But apparently it had only been a couple of them, because two stayed behind and now were leaning against the driver's side of the Camaro. The taller, wider one had a baseball bat and was sort of thumping it against his leg as we walked toward them.

"Hey," James said, real friendly, like he'd never seen a pair of thugs about to jump him before.

"Hey yourself," said the one with the baseball bat, sounding considerably less friendly. They both wore Carhartts, and wife beaters that showed off their farmer's sunburns. They looked real young, not much older than me, and truthfully I felt a little sorry for them. As we'd driven off the highway to this barbeque place, the area had looked real depressed, lots of broken-down motor homes and sad little houses. Thinking of all the people who'd fallen on hard times back in Caldecott, I could almost sympathize with their wanting to jump us — weird-looking strangers flashing around fistfuls of cash. Which is not at all to say that I felt like getting smacked with that baseball bat.

Meanwhile James stood there looking as friendly and relaxed as a person possibly could, just waiting for them to move so we could get into our car. He did not look like he had any intention of putting his considerable size and muscle into protecting himself, let alone me. Finally he just said, "Well, that's our car."

The two of them laughed, and the smaller one — he had real bad acne — spit on the ground.

"Is it?" said the one with the baseball bat. He lifted it up and gave his palm a couple slow whacks. "Maybe now you can tell me something I don't know. Like whether you'd like to part with that wad of cash in your pocket."

"Oh," James said, still not sounding afraid, or even bothered. "Do you need some cash?" It took every ounce of effort I had not to slap my forehead. Or slap him, for that matter.

"Look," I interrupted. "It's real nice of y'all to welcome us to town this way. But it so happens we need that cash for our travels. So if you wouldn't mind moving so we can get into our car, we'd sure appreciate it."

"Would you now?" said the one with the baseball bat.

"Yeah," I told him. "We would."

Not so long ago, when I had normal clothes and hair, this small town Southerner would have recognized me as one of his own. Back then I might have stood a chance of convincing him to let us go. But this was now, and I knew I looked to him like a citified freak. I decided in that moment to just go ahead and hand the money over, then get in the car and burn rubber.

But I guess Baseball Bat Man didn't realize I was about to surrender, because he stepped away from the car and drew that bat back over his shoulder and started to swing it straight at James.

Now, I'm sure what happened next only took a couple seconds. But for some reason I could see every little piece of it, even at the time, just like a slow-motion replay. I remember that I expected James to do something, but he didn't put up a fight at all. He just stood there, like he had no idea the bat swinging his way could break his skull wide open. So I knew that if we were going to move on to the next part of our journey, it would have to be me that did something. And all that something had to be was taking off my gloves and reaching out to touch these fellows, these men with their bare arms and shoulders, and both of them would be lying flat on the ground. After that they'd be in comas, all the things that made them *them* transferred into me.

It wasn't just because I didn't want their memories that I did not go straight to that course of action. Because even as this all happened so fast, and at such possible harm to me and James, I also didn't want two more bodies on my conscience.

You couldn't call it luck. But it did work out in our favor that I had Cody inside me, because Cody was fast, and strong, and knew how to use a baseball bat. So before the thug could connect with James, I stepped forward and kicked him in the stomach, my thick-soled boot protecting him from worse damage than losing his wind. The baseball bat clattered to the ground and I picked it up and held it over my shoulder.

The thug with the acne took a step toward me and I didn't hesitate, though I did hold back a little. I aimed for his knees, taking a low swipe like I was hitting a ground ball, and next thing both of them were lying on the pavement, but not for long.

"Get in the car!" I screamed at James, who had pretty much just stood back and watched the whole thing. I tossed the bat and dove for the driver's seat while he hustled around to the other side.

"Jesus Christ!" I yelled at him. "You think you could've helped me out a little there?" As we pulled out of the parking lot, I could see Gramps, standing in the doorway with a shotgun in one hand and a phone in the other. You could bet when the local police arrived they wouldn't be hearing our side of the story, and I knew I'd better hightail it out of West Virginia as fast as humanly possible.

"I'm sorry," James said, after a few minutes had gone by. "I just had no idea. I couldn't see it coming, not until it was happening."

"Look," I said, trying not to yell, "I don't know how things work where you come from. But around here you can't flash money around like that. Got it?"

From the corner of my eye I could see him nod. I checked the rearview mirror for flashing red lights and felt slightly comforted. If the police hadn't started chasing us by now, chances were the incident hadn't been reported. Probably the guys who attacked us had as much reason as us to avoid the police. I took my eyes off the road for a second, because James's face had gone white, completely white, like something very serious grieved him.

"Next time I'll be prepared," he said. "I promise, Anna Marie. That's the last time you'll be the one protecting me."

I couldn't be so sure about that one, but I nodded to make him feel better. "Let's just leave it in the past," I said. The thing was, James didn't seem cowardly, or weak. He just seemed innocent. New. So I couldn't find my way to being angry at him, or even disappointed.

After a long silence in the dark car, the hum of the engine the only sound surrounding us, James said, "They were hungry. Those men. Weren't they?"

I thought of the great big plates of barbeque we'd seen them eat with our very own eyes. "Not hungry for food," I said. "But yeah. Hungry is the right word for sure."

"This is a very violent world," James said. His voice broke like he'd never noticed anything sadder.

And even though I hated to quote our near-assailants, I couldn't help myself. "Tell me something I don't know," I said.

BY THE TIME WE GOT TO PENNSYLVANIA, IT HAD BEEN DARK A long while, and I knew we should stop and get some sleep. I'd never stayed in a hotel in my entire life, but I figured the wad of cash that had made us targets would buy an awful nice room, so I pulled up in front of the one that I thought looked fanciest.

Something else I'd never done in my life? Sleep in the same room as a man. Thank goodness there were two beds is all I can say. While James went into the bathroom, I turned on the TV, trying to find some news. By now I'd stopped worrying about the men in the barbeque parking lot. And of course even if Wendy Lee were dead, and it was considered a murder, it seemed unlikely that the story would be on the news all the way in Altoona, Pennsylvania. So I gave up after a minute and decided to go downstairs and use the computer room I'd seen connected to the lobby. From inside the bathroom I could hear James running a tub. I knocked, trying to stop myself from wondering what state of undress he might be in.

"Yes," James said, from the other side of the door. I told him I was going downstairs to check the computer. "OK," he said, like we'd been married twenty years. "See you in a bit."

The hotel computer room had a window that overlooked the outdoor swimming pool. It was dark out there, but I could see the shimmer off the water. How nice would it be to slip on a bathing suit? The last time I'd worn one, I'd gone over to Emma Deane Wilford's house back in Caldecott. They had an aboveground pool in the backyard, and Emma Deane and her cousin and I had sat in the water wearing bikinis and drinking lemonade.

What would I have done different that day if I'd known it was the last time I'd ever get to do such a thing? Sit beside friends in the cool water, our harmless skin hovering next to and sometimes brushing against one another's?

I turned my mind away from those thoughts and went to the *Clarion-Ledger*'s website. Surely if Wendy Lee were dead — a respectable, churchgoing business owner assaulted in her own bakery — it would be front page news. But all I could see was a bunch of articles about the Baptists opposing gay marriage and the football stadium expansion — pretty much the same boring stuff I read anytime I picked up that paper, which wasn't very often. I clicked on the obituaries. Nothing. Of course there hadn't been any obituary for Cody either. Not yet, anyway.

• • •

BACK IN THE HOTEL ROOM, JAMES SAT ON ONE OF THE BEDS, bundled up in a white robe, flicking through the channels. He'd cranked up the radiator so it was good and musky in the room. I sat down on the other bed, my feet on the floor, my knees just a few feet from his bare elbow. I took off my jacket. It felt good being with someone who knew not to touch me, even if he didn't know why. I tried not to think about all the things I suddenly knew how to do, things I'd learned from Wendy Lee, and what all would happen if I reached over and pulled that robe off him. James flicked off the TV and tossed the remote onto the bed.

"That was quite something," he said. "The way you handled yourself back there. With those men."

I knew he meant it as a compliment, but I sure didn't feel like saying thank you. "You mind if we don't talk about it?" I said instead.

"Sure," he agreed. And then, out of the clear blue sky, he said, "You don't look like an Anna Marie."

I snorted. "Really. Sorry to tell you I've been an Anna Marie since the day I was born. What all do you think I look like?"

"I'm not sure. I'll have to think about it."

I smiled. Then I did something I hadn't done in the presence of another person in what felt like forever. I took off my sweater. I had on a tank top underneath, so it's not like I was naked, though considering the change that came over James's face, you might have thought I was. He wasn't shy about letting his eyes roam across my bare shoulders, my collarbone. I closed my eyes and imagined his hands doing the same. But not for long.

"Hey," I said, coming to my senses. "Aren't you ever going to ask me why I'm on the run?"

"Aren't you going to ask me why I am?" he answered.

This took me by surprise. I hadn't thought of him as on the run. I thought of him as the person helping me escape. Probably it had to do with being on my own so long, not having to worry about anyone else.

Or maybe because he'd seemed like such a misfit — such a visitor — there in the first place. I'd forgot he must have reasons all his own for just up and driving out of Jackson.

"Well then," I said. "Why are you on the run?"

"I can't tell you that." He put his hands behind his head and kept on looking at me, like I was a great big milkshake he wanted to slurp right down. He had this real nice twinkle in his eye, and it was hard to imagine he was running from anything.

"So, Anna Marie." He said my name like it was the most ridiculous thing in the world, like I was named Hydrangea, or Moonbeam, or some such nonsense. "Why are *you* on the run?"

I took a deep breath. For all James didn't seem to mind the thought of scamming the welfare office, or stealing from a bank, he didn't seem like the kind of person who'd cotton to hurting anyone, especially if I took what had happened in that parking lot as an example. So I needed to choose my words real carefully.

"I think I might've hurt my old boss, Wendy Lee," I said. "Not like those guys in the parking lot. I mean, not on purpose or anything. On accident. But the police might not see it that way."

"You think you hurt her, but you're not sure?"

"Yeah. That's what I was doing just now. Trying to find news about her in the paper. When it happened, I got so scared I just ran off. That's pretty much when you found me."

"Huh," James said. "Why don't you call her?"

"Call her!"

"Sure." He jutted his chin toward the hotel phone on the nightstand in between us. It had about a million buttons. "That's a phone, right?" Anyone else I would've considered this a figure of speech. But with James, I couldn't be sure he actually *did* know for sure that was a phone. "Just pick it up and give her a call. See if she answers."

He took his hands out from behind his head and rested them on his bare stomach. I didn't know Wendy Lee's number at home, but of course in the morning I could just call the bakery. No one up there knew my voice so well that I couldn't disguise it a little. If I asked for Wendy Lee, they were sure to let me know something about what'd happened to her.

I stood up and crossed over to the window, feeling James's eyes on my every move. I pushed the heavy, green curtains aside and looked down at the pool. It had to be close to midnight, and not a soul was down there. The clerk who'd been at the desk looked about fourteen years old. Probably he'd just sit in the office reading comic books, not paying much attention unless someone wanted to check in, which at this hour seemed unlikely. Altoona seemed to me a whole lot sleepier even than Jackson.

"You know," James said from the bed, "I think I'm finally getting used to this climate."

"That's because you got the temperature in here at about a hundred and ten degrees," I said. "I think I might go down for a swim."

"Want me to come with you?"

"No," I said. I let the curtain fall shut. "It's only about eighty-five degrees down there. You'd probably freeze to death."

NOBODY WAS AT THE POOL. THERE WERE ORANGE HALOGEN lights all around it, kind of half-lit. I'd been living so carefully, keeping myself so much under wraps. Now I felt reckless. Reckless enough, anyway, to shimmy out of my leather pants, and the sweater I'd put back on for the elevator ride. It didn't seem to me there were many people staying at this hotel; I couldn't see any lights on in the rooms, except for one on the third floor where James must still be lying on the bed, flicking through the channels. In my tank top and panties, I dove right into the deep end.

That water felt so good on my skin, clean and cool and crisp. And familiar, like a hug from an old friend. So what if I was on the run?

I was traveling! I was in a northern state. And I was swimming. Maybe life didn't have to be so lonesome and pleasureless after all.

I lay back into a dead man's float and stared up at the stars. They twinkled back at me. *Where you been so long, Anna Marie?* they seemed to ask. I smiled.

My eyes wandered back to the hotel, back to that one lit-up window. And I saw a figure standing there, all bundled up in his white robe, looking down at me. He lifted his hand and waved.

Making the barest little splash, I moved out of my float and treaded water. This was the closest I'd felt in ages to that girl I'd left behind in Caldecott. I stared back up at James, those cat eyes of mine adjusting to the dark and distance with no trouble at all.

The cotton tank clung to my skin. It felt itchy. It was getting in the way. So I pulled it up over my head and tossed it aside. It floated on the surface of the water for a moment, then started heading down to the bottom as it got more and more waterlogged. Myself, I let my arms fall out by my sides, and leaned my head back, returning to my dead man's float. I could feel my breasts, bobbing just a little bit out of the water. Better than that I could feel James, standing up there in the window, looking down at me.

When I got back upstairs, the room was dark. James lay in bed asleep — or at least pretending to be asleep. His breathing sounded a mite too shallow to be convincing. I tiptoed into the bathroom, quiet as I could.

WITH THE DOOR CLICKED SHUT BEHIND ME, I PEELED OFF MY wet clothes and hung them over the shower door to dry. Then I toweled myself off. James had left one of his many layers, a white T-shirt, hanging on the towel rack. I pulled it down and brought it to my face. Breathed in. It was nice to smell him up close like this, not from across a room or the seat of a car. He had a good scent, nicely spicy, like ginger and jasmine mixed together with baby shampoo, and just enough sweat to make that manly. I pulled the T-shirt over my head, brushed my teeth, and headed on out to bed.

I really can't begin to tell you how much I wanted to crawl under the covers with James. At the same time it felt so much better than anything had in a long time, sleeping in a room with somebody else breathing, wearing somebody else's clothes. It felt so personal. My throat filled up with a kind of sadness. I hadn't realized just how lonesome I was.

Bam! Crackle!

Even in the dark room, with my eyes shut, I could see the blinding white light that suddenly surrounded us. The crackling kept going, softer now, like something electric had shorted out, or else lightning had struck right in the middle of the room.

James was on his feet before I could open my eyes. By the time I sat up he was already gathering his things, throwing them into his little leather satchel.

"We have to go," he said. *"Now."*

Even a curious person like myself could see this was no time for questions. Obedient as I'd never been in my life, I threw on all my clothes, including gloves underneath one of my new sweaters, and shoved everything into my duffel bag.

"No," James said, when I started to head toward the elevator. And it was a good thing I'd taken the time to gear up, because in his frenzy, he reached out and grabbed my arm. He had big, powerful hands, and his fingers closed full around my upper arm. He looked down at the contact for a moment, taking it in, and I could tell he thought maybe I'd been lying to him.

"Not that enclosed space," he said. "We'll take the stairs."

He let go of my arm and we ran down the hall in the other direction, down the stairs, and out into the hotel parking lot. James got into the driver's seat and turned on the ignition. The car made a terrible, whining, downright pathetic sound. And then it just sputtered and died. I looked up through the windshield at the window of our room. Neither of us had turned on the light, but something in there was crackling and flickering, like fireworks being set off indoors.

I unzipped my duffel bag and pulled out the screwdriver I'd packed when I left my apartment in Jackson. "Not to worry," I told James, holding it up in the dark car. "I've got it covered."

BEFORE, IN MY MIND, I'D BEEN HEADED TOWARD MAINE. THAT was a place I'd always wanted to see. I'd never seen a lighthouse or the ocean, or eaten a lobster. And I'd always heard how cold it was, so maybe even in the summer I wouldn't be broiling to death wearing all these clothes. But I figured the best thing to do when someone's chasing you is to change up your direction, so I headed west on 80. Maybe I could shift back a little later and head northeast again.

My heart was beating fierce and fast, and James had turned this shade of white that reminded me of the waxy magnolias that grew all around Caldecott. We'd taken the first car we saw, a little blue Scion that was hardly bigger than a golf cart. Bucket seats, which I guess were safer, but seemed kind of lonesome after that ratty old bench seat in the Camaro.

"It's OK," James said. "We got away in time. The tracking might not even register. Having you there probably confused it."

"Tracking?" I said. "Is that what that was?" The word shouldn't have comforted me, but it did. It sounded technical, like an electronic device, and not so supernatural as how the eruption of light had felt.

"Yes," he said. "The people I'm running from. They're pretty . . . sophisticated."

I nodded and kept my hands square on the wheel. Clearly James wasn't telling me everything, but I didn't mind so much as you might think. The whole thing was coming together in my mind, and starting to make some kind of sense. Another girl might not have jumped to the same conclusion so easily. But after all I'd been through, it didn't seem like much of a leap.

"James." I said it pretty careful, because if I was wrong he might get offended. But I had this strong feeling I wasn't wrong at all. "You're from a different planet. Aren't you?"

He sat quiet for a full minute. Finally, he nodded. "Yes, Anna Marie," he said. "Yes I am."

·4·

WHEN I WAS ABOUT TEN YEARS OLD, THE PREACHER AT AUNT Carrie's church, Reverend Otis P. Johnson, made plans to wallpaper his front hall. He lived in a big old house on Main Street, just a few doors down from his church, and that hall went all the way down from the front door, past a living room on one side and a sitting room on the other (don't ask me the difference), past a powder room and on down to a great big kitchen. In other words, there was a whole lot of wall. Before they started into pasting on the new, stripy wallpaper, he invited all the kids in the congregation to come over and draw on what it would cover up.

Aunt Carrie was real conflicted. On the one hand, drawing on walls was the sort of habit she'd worked hard on ridding me of, and I had the welts to prove it. On the other hand, it was an invitation to Reverend Johnson's own home. We folks living on the outskirts hardly ever got invited to the homes in town, especially not the preacher's. So in the end Aunt Carrie couldn't resist letting me go, knowing all the while she'd be setting in the kitchen, drinking coffee and eating baked goods with Mrs. Johnson and her friends. So Aunt Carrie loaded up a basket with fruit from her own garden, and even bought me a brand-new box of sixteen Crayola crayons. I remember that last part very well on account of in the past I'd only ever had the box of eight classic colors. This box had burnt sienna, plus a particular shade of red called razzmatazz.

While the other kids drew pictures of dogs and horses and dinosaurs, I set to drawing a great big razzmatazz spaceship. Underneath it I drew lots of green grass, and some black-eyed Susans. Two people stood on the grass — a lady with marigold hair and a man with burnt sienna hair — kind of bathed in a classic yellow light that was shooting out from the ship. And off away from the light there was a little girl with the same burnt sienna hair as the man.

"What's happening in your picture, Anna Marie?"

I turned from my work to look at the very serious, very chubby face of Lula Johnson, the preacher's daughter. She would've been about four years old at the time.

"It's my mama and daddy," I told Lula. "You see? It's their last day on Planet Earth. This spaceship's come to take them to the Far Banks."

Lula opened her mouth to ask what the Far Banks were, but before she got a chance — let alone before I got to answer — Aunt Carrie came flying out of the kitchen like an angry crow. She grabbed my wrist and dragged me right out of the house. I guess we were about halfway home before she realized that by doing so, leaving her half-eaten pickled peaches and her cold cup of coffee behind, she'd brought a lot more attention to my drawing than if she'd just ignored it.

"What comes into your head, Anna Marie?" she said. My butt was already stinging just looking at the way her knuckles had turned white on the steering wheel.

"I dunno," I said, slumping in the seat. No way on God's green earth would I let her know I was scared of her. Even when I was ten I knew it was unfair, and mean, to get angry at a kid for thinking on how her parents left the world.

"Was it Uncle Gillis told you about the Far Banks?" she said.

Uncle Gillis had come to visit a few weeks before. He was my daddy's older brother. He told me that back at the commune, my parents got it in their heads to go to this other realm, a mystical place called the Far Banks. That's how they disappeared. Trying to get there.

Without waiting on an answer from me, Aunt Carrie muttered, more to herself than me, "Gillis had no business to do that."

"But Aunt Carrie," I said. "It's my own mama and daddy. Why can't I know what happened to my own mama and daddy?"

"They were foolish and godless and that got them into a whole mess of trouble," Aunt Carrie said. "That's all you need to know."

After another minute she added, "I can tell you one thing. They didn't go anywhere in a spaceship." Her voice had got kind of dreamy, a little bit softer than usual, and I could tell this was a good time to keep asking questions.

"Well how did they go?" I pressed her.

"I don't know how to explain it. They just . . . went."

"Disappeared right into thin air?" By now we'd pulled into our own driveway. Aunt Carrie shoved the car back into park like she'd remembered she was mad.

"People don't disappear into thin air, Anna Marie," she said. She didn't look at me, just sat there frowning through the windshield. A mess of Canada geese had landed on the pond. I waited for her to tell me to go on into the house and get the belt. But she didn't. She just sighed and told me to go to my room. I hightailed it in there before she could change her mind, then lay on my bed, staring at the ceiling, trying to think on how two grown people could just vanish into another realm.

No, I decided. They must all have it wrong. It must've been a spaceship that came to fetch them away.

SO YOU SEE IT WASN'T ONLY ON ACCOUNT OF MY AFFLICTION that I could make that leap, to James being from another planet. Long before that kiss with Cody, I had it in me to believe that life wasn't just what you could see with your eyes. Other things went on. Things you couldn't make sense of with logic or even religion. Not just magic things, but unexpected and unexplained.

When James and I had driven on through the darkness, past morning into midday, he started to relax a bit. Before that I'd felt so bad for him that I'd even cranked the heat myself — I had to struggle out of my jacket and sweater as I drove to be able to stand it.

By noon he said, "If they haven't found us now, I think we can comfortably assume they lost track. It took them weeks to find me. So even if they cut their time in half, we've got a little room to breathe."

"But James," I said. "Who's *they*, anyhow? And what happens if they find you? Us."

"It's a long story," James said.

I threw my hand out to point at the highway, stretching on endlessly into the day. "Sugar," I said, "we got nothing but time."

"Let's eat first," James said. He pointed to a GAS-FOOD-LODGING sign up ahead on the right, and I eased the little car over into the exit lane.

BY NOW WE'D REACHED A TOWN CALLED LA PORTE, INDIANA. I drove the little Scion all the way to the end of a road where there was a sports bar on a lake. Now, I've seen plenty of lakes in Caldecott County, and the bayou, too. But this lake looked more to me like I'd imagined the ocean. It went on and on so far you couldn't see the end of it. James and I sat by a big window, looking out at the water, and ordered a couple plates of chicken wings.

"Well," I said. "I guess I don't need to ask what the temperature's like where you come from." James sat across from me, all bundled up and shivering a little, while I was sweltering in my sweater and jacket. You never did know when a friendly waitress might want to pat you on the back, so I had to keep covered up no matter what.

James laughed a little, but he looked tired and worried. We hadn't got a chance to sleep at the hotel, but the adrenaline of escaping and discovering my companion was an extraterrestrial being had perked me up quite a bit. I decided I'd save questions about why he was on the run for later and stick to more general topics. Maybe it would make him feel comforted, talking about his home.

"How'd you know to bring warm clothes?" I said.

"I didn't," he said. He didn't go into more of an explanation, so I figured he must have stolen them. Judging from that long leather jacket, he'd stolen them from a very nice place. But before I could ask anything more, he said, "The thing is, I can't talk about it too much. Up till now they were tracking me through the universe. Now they've got it narrowed down to one particular place. Things like key words, pertaining to my situation, can help them zero in."

Something in my stomach bottomed out. For a moment I felt almost as scared as I had when Cody'd hit the ground under the tupelo tree. It must have shown on my face because James said, "Look, it sounds a lot easier, but they still have to travel back and forth to get the right bearings. It takes time. If we keep moving, we should be able to stay ahead of them."

"What will they do if they find you?"

Something kind of funny came over James's face. It might have been fear. But it might have been something else. You know the look a man can get when you ask him a question he doesn't want to answer?

"Let's not worry about that right now," he said. "Let's just concentrate on staying a few steps ahead of them. And the best way to do that is not talk about it."

"What if we write it?" I said. "I can write questions on a piece of paper and you can write the answers."

His eyes got the tiniest bit narrow, then flickered away from me, in a way that made me think his answer might or might not have been the truth. "Language is language," he said. "I'm telling you, the less we say about it — by any means — the safer we'll be."

"But how can they even understand?" I said. "You say language is language. You speak and read English so perfect. That can't be the same language as on your planet."

James reached into his pocket and pulled out what looked like a tiny red marble. He put it on the table between us, and when I looked closer I saw it wasn't a marble at all, but a little dot of energy, shot through with shades of yellow and orange, spinning away. "It's a translator," James said. "Carry it with you and any language sorts itself out in your brain, written or spoken."

That made sense of it then, how come James could speak English so well but not know words for things they must not have on his planet, like fans and air conditioners. I wished I'd had it when I took that AP Spanish exam.

"I should get rid of it now," James said. "Since I've got the language more or less down. It's just one more thing that makes it possible to trace me."

Remembering that crack of light, and the look of terror on James's face, I said, "Well then for sure. Let's get rid of it."

AFTER WE FINISHED EATING, WE WALKED OUT TO A PIER. JAMES let me hold the little red ball in my hand a minute. I wished someone would start speaking French or Chinese so I could see how it worked. It felt like a damn shame to toss such a useful device.

James knelt down and stuck his finger in the water. Then he tasted it. He looked surprised. "Salty," he said. "Is this an ocean?"

"No. I think it's one of the Great Lakes." Honest, I'd never seen the ocean before, and this looked so much like I'd pictured it — sandy shores and everything — I didn't feel entirely confident in my answer. I wish I'd paid more attention in my geography classes, although I had paid enough attention to know there weren't supposed to be any oceans in Indiana.

I raised my hand in the air and pitched the little ball of light out into the water. For a second the waves above it turned red, yellow, and orange. Then the light narrowed and petered out altogether. Once I realized it was gone I felt a strong wave of fear. "Are you going to be able to understand me now?" I asked James.

He smiled. "Sure," he said, and tapped his temple with one finger. "I'm a fast learner. It's all up here now."

I let out a good long breath, relieved that I could add "fast learner" and "linguist" to James's growing list of talents. "You got oceans where you come from?" I said.

"Where I come from, we've got practically nothing but ocean. Ninety-five percent of the planet's surface."

"You must be good sailors," I said, and he laughed.

Then he said, "Anna Marie. Back at the hotel. When I grabbed your arm . . ."

He was still kneeling down on the pier, and he looked up at me, those great big blue eyes, looking like he'd got his feelings hurt again.

"Well the thing is," I said. "The problem, I mean, is my skin. You can't touch it, not with your own skin. But it's OK if you touch me and there's some kind of barrier. Like our clothing."

He didn't ask why, and that made me glad. I wasn't ready for him to think I was some kind of monster. He just said, "So I *can* touch you if there's something between my skin and yours."

"Yes," I said. My voice suddenly sounded like a big old toad had hopped into my throat. "You can."

James stood up. He looked down into my eyes, and I could tell he wasn't thinking about his home planet, or who was chasing him.

"Good to know," he said, and I decided one of my favorite things about him was that little bit of devil in his eyes.

JAMES AND I GOT OURSELVES ANOTHER HOTEL ROOM. HE FELL on his bed, totally spent, almost as soon as we walked through the door. I hadn't got any more sleep than him, but I still felt jumpy, so I went downstairs. Across the street from the hotel was a gas station, and I went over there and bought myself a phone card. Then I used the pay phone outside the store. It took three rings for someone to pick up.

"Sunshine Bakery," said a man's voice. I didn't know who all it was, but then I never had been permitted to spend much time aboveground.

"Hello," I said. "May I please speak to Wendy Lee?"

There was a very solemn kind of quiet on the other end. My heart dropped clear on down to my toes, leaving a scared, empty place in between.

"Who's calling?" He sounded just a tiny bit suspicious.

I reminded myself that there was no way he could recognize my voice. I said the first name that came into my head. "This is Emma Dean Wilford. I spoke to Miss Beauchamp a week or so ago about maybe ordering a cake for my wedding."

"Well honey," the man said, suddenly sweet as sugar. "I'm sorry to tell you this. But Miss Beauchamp, she's had . . . an accident."

"Oh dear," I said, sounding just like prissy Emma Deane. "I do hope she'll be all right."

"Only the Lord knows," the man said. Suddenly I recognized his voice. Not that I'd ever met him. But I heard him with Wendy Lee's ears. She'd hired him a year ago to work the register and take cake orders. He had a wife and three children at home, but that didn't stop him and Wendy Lee from closing the door behind them in the dry pantry downstairs. I shut my eyes against the image of his great big bare belly and tried to concentrate on how Wendy Lee was doing now.

The man went on talking. "She's been in the hospital for days," he said. My heart traveled back to my stomach and started in fluttering. I thought he should sound a whole lot more cut up about it, considering what all the two of them had done together.

"What's wrong with her?" I blurted out. I wanted to say, *Is she in a coma?* But that didn't seem like a question a normal wedding cake customer would ask. Probably bad enough to ask what was wrong.

"She was attacked," said the man. "By a disgruntled former employee."

"Why, that's terrible," I said. And then I said again, "I do hope she'll be all right," hoping he would translate this to *Tell me what's wrong with her.*

This man, Curtis was his name—I could hear Wendy Lee's voice giggling and simpering, *Oh, Curtis*—Curtis didn't need James's little red ball to read between the lines. He said, "The doctors can't say yet if she'll wake up. They can't say she won't though, so we're putting our faith in small miracles."

I DIDN'T THINK I'D BE ABLE TO SLEEP A WINK, BUT WHEN I crawled under the sheets back at the hotel it came over me like someone pulling me underneath the water. It was only about mid-afternoon, and the last thing I saw was orangey daylight behind the thick gold hotel curtains.

Hours later, when I woke up screaming, the room was completely dark. I'd been having the dream. The same old dream I'd had what seemed like a million times before. Except this time it wasn't Cody in the dream but James.

The two of us had been out sailing on a wide, rumbling body of water. "I could swear this is the ocean," James said, and I told him no, it was just a saltwater lake. In my dream I remembered what I'd learned in school, that it was Lake Michigan, and that some of the smaller parts were salt water, just like the sea.

James smiled at me like I was the brightest creature on any planet, mine or his. He smiled at me like I was wise and beautiful and very desirable. I smiled back, hoping my smile communicated the same things his did. He reached out to touch my face. I knew I ought to stop him. But I wanted it so bad, to feel the palm of his hand against my cheek.

His hand came toward me, cupped lovingly. I knew I couldn't let it happen. At the top of my lungs I screamed "NO!" — in my dreams and I guess also in the hotel room. When I opened my eyes, someone from the other side of the wall was knocking their complaints. But I couldn't stop screaming, even though I knew it had only been a dream.

My eyes had started to adjust to the dark. And I saw James, sweeping from his bed over to mine. I could feel my hair, spilling down over my bare shoulders.

"No!" I screamed again, this time in real life, for real reasons.

But James had come prepared. He had the hotel blanket in his hands, and he spread it out over me. It covered my hair and my shoulders, and protected his hands as he wound it tight around me, and rocked me close, and even kissed the top of my head through the itchy fake wool.

I could feel his chin on top of my head. His arms around me were every bit as strong as I'd imagined they'd be. James leaned back against the headboard, and I leaned against his chest, still with his arms around me.

"James," I finally said, after a long time. "The name James. That's an American name. A Planet Earth name. It can't be your real one."

"No," he said. I could feel his lips moving against the blanket over my head.

"Well," I said. "What's your real name then?"

"You wouldn't be able to say it. Our speech is very different from yours."

I didn't want to argue with him, but I really wanted to hear his name — his real name. I wanted to *know* him, in a way I'd never known anyone else in the world. After a couple minutes of silence he must have been able to tell how much I wanted to know because he gave in, and made a noise that sounded a little like a song and a little like a very low whistle.

"That's beautiful," I said, and I meant it. The sound made my heart hurt a little, with its prettiness and also because I knew I'd never get close to imitating it. "Does it mean something?"

"It does," he said. "But you wouldn't believe me if I told you."

"Try me."

"It means touch," he said.

I sat up and turned my head to look him straight in the eye. "Touch?"

"Touch."

"No shit?"

He looked at me, perplexed, then smiled. Sure enough he'd got past needing his translator. "No shit," he agreed.

I flopped back down on his chest, the blanket firmly around me. I couldn't let myself fall asleep this way — it would be too dangerous. At the same time I couldn't give him up just yet.

Touch. Fighting hard to keep my eyes open so I could make this last just a little bit longer, I knew I never would call him anything else again. It didn't take long for him to fall back asleep, and worried I would do the same, I tore myself away and crawled into the bed where he'd been sleeping. I pressed my face hard as I could into the pillow, breathing in his fragrance like it was oxygen, and feeling the warmth he'd left behind like it was luxury.

WE DROVE OUT OF LA PORTE IN DUSKY MORNING LIGHT, HARDLY any other cars on the road. Touch took the wheel. As he pulled onto 80 West, the glove box flew open and the owner's manual fell out, along with an envelope of photographs from CVS. I leafed through them, all these pictures of some kind of office party. There were a lot of photos of one person in particular, this smiley brunette woman who looked about thirty. I figured it was her car, but when I looked at the little registration card it said "Franklin Faxon." That seemed like a funny name to me. Franklin Faxon must have a crush on this girl in all the photos. She could've been his girlfriend, but something about how she smiled at the camera, looking flattered but not totally comfortable, made me think she wasn't and never would be. Now on top of that he'd got his car stolen. How must he have felt when he came on out of the hotel and found it gone? Even if we did steal it as a matter of life or death, I felt awful sad for Franklin Faxon, and guilty, too. The car was so clean and neat. Everything about it screamed Man on a Budget.

Touch and I talked about it for a bit. According to the registration, Franklin lived in Napoleon, Ohio. Maybe he'd been in Altoona on business, or on the way from visiting someone. We decided we'd backtrack to Ohio and leave the car someplace in town, then send him a little postcard telling him where to find it. Then we'd get another car, which we'd also have to steal, but we'd take this car from a dealership.

"But that's stealing, too," Touch said.

"Yeah, but it's stealing from a corporation," I said. "We won't steal from a little lot, we'll go straight to a big dealer." I filled Touch in, on how bad corporations were on account of only wanting to make money and not caring about the people who worked for them, or the people who bought things from them. He nodded like he could take this idea personally. "Is there anything like that where you come from?" I asked. Despite my quick acceptance of the general concept, I couldn't quite bring myself to say *on your planet*.

"If you'd asked me that a few weeks ago, I would have said no," he told me. "But right now . . ." He let his voice trail off, like for some reason the answer had changed to yes.

IT WAS STILL AMAZING TO ME, AFTER ALL THE YEARS OF MY LIFE wanting to travel and see sights, how fast they were all passing me by in a blur of pavement and green grass. We got to Napoleon in the late afternoon and left Franklin Faxon's car in the parking lot of a Super Walmart store. Then we walked down along the busy main thoroughfare till we found a hotel to check into. Neither of us was hungry, but we both felt kind of restless, so we went for a walk beside this wide, pretty river. So far every town we'd stopped in had something neat — like this river, or that great big lake in La Porte — but nothing I'd seen had blown me away, or been different enough from what else I'd seen my whole life.

Oddly, Touch seemed to be thinking the same thing. He stared out over the water and said, "This is just like the rivers where I come from. I mean the landscape is different. It's colder, and there are a lot of trees I don't recognize."

He turned toward me, like he meant to say something else, then got distracted. He smiled, and looked me up and down, head to foot and then back again. I liked that feeling, that just the sight of me could derail him, get him off whatever subject he had on his mind. So I let myself smile back, trying not to think on how looking at me was about all he'd ever have.

Touch and I kept walking along the river. He told me how where he came from, it wasn't unusual at all to visit other planets. In fact one of the things Touch did there was build ships for interplanetary travel, and devices like the little red ball that translated for him.

"So, you're like an inventor," I said.

"Yes. I make things that let people travel places they wouldn't ordinarily be able to go. The device that brought me here . . ." He trailed off and looked around us, almost like he was worried someone would hear. "Let's just say I miscalculated."

TOUCH WAS ALMOST OUT OF CASH, AND HE DIDN'T WANT TO use the ATM at the hotel lobby, so we stopped at a gas station. You can bet the clerk kept a close eye on us, two freaky leather-wearing strangers. Good thing the two of us standing there blocked Touch's method of retrieving cash. He reached into his pocket and took out another tiny little ball. This one was blue. He held it out in his palm, then released it just in front of the slot where your card was supposed to go. The ball hovered for a moment and then whooshed on into the slot. The screen lit up, but didn't ask for any pin number or amount or anything. It just started spitting out twenties, one after another, a little pile of them getting fatter and fatter till I didn't think the tray could hold them.

"Touch," I said, elbowing him. "I think that's enough."

He tapped the card slot and the little blue ball flew back to him. He put it in his pocket along with his bills. On the way out we bought a Coke for me and hot tea for him, then started to walk back to the hotel.

"What about the food?" I said. "Do you eat the same sort of thing where you come from?"

"Pretty much the same," he said. "We've got the same kind of animal life, so the meat's the same, and the fruits and vegetables, too. Your preparation is more primitive. I can taste chemicals. But what about you? Now you know why I'm cold all the time. Are you going to tell me why I can't touch you?"

I put my hands in the pockets of my jacket. Although Touch had a big secret, there was no denying it, it seemed like it fell into a different category than mine. For example, he came from a whole world of people just like himself. Whereas I was the only freak like me anywhere in the galaxy. What's more, Touch might present a kind of danger in the form of that crackling light that had filled up our room. But the danger I presented came directly from me.

"I got a skin condition," I told him. The words sounded pretty hollow coming out of my mouth. By now we'd come back to the business section of town, all cement and stores and cars whizzing by. "If you touched me, you could catch it."

Touch cleared his throat. "I don't want to contradict you," he said. "But at this point I've seen a good deal of your skin, and the only condition it appears to have is extreme touchability. So you might have to provide a more convincing reason. If you really want me to keep my hands off you."

I stopped walking, and so did he. He smiled down at me. And because I wanted to make my point, make it clear, I closed my double-gloved hand around his arm, which was also covered in several layers of clothing.

"Listen," I said. "For now could you please just take my word for it?"

He stood there blinking at me, and I looked back at him with eyes that didn't even belong to me, not rightfully. But he nodded, as if he believed I were someone to trust, which made me feel a little sad. Then I noticed the store we were standing in front of. REI. Cody used to stock up on supplies there for hunting trips with his daddy.

"Hey," I said. "Let's go in here and put some of that money of yours to practical use."

• • •

AT THE HOTEL ROOM WE UNLOADED EVERYTHING WE'D BOUGHT for Touch at REI — different kinds of long underwear, a fleece vest, a down vest, and a down parka. Cold as he was, he hadn't quite got to a point where he needed the last, but it seemed smart to be prepared. No telling how long we'd be on the road or how far we'd end up traveling. I also bought myself a wool cap and a balaclava, which was a kind of wool hat that covered my whole head and face except my eyes. It might come in handy down the road.

"It's funny," I said to Touch. We sat on the hotel bed, on either side of the big shopping bag, sorting through the new loot so he could put his silk long underwear right on. "My whole family's from the south, but I always hated the heat. I always wanted to go somewhere cold, even see snow."

"Snow?"

I had to laugh. "I've never seen it either," I said. "Up north, where it's cold, in the winter, rain turns to snow. This white fluffy stuff." I showed him the tag on his down jacket, which had a picture of snow-topped mountains. Touch shivered just looking at it.

"That's how the rest of my family reacts when they talk about cold weather," I said. "But to me it sounds just glorious. Must be some kind of rogue gene, I guess."

Touch looked at me, real thoughtful. After a while he said, "I guess."

When he went into the bathroom to take a hot bath, I went downstairs to the lobby to use the computer. This time, I found what I'd been looking for in the *Clarion-Ledger*: a whole article on Wendy Lee and her coma, and the "disgruntled employee" who put her there:

When a bride in Jackson wants the very best, she knows who to call for her wedding cake. But summer orders are going unfilled as Wendy Lee Beauchamp lies lifeless in a coma, brought on by an attack from the night baker she'd fired just days before.

"We all knew there was something sinister about that girl," says Maybelline Morling, owner of the business adjacent to the Sunshine Bakery. "I was so glad to hear Wendy Lee'd let her go. And now this has to happen."

The article went on to give my name and a description. It said I was six feet tall (as if! Maybelline must've made this estimate, she was like a human Chihuahua) and considered "armed and dangerous." It also said that a phone call I'd made had been traced to Altoona, Pennsylvania, and since I'd crossed state lines the FBI might get involved. Dang. I guess I shouldn't have made that call. But how else was I to know what all had happened to Wendy Lee? And didn't it at least show I cared? Damn Curtis. Did he happen to mention to the reporters or police that I was asking after Wendy Lee's health?

By the time I got back to the hotel room, my heart hadn't slowed down at all, it was thwacking against my chest so loud I figured Touch could hear it from across the room. He stood there, wearing blue jeans and plaid and his new fleece vest. I could see the blue silk long johns poking out of his sleeve, and he also wore a wool skullcap over his long hair. I'd talked him into the hat. I had this memory of Joe Wheeler, Wendy Lee's ex, telling her the secret to staying warm is keeping your head covered.

"You feel better?" I asked.

"I do feel better," Touch said. "I feel like I'm getting used to the cold anyway, slowly. But these clothes help me along. They definitely do."

Surprisingly, just hearing his voice did what I thought couldn't be done: it made me feel calmer. I sank down onto my bed and took a deep breath. Where would I be now if he hadn't come rumbling up beside me in that old Camaro? I felt a deep wave of nostalgia for that car. Already I'd noted the Chevrolet dealer down the road. Maybe when we snuck over there tonight as per our plan, I'd see if they had a used one on the lot.

Touch hadn't turned on the heat this time, but of course he hadn't turned on the air conditioner either. It might not have been Mississippi anymore, but it was still summertime, and even in Ohio that meant it was much too warm for wool and leather. I took off my coat. Touch still stood over by the window. He pulled the curtains shut. Then he turned back toward me and kind of thrust his chin in my direction. He had a cleft in his chin; you could hardly see it on account of a day's worth of stubble. It was one of the sexiest gestures I'd ever seen, or even dreamed of.

"Go on," Touch said. "Keep going."

Maybe if my skin hadn't set into tingling I would've listened to him. At first it felt good, that tingling, but then it just felt so yearning to make contact, and so dangerous, that I couldn't stand it. I pulled my jacket back up over my shoulders.

"I can't," I whispered. "I really want to. But I just can't."

His face didn't move. He just stood there, stock still, blue eyes wide and impossible to read. Then he walked over and sat on the bed next to mine, what was getting to be our classic pose, sitting on different beds, face-to-face, our knees just inches away from touching.

"Rogue," he said.

"Rogue what?" I asked.

"That's what I'm going to call you. Instead of Anna Marie. After that rogue gene that keeps you from enjoying the heat."

Of course I could have taken this as an insult. Part of me, the contrary part, wanted to tell him he had no business changing my name. Then I thought on how the people who'd given that name to me — my mama and daddy — had disappeared searching for something they considered a whole lot more interesting than me. And I also thought on that girl I used to be, the one who dreamed of traveling, the one who had her skin exposed to the wide world because no harm but sin could come from it. That girl was a million miles and a million years away. She'd stopped existing the second Cody Robbins hit the ground underneath the tupelo tree. So why not give her a new name along with everything else? Rogue would suit me just fine.

I sat there on the hotel bed, Touch just inches away from me. He might as well have been five states away for all the chance I had of feeling his skin on top of mine. The way I wanted to.

"Rogue," Touch all but growled. "This is going to take some imagination."

I paused a minute, then nodded. I knew exactly what he meant. And while Anna Marie didn't have a whole lot of imagination to spare in that department, Rogue was starting to build up a whole, wide reservoir.

THE CHEVROLET DEALERSHIP WAS ON A STRETCH OF ROAD THAT had nothing but car lots, one after the other. Some were big brands, like Volkswagen and Toyota, and some were little secondhand places with cars that would likely break down soon as you got halfway down the street. They all had the same kind of lighting as the pool back in Altoona — wide and orangeish, casting shadows that were easy enough to slip through in the very early morning. Touch and I walked through the rows of Chevys like we were shopping, both of us bundled up for different reasons. I could believe Touch was getting used to the climate here because of the way I'd become used to wearing piles of clothes and being hot all the time. People, I guessed, were made for adapting. That warm night I even wore my wool cap, figuring it would at least cover up the white streaks in my hair in case anyone saw me.

"Let's go look at the used cars," I said to Touch. "We don't want to choose anything too flashy." Secretly, of course, I had my heart set on another Camaro, which had to be the Cody part of me. We headed onto the back part of the lot, where I saw something that made Cody's heart take over in full force. It wasn't a Camaro, but a cherry-red 1965 Mustang. Hardtop. Dang but I wanted that car.

"This one," I said. "Let's take this one." I put my hand on top of the roof. From what I could see it looked like original everything.

"I thought you said we didn't want anything flashy."

Dang. I'd thought maybe he wouldn't be able to tell. Like maybe this would be a modest vehicle where he came from.

"What do you drive where you come from?" I asked him.

"We don't really drive. It's a little bit more . . ."

"Sophisticated?" By now I had noticed that when Touch talked about his planet he used the word "sophisticated," and when he talked about mine he used the word "primitive."

He laughed. My duffel bag was slung over my shoulder, and I unzipped it to get my screwdriver. Anna Marie would never have taken a risk on a shiny '65 Mustang. She would've taken a Ford Taurus.

Bam! Crackle! Boooom!

It was about three times louder than when it happened at the hotel room. Along with the noise came a flash of bright, white light. Touch and I both hit the ground. We were on opposite sides of the car, but luckily I had a good view of him from underneath the Mustang's carriage. He had his hands on the pavement, and he had turned that same waxy magnolia color. But his eyes fixed on me, like he hardly cared about himself, and the most important thing was protecting me. It hit me that the two of us would have to trade off. When it came to threats in this world, like thugs in a parking lot, it was my job to protect him, and vice versa when it came to threats from his world. I could tell from the expression on his face that he meant to do just that, and scared as I felt in that moment, I also felt precious. I knew he wouldn't leave me behind.

Bam! Bam!

The orange hue from the manmade lights was completely drowned out by the wash of white brightness that had come with the noise, these great explosions of sound, and I couldn't believe the whole town wasn't waking up and running in this direction. The light itself, despite the great glare it created, didn't hurt my eyes at all. It only made everything around us super-clear — the darkness had disappeared along with the orange glow — clearer and more in focus than anything I'd ever seen. And then suddenly — so immediate I had no sense of them ever not being there with us — three figures appeared. As soon as they arrived the light went away, returning us to the haze of middle-of-night-on-Earth and regular old halogen lights.

My heart had stopped beating for a good minute. It started up again reluctantly, with an awkward sort of lurch.

Those figures — three men, I'd just had time to make out — started moving around the cars, searching. I guessed they were looking for Touch. They all had bare, muscular arms and long hair. I couldn't make out their faces, but they looked very determined, like they were on a mission, and they were headed directly toward us.

I pushed up on my elbows to get a better look at them. Then Touch did something I wouldn't have expected. He stood up. Wanting to follow his lead, I started to get to my feet, too, but he gestured to me to stay down. So I kept my belly flat to the pavement and wriggled underneath the car. From that position, I saw Touch walk straight toward the men with his hands up in the air. It wasn't a "don't shoot me" kind of gesture. More like a "listen to me" one. And then he started speaking in that whistly, unearthly language of his. It was hard to read the tones of a language that was so unfamiliar. But something about Touch's body language told me he was trying to placate the other men. Not only that, but he knew them, and his main goal was to divert attention from me, my presence. I inched my way farther underneath the frame of the car, hoping they wouldn't see me.

The men didn't look placated. They looked downright pissed.

They also looked cold. None of them was bundled up the way Touch was, which seemed like a good thing. Maybe being too cold could slow them down. The one in the middle, with blond hair, seemed to be in charge. He was kind of hugging himself as he talked, if you could call it talking — that musical rush of whistles, lower and harsher than when Touch spoke. Of course I couldn't understand what he was saying, but I could tell it wasn't very friendly. Touch answered, gesturing like he was trying to convince them of something. Then the guy to the blond one's right stepped forward. Touch stepped backward, real immediate, and I knew it was important — very important — that these people not get ahold of him.

But they didn't seem to want to get ahold of him. They didn't try grabbing him, or hitting him, or anything like that. The one who stepped forward was smaller than the blond guy, but he seemed a whole lot angrier. Something about his whistles and hoots sounded sharp and demanding. Touch stepped back again; probably he was working hard not to look back at me, give my location away. I wished he would say something in English so I could understand, but maybe that would be too dangerous.

Suddenly, as the smaller guy lectured Touch, the blond one turned his head sharply, directly toward me. As Touch stepped forward to stop him, the blond guy reached into his pocket and pulled something out, then threw it in my direction. From the way his fist closed and then opened, I thought for a second that he'd released a bird. Then I realized it was a big ball of flaming red light. When it hit the Mustang the whole thing crumbled above me in a blast of light. No noise, no explosion. Just a great, blinding flash of whiteness. And then what had been a beautiful, perfectly restored old car was no longer sheltering me, hiding me. Instead it had coated me with sharp, metallic dust. Above me there was nothing but air.

"Run," Touch yelled, still not looking back at me. "Just run."

Don't ask me when I got so obedient. Maybe it came out of not knowing what the hell else to do in the face of silent, vaporizing weapons. I started out in a crouch and then set to running, fast as I could, my footsteps pounding in my ears.

Behind me I could hear the three men speaking at once, yelling at Touch, who I guess was trying to prevent them coming after me. I didn't look back to see. By now I'd reached the Toyota lot. I ran around the building, pulling at all the doors in case one had been left open. No luck, so I started running again, toward the Jeep dealership.

And goddamn if just when I got there, those three men from Planet Touch stood right in my path, waiting for me. I skidded to a halt, with no time to wonder how the hell they'd got there when I hadn't even heard them running behind me. Since I didn't have whatever de- and rematerializing device they apparently did, all I could do was turn around and start running in the other direction. I don't know if I could accurately say I was capable of feeling relief in that moment, but amid all the panic I did feel glad to see Touch running toward me.

At the same time, somewhere inside me, I did manage to think: *Hey. They're supposed to be chasing Touch. So why do I get the feeling that they're chasing me?*

There wasn't a whole lot of time to ponder the issue, because before Touch got within twenty feet of me another of those orange balls came spinning in my direction. I put my hands over my head, ready to shatter into a million pieces, but Touch reached into his pocket and threw his little blue ball into the air. It was one of the best throws I've ever seen in my life. The blue ball hit the orange ball, and the two pieces melded in the air right over our heads.

"Catch it!" Touch yelled. I held out both my hands and the ball landed in my palms like it knew exactly what to do. Those three men were running in our direction, shivering all the while, and meantime a kind of warmth was pulsing through me on account of the swirling lights I held in my hands. For a second I felt afraid that I would dissolve and disappear, but then it was like the lights were speaking to me, and I knew exactly what to do. Touch wasn't running toward me anymore, he was running toward the Toyota building, and I lifted up my hand and threw the orange/blue ball at the front door. In that very instant the door disappeared, letting Touch through.

As I ran toward the open door, the three Planet Touch men seemed to be coming toward me in slow motion. Touch must have done something to them to slow them down. But from the way he was moving, that effect wouldn't last forever. I saw him scoop the little ball up off the floor and then dive behind the wheel of a Prius that sat in the middle of the display room. The next thing I knew, he was breaking glass walls the old-fashioned way: by driving right through them. The front wall of the dealership shattered, raining glass down on the car. I could feel a few shards scrape my face as I ran to the passenger seat. Touch floored the gas and we went flying down the road.

"How come they didn't just grab you?" I yelled. "How come they didn't just rematerialize right in front of us?"

"Rogue," Touch yelled back. "Do you ever stop asking questions?"

That shut me up for a minute, which made me remember that I needed to catch my breath. While Touch drove, he searched his inside pocket, then pulled out a gold ring — about half the diameter of a pie plate. He held it out in front of me.

"Grab on," he commanded.

I hesitated. It would bring our knuckles awful close.

"Grab on!" he yelled again. Through the rearview mirror I could see those men had disappeared, which I guessed meant they were going to reappear right in front of us, in the road, or maybe even in the car. This was no time to ask questions, or to argue. I grabbed on to the other side of the ring and closed my eyes. A whirling sort of sensation came over me, and for a moment I felt terrified that I had somehow touched him.

When I opened my eyes, Touch sat in the driver's seat, both hands on the wheel. I held on to the golden ring all by myself. I dropped it onto the seat next to me and brushed glass off my shoulders.

We were driving down the same road. That much hadn't changed. Now we were past the car dealerships, in the land of box stores and chain restaurants. But the light had totally changed, from dark to dawn, rays of the sun rising up over the pavement and the asphalt roofs. There were no tall, long-locked men to be seen anywhere. Except the one sitting beside me.

"What did you do?" I whispered.

"I bought us a couple hours," Touch said. "That's all." He pulled the car over to the side of the road. "I need you to drive," he said. "That took everything I had right out of me."

I wasn't exactly feeling chipper myself, but it didn't seem like the time to argue. We got out of the car and switched places. When I'd buckled myself in, I turned toward Touch. Somehow we'd made a silent agreement that for now, anyway, he was in charge.

"West," Touch said. "Drive west."

This surprised me since he hadn't seemed to know or care about directions up till now. I wasn't sure which road led directly west from here, so I headed south first, figuring we could cut over on 70 and start making our way west.

As I pulled onto the highway, the engine of the bright red and brand-new Prius revved high and the sun rose in earnest, shedding its light on the pavement, the trees, and the white lines of the highway. Car-wise, it's not like Touch had had a whole lot of choice. The Prius was red, but at the same time it was just a regular sedan, something like any soccer mom would drive, plus it would save us a whole lot of money and stops on gas. Soon as I had a chance, I'd pull over and rip the dealer price sheets off the window, but for now I couldn't stop checking the rearview mirror to see if those men were following us in a manner more *sophisticated* than this primitive vehicle. When I looked back at the dashboard, I saw the speedometer registering 94, and I lifted my foot up off the gas. It was important to remember that Touch wasn't the only fugitive in the car. If I got pulled over, that could be the end of our little road trip.

"Hey," I finally yelled. "You know how to travel in time?"

"Not really," he said. And then, because that was clearly a lie, he added, "It's complicated."

"Complicated," I whispered. By now I'd started to wonder if Touch's reasons for not talking about his past — not to mention what all he was doing here — were just a mite too convenient. "That ring," I said. At some point Touch had picked it up off the seat and put it back in his pocket. "It's some kind of time travel machine?"

"Some kind," Touch admitted, though I could tell he didn't want to.

"Listen," I said. "Listen. If that thing works. If you can travel in time . . ."

"I can't," he said quickly, sounding harsher than I'd heard him.

I sucked in my breath and tried to focus on the road. No matter what he said, I knew that golden ring could help me travel through time. I'd seen it with my own eyes, felt it with my own body. And if I could travel through time? That meant I could go back to Jackson, before I'd hurt Wendy Lee. Better yet I could go back to Caldecott County and stay away from Cody. Hell, I could go all the way back to the hippy commune and stop Mama and Daddy from trying to get to the Far Banks!

Touch must've been able to read the excitement building in my face. "Anna Marie," he said, and then he corrected himself. "Rogue. It's not like that."

"What?" I said. "Can you only go forward and not back? Is that it?"

"I don't know," he said. "I mean I do know, but not exactly. That's why I didn't take us any farther than a couple hours."

He took a deep shuddery breath. Then he put his hat back on and turned the heat up. I didn't stop him. I didn't even take my own hat off, though I was starting to sweat. Better to be uncomfortable than to risk not getting his explanation.

"You see," he said, "back home, I work for . . . I don't know what you'd call it here, but I work for, what we think of as . . ."

"The government?" I said.

He shook his head. "No. Not exactly. We think of it more as one whole. Arcadia, you might call it. A simple and peaceful place, where everyone has enough. Everyone fulfills his or her purpose. I come up with ways to travel. Our world is small. Very, very small, at least in terms of landmass. Like I told you, we're mostly water. Salt water. So I invent ways to travel on the water, and underneath the water, and sometimes to other planets. To get more resources."

"And also through time," I said. As I said it, for some reason, I felt newly afraid.

"Well, yes," he said. "But that's new. Not the concept of course — that dates back to our earliest poetry and fiction. But no one's ever done it before. I've been developing this device, and I brought it with me so it wouldn't fall into the wrong hands." He rolled his eyes, like he wanted to communicate exactly what was going on but didn't know how. "The thing is," he said, "we shouldn't talk about it. There are certain ideas, certain key words, that will lead them to us. Even in your language."

"OK," I said, and then added, "Just let me ask one question."

His face looked hard, but he nodded.

"If Arcadia is so peaceful, what's with those guys blowing up cars?"

"They don't work for Arcadia."

"But you do."

"Yes."

"You came here," I said, "working for Arcadia. And now those bad guys, the ones who don't work for Arcadia, want you to go back. Right? They don't want to kill you, but they want you back."

"Yes," he said. "At least for now. Eventually they might content themselves with killing me. But at the moment they want to bring me back."

"But you don't want to go back."

He paused for a minute. "Let's just say I don't want to go back with them."

"So how come it seemed like they were chasing me instead of you?"

He paused for the barest second, long enough for me to suspect that he might be putting together an answer for me. Then he said, "They brought firepower of their own. But I've got firepower, too. You don't. Maybe they thought if they caught you, I'd surrender."

"You made them slow down like that? You made it so they couldn't do that dematerializing thing twice?"

"Yes," he said.

I reached over and put my gloved hand on his shoulder. He jumped, like that surprised him a little. "Sorry," I said, drawing my hand back. "I didn't mean to startle you. It's just . . . I'm glad you're here. With me."

"Even though I might get you killed?"

I thought, *Just let them try.* Touch had this most worried look on his face, all scrunched up between his eyes. He had a little more color to him, but still looked pale.

"Can I see the ring?" I asked.

I expected him to say no, but he reached into his inside pocket and pulled it out. It looked very ordinary, not even particularly shiny. Touch stared down at it in his hands, like he didn't know whether to be proud of it or chuck it out the window of the moving car. "We'll hold on to it," he said, as if he was making the decision then and there. "I don't want to risk using it unless it's an emergency. Unless there's no choice."

"Hey," I said. "Hey, Touch."

"Yes, Rogue?" For the first time today he sounded kind of relaxed, kind of jokey. Like his old self.

"You don't have to worry about those men coming to get you. Know why?"

"Why?"

" 'Cause I'm here to protect you. Remember those guys in West Virginia? All I need's a baseball bat."

He smiled and nodded. In his head this was just a little joke, a flirty way of comforting him. Still, I could tell, it moved him all the same.

EXCEPT TO STOP FOR GAS AND SWITCH OFF DRIVING A TIME OR two, we drove straight through till the sky got dark again. All of a sudden Touch seemed to know where he was going. Not the names of the states or anything so specific as that. But he sure had become aware of the direction he wanted to go. "West," he kept saying. "Head west."

Much to Touch's relief, I'm sure, we drove back down into the sultry heat of Missouri, and made it almost all the way to Oklahoma. I wanted to figure out a way to slow down, to see some sights. Hell, to just go to a zoo or something! At least I'd seen that famous arc, driving through St. Louis, which I'd only ever seen in pictures. I pointed it out to Touch, and he'd perked up because I was so excited, but I could tell he wasn't particularly impressed.

We parked at a McDonald's just outside of Joplin and sat in the dark of the parking lot. Touch reached into his pocket and pulled out the blue ball of light whose special power was emptying out ATMs and making doorways disappear. I wondered what all else it would be able to do by the time we were done with it.

"The truth is," he said, "I should get rid of this, and the time travel ring. I'd hoped getting rid of the translator would be enough. But obviously it wasn't. And now this has absorbed one of their weapons."

"Isn't that a good thing?"

He shrugged. "I have no way of knowing what sort of advances they're making when they're not here."

"But listen," I said, "you already said you can't get rid of the time travel ring in case of an emergency. It's your last resort. A person on the run doesn't just toss his last resort. And as long as they can track you through the ball, you might as well hold on to the ring."

I reached out to put my hand over that swirling blue/orange ball. Touch stared at it a minute. Then he moved his hand over it, like that helped him figure something out. He closed his fist around it for a minute, and when he uncurled his fingers it was two balls again — the blue and the orange.

"Wow," I said. "You're like a magician."

He pushed the blue ball back into the inside pocket. Then he handed me the orange one. It made me feel uncomfortable holding something that could make cars and doors crumble. As it was, I started out with enough destructive power on my person.

"What am I supposed to do with this?" I asked.

Touch said, "Flush it."

He waited in the car while I went inside. In the bathroom that orange ball traveled through the eddy like some kind of supersonic toilet bowl cleaner. I expected the whole bowl to light up and maybe even disappear when the ball went down, but it didn't.

At the sink I splashed my face with water and stared hard into my own strange eyes. The rare moments I got away from Touch, all these doubts would come flooding over me about the various things he'd said, the way some of his explanations just didn't add up. I grabbed a paper towel and dabbed at my face. The paper felt hard and crackly. Probably my suspicions came from having Wendy Lee inside me, on account of her sorry history with so many sorry men — starting with that husband who seemed like he loved her and then jumped ship.

Back inside the Prius, I handed Touch a carton of fries and a Filet-O-Fish sandwich. That's what Cody always liked to order at McDonald's.

"Were you kind of rich, where you come from?" I asked. I bit into a fry, hoping I didn't sound like I'd mind if the answer was yes.

Touch sighed. "You know what?" he said. "I'm a little spent from talking about it all so much. Do you mind if we give it a rest? At least until tomorrow."

THE ORANGE BALL WAS GONE. ALTHOUGH CLEARLY WE WERE not in a position to get rid of that blue ball, we decided it was best to budget so we wouldn't have to use it for a while. So after Joplin we just kept on going, taking turns sleeping while the other one drove, and using the cash we had to buy gas. Truthfully the cash in Touch's pocket was more than I'd ever seen in one place in my entire life. This might not be saying much, but I figured it would keep us a good long while. In the light of day we could count our money, and then maybe buy a tent somewhere in town. Couple hundred dollars for a tent would save us a whole lot of money on hotel rooms. We could head into the wilderness and camp out for a few days, think about what our strategy should be.

Touch liked my idea of camping out. He thought maybe we'd be harder to trace the farther we got from civilization, and the less electricity that surrounded us. "It's obvious that they haven't put together any kind of command center here," he said. "They're operating from my world, which means they have more information than I do, and more resources. But it also means they're tracking across a great distance. There are enough variables to make it difficult. Not impossible, obviously, but difficult, as long as we keep moving."

By the time businesses started opening their doors, Touch and I had driven well through the night, all the way to Pueblo, Colorado. Now I was seeing something that looked a whole lot different than Mississippi. It wasn't as green for one thing, and for another, the mountains! I had never seen anything close to these kinds of mountains, looming up so high, all snowcapped even in summertime. Touch looked plenty impressed, too.

"Have you ever seen anything so pretty in all your life?" I said.

He looked over at me and smiled. "Not until lately," he said, and my heart did this little somersault. Then he looked back out the car window. "Actually," he said, "those mountains remind me of home. Minus the snow."

"Must be pretty there," I said, and he nodded.

We drove up and down the main street a ways and couldn't find an outdoor store, so we went to Walmart. In the parking lot we counted out what money we had left — a little more than two thousand dollars.

"Is that a lot?" Touch asked.

"Small fortune," I said. "We have to give up the fancy hotels, that's all. And right here's the right place to shop."

We loaded up our cart with a tent and a lantern, some sleeping bags, a cooler, and a bunch of food. I tossed a few artificial logs in there, too, since I never had been much good at making fires. As we passed the book section, I grabbed an atlas, which would come in handy — so far I'd just been zigzagging from one road to another, hoping for the best.

"Look," I said to Touch, standing in the checkout line. There'd been a whole mess of motorcycles in the parking lot, and the entire store was swarming with people wearing leather, so the two of us didn't draw as many stares as usual. "We can go here," I said, placing my finger on a big green spot that said SAND DUNES NATIONAL MONUMENT.

He looked real hard, like he wasn't sure, so I said, "It's west of here."

"Fine with me," he said, with a little shrug.

Sometimes being with Touch reminded me of my first days on the run from Caldecott County. I remembered how lost I'd felt, almost like I was in a daze. I cared about what happened to Cody, and I hardly cared at all what happened to me. At the same time I felt so scared about what the future held. All those feelings kind of butted up against one another, so it was like I didn't have any feelings at all. I just went numb. Almost like I'd become an animal, I only thought of living one minute to the next. Touch seemed like that, almost like he'd stopped caring about everything but the most basic survival. The only time he didn't seem like that was when he took a moment to look straight at me.

Touch took the wheel driving out of Pueblo so I could navigate — he said they didn't have maps like this where he came from, so he didn't know how to read one.

"TOTO," I SAID, AS WE DROVE UP THE LONG DIRT ROAD INTO THE national park, "I've a feeling we're not in Mississippi anymore."

Touch looked over at me like I'd gone and changed his name again. "It's an expression," I said. "From a movie."

Clearly they didn't have movies where he came from, because he got that quizzical look, with a line between his eyes. Suddenly I got to wondering exactly how old he was.

"So how old are you, anyway?" I said.

"Twenty-five," he said. "And how about you?"

"Eighteen," I said. "But shouldn't you know that? How'd you know my name, anyway, before I'd even told you?"

He laughed. "Nothing mystical," he said. "And I didn't use any otherworldly technology, either. I just went into the bakery and asked about you."

My heart sank. That made one more of us the police would have a description of.

"Look," Touch said. He rolled down his window. The land here was like nothing I'd ever seen in my life — rolling hills made up all of sand, surrounded by grassy meadows, and in the distance, those tall, rocky, snowcapped mountains. Just behind the road, in a wide and grassy meadow, about a hundred little creatures munched under the hot sun. They looked like deer, but they were smaller, more delicate, with little horns and white fur mixed in with pale fawn.

"Fleetdeer," Touch said. "We have them where I come from."

"You do?" I stopped the car. There was no one behind us, and I'd never seen such pretty animals before. A mile or so back we'd passed a sign that said PRONGHORN ANTELOPE CROSSING, so I figured that's what we called them here. I didn't mention that, though. Instead I said, "It's weird, thinking about this whole other planet that's so much like ours. How far away is it, anyway?"

Touch frowned like this was something else he didn't want to talk about. I'd noticed lately that he'd stopped saying "planet" altogether. Instead he'd say "world," or "where I come from." Sometimes I had the feeling he wasn't giving me anything close to the whole picture, and not necessarily for the reason he'd given me — that talking about it would summon his enemies.

"It's really far," he finally said, which didn't seem like a very scientific answer, but I decided to let it go. It wasn't exactly like I was telling him everything there was to know about me, either.

WE SET UP CAMP A WAYS PAST THE FAMILY CAMPGROUND, which was mostly empty. I realized that by now it was late enough in August that kids had started getting ready to go back to school. This worked out well for us — not so many vacationers to take notice of us. I channeled Cody's old Boy Scout days and put up our tent. We'd splurged and bought a four-person Coleman. That way I'd be able to set up some sort of barrier with pillows and maybe even the cooler, so Touch wouldn't accidentally roll into me during the night. Of course I'd zip myself tight into my sleeping bag, too, but I couldn't be too careful. The smartest thing would've been to buy two one-person tents, but I had to admit, I'd started relying on all this togetherness. I might not be able to actually touch him, skin to skin. But at least we could share the same oxygen.

While Touch walked around investigating the place, I laid out our sleeping bags in the tent. Later on I'd work on that barrier, but for now I liked the look of the two of them, lying there side by side.

Outside of the tent, it was fun just kind of bustling around — finding a place for the cooler and throwing an artificial log on the fire pit. I walked around collecting real logs and kindling, too, feeling like I was getting a little house in order for the two of us.

Touch came around the corner, dragging a pair of sleds. Now, we don't do a whole lot of sledding in southern Mississippi, but of course I knew what they were from pictures and movies and such. A blue sled and a red one. Touch handed me the rope for the blue one.

"I found these in one of the empty campsites," he said. Then he turned around and started trudging up toward the top of the nearest sand dune. I stood watching him a minute, then when I figured out what all he had in mind I trotted on after him, dragging my little blue sled behind me.

As a kid I used to dream of snow and all that I'd do if I ever got to it. Of course one of those dreams was sledding. Touch and I set our sleds at the very top of the sand dune. I watched him push off with a little whoosh and then go screaming down the hill.

"How do you stop?" I yelled after him. "How do you steer?"

All I got in reply was the wind and his happy shouting, so I just pushed off myself and hoped for the best. The wind blew back my hair, and hot sand blew up against my skin. I swear I left my stomach way back at the top of the dune, and before I hardly knew it I could hear my own screaming in my ear. But they were happy screams, scared and excited at the same time. When I was almost at the bottom, I saw Touch already out of his sled and standing there waiting for me. It seemed so certain that I'd ram straight into him that I put my feet out to stop myself, but I guess I was going too fast, and I ended up tumbling head over heels, then flying. I landed on the soft sand a good four feet beyond him.

"Ready to go again?" he said.

"You bet," I told him.

I COULDN'T REMEMBER A HAPPIER DAY IN MY WHOLE LIFE. WE dragged our little sleds all over the sand dunes, hardly running into another living soul. Most of the day it felt like the whole world had up and left the planet. Like Touch and I had inherited the whole place lock, stock, and barrel. If that had been the case, I would've been glad to stay just exactly where we were forever, climbing to the top of different dunes and screaming all the way down. By the time we made it back to our campground, my legs ached from all that hiking, and my skin glowed pink from all that wind and sand.

The cooler sat full of hot dogs and sodas and potato salad. I sent Touch off to find sticks for roasting the hot dogs, and I lit the paper on the fake log. Here in Colorado it was awful hot — almost as hot as Missouri had been — but at the same time the air was so dry I didn't mind it near as much. And now that the sun was on its way down, the air got about fifteen degrees cooler. Nice. I felt a little guilty thinking it was nice, as I saw Touch shivering his way back with two sticks, nice and green like I'd told him. But then the fire would take care of that.

He sat down on the log next to me. Not too close, but just close enough. I smiled at him, and he smiled back, and handed over the sticks. I set up our hot dogs and handed one back to him, and showed him how to turn it round and round over the fire.

"You know," I said to him, "if that was my last day on Earth, I couldn't think of a better way to spend it. I don't think I ever had more fun."

Touch had finished cooking his hot dog and was blowing on it so he could take his first bite. "We have a place like this at home," he said. "It's called the Sledding Sands. I always thought I'd take my son there someday."

When he said that, I thought he was speaking metaphorically, futuristically. The way I sometimes used to think that when I had a daughter I'd name her Lily and take her to Disneyland. So I just kind of nodded like I understood what he meant. I didn't say what I was thinking, which was maybe one day he and I could take *our* kid back here. It didn't worry me in the slightest, in my happy haze, that we couldn't touch. Who needed to touch to make a baby in these modern times? Hell, all we'd need is a thermometer and a turkey baster.

Touch loaded up another hot dog and set to roasting it. I'd barely taken my first bite. "It makes me sad being here without him," he said.

"Wait. You have a son? A real, live, actual son?"

He nodded. "He's six. His name is Cotton. I couldn't help thinking about him all day. He'd love this so much." Touch kind of gestured with his hot dog to show he wasn't just talking about the sledding, but the camping, the fleetdeer, the fire. All of it.

It hit me in that moment that no matter how many strides the science of fertility had made, a mother couldn't take care of a child she couldn't touch. Who knew if a baby could even survive inside my body?

"Touch," I said. "I know we haven't discussed the culture on your home planet. But here on Earth? When a man has a son? Generally speaking, he also has a wife."

I waited for him to get that foggy look, with the wrinkle between his eyes. *Wife?* he would say. *What is this word, "wife"?*

But no. Judging from the look on El Creepo's face, he knew exactly what the word "wife" meant, and it meant the same damn thing on his planet. I stood up, threw my hot dog into the fire, and marched on over to the car.

"Wait," he said. "Rogue."

I slammed myself into the Prius and crawled into the backseat. Soon as I found myself lying there, I wished I'd taken the time to get a pillow and sleeping bag out of the tent. Damned if I were getting out now.

Touch peered in through the window. He actually looked a little relieved, like he'd thought I was going to drive away, and now he realized I just planned on sleeping in there instead of in the tent. Thinking on how happy our sleeping bags had looked lined up next to each other, I almost let myself dissolve into a good, long cry. But hell if I'd do that while he stood out there watching me.

He banged on the window. "Come on," he said. "It's not what you think."

"Oh, what is it?" I yelled. "Doesn't she *understand* you?"

Wendy Lee's thoughts and memories filled my head. She'd had a whole lot of arguments exactly like this one. I put my hands over my ears, like that would drown out the sound of them. Then I closed my eyes, and felt the most powerful rush of sadness, remembering what it felt like to lose a baby.

Damn, damn, damn. My most perfect day of my whole life, ruined.

Finally Touch gave up and walked away from the car. After fifteen minutes or so I peered out the window to make sure he'd put out the fire. It was totally dark. I guess they had wildfires where he came from, too. Of course they would. Apparently it was just like here — with sand dunes and mountains and sons and wives and cheating husbands.

• • •

DON'T ASK ME HOW I FELL ASLEEP, BUT FINALLY I DID, JUST UN-fortunately not for long. I woke up about an hour later with my teeth chattering together, the first time I'd been cold in what seemed like forever. I hunted around the car for some kind of blanket, with no luck. Everything had been hauled out to the tent when I was playing house. Like a good little extramarital girlfriend.

I took one last, hopeful look in the way back of the Prius. Nothing there except the plates we'd taken off a car at the Pueblo junkyard. We'd have to remember to put them on tomorrow and get rid of the dealer's tags. Just thinking that word, "We," made me powerfully sad. I shivered. My breath came out in a thin little gust in front of me. If I didn't get into that sleeping bag, I'd freeze.

Touch hadn't slept a wink. I could tell that as soon as I unzipped the tent flap. He just lay there, with his hands under his head, staring at the nylon ceiling. Mad as I was, I still had no wish to kill him, so I moved around the small space with a whole lot of care. I didn't say anything, just zipped the tent back up and crawled very gingerly around him. I fished the balaclava out of my duffel bag, pulled it on my head, and crawled into my sleeping bag.

"You cold?" he asked. He sounded surprised, like he didn't think it was possible for me to be cold.

"Freezing."

"Here." I could hear him more than see him, taking his arm out from behind his head and setting to wrap it around me.

"Don't," I hissed. "Don't touch me."

"It's OK," he said. "I'm wearing gloves and—"

"Don't. Touch. Me."

"Oh," he said. Those hurt feelings again. "OK."

He pulled his arms back and put them in his sleeping bag, maybe to show he respected my wishes. For a while I just hunkered down in my sleeping bag, working on getting warm. When my teeth started chattering, I found myself wondering about his wife, what she looked like, how old she was, what kind of mother she made. Did he like her cooking? Now that I had all Wendy Lee's abilities, I bet I could cook better than her. I wondered what kind of job Touch's wife had, if she made a lot of money — or whatever the thing in his world would be that was the same as making a lot of money.

The only thing I knew for sure? Whoever his wife was, whatever she did, whatever she looked like, whatever her faults and failings, she could touch him, and she could let him touch her. They had a child to prove it.

"Rogue?" he said. By that time he must've figured I was never going to talk at all. "It's not what you think."

"That's what married men always say." I'd seen my share of soap operas, plus I had all Wendy Lee's experience bundled up inside me. He didn't answer, so I said, "What's her name? *Mrs.* Touch?"

"We're not together anymore."

"Oh." I hated to admit it, but this sounded promising.

"She's not . . . I can't explain it thoroughly enough. It's not safe."

"Anytime you don't want to talk about something," I said, "you say it's not safe. That's getting old, Touch. Mighty old."

Our tent was light blue, and through the ceiling I could see shadows of tree branches. The trees here were pretty, a lot of them looked like little birch trees, but with these tiny green leaves shaped like circles. I'd noticed them shimmering in the daylight, and now their shadows shimmered, too. In Mississippi, there'd be about a million bugs gathering on the outside of the tent. But here I didn't see any bugs at all, just the shadows of branches, and I felt like if I squinted I might see the stars, too.

"I like it here," I said, after a bit. "It's pretty. And it feels like . . . I don't know. Good spirits or something."

When I let myself look over at Touch, he was propped up on one elbow. His eyes looked darkly blue and troubled.

"I really wish I could tell you everything," he said. "Eventually I'm going to find a way to do exactly that. But for right now, let me tell you this. Where I come from, there's this thing, like I told you, called Arcadia. Nobody goes hungry. Nobody gets sick. Nobody has more than anyone else. You know how you asked me if I was rich? The truth is, I am and I'm not. I have everything I need, but so does everyone else. It's all equal. But it wasn't always like that. And some people — people who're descended from the people who ruled in the time before Arcadia — they want to make things the way they used to be. They want to bring us back to a time when some people had more than they needed, which meant that other people didn't have enough."

"So those men in the Chevy dealership?"

"They're working against Arcadia. It's the first time in five hundred years anyone's opposed it." Touch lay back down, but on his side, still looking at me. By now he had a few days' worth of stubble across his jaw. Even in this light I could see how sharp and sculpted his cheekbones were.

When he spoke again, his voice sounded very low, and also very matter-of-fact. It was a voice that conveyed simple truth. "If you could translate my wife's name into your language, it would be Alabaster. She's very fair, with pale skin and white-blond hair. Blue eyes. She's small. Like a pixie, I used to think. I've known her since I was a child. But we're not together now. And the reason for that is, she's one of the people working against Arcadia. That's why I don't want to know her anymore."

Inside my head, all Wendy Lee's memories told me not to believe him. She'd heard it a hundred times before and it never did turn out to be the truth. But there lay Touch, all earnest and so damn handsome. Besides which, my choice in the world was pretty much to forgive him — trust him — or be completely alone for the rest of my livelong days.

"What about me?" I said. "Do you want to know me?"

He smiled. A slow, sexy smile that just about melted me from the neck on down. "I certainly do," he said.

I pulled that balaclava over my mouth. Then I leaned forward and kissed him on the lips. Hard. It mostly tasted like wool. But beyond that I could feel his lips, and smell his breath, like being held just one step away from the most wonderful thing in the whole wide world.

I kept that balaclava up over my face, only my eyes showing. He threw his arm over my sleeping bag. And the two of us fell asleep, the first time in my life I'd come close to sleeping held up in someone's arms.

·6·

ROGUE. AS OF YET I HADN'T GIVEN MUCH THOUGHT TO THE NAME
Touch gave me. But the next morning in the tent, it was the first thing
that came into my head when I opened my eyes. Touch still lay sleeping beside me, and my heart set right in to thumping happily at the
sight of him. He had his hat pulled down almost over his eyes and his
sleeping bag up to his chin. We'd gone ahead and bought him the
most expensive one at Walmart. It cost eighty dollars and the tag said
it would keep a person warm down to ten degrees. His sleeping face
looked so dear to me in this morning light. I wished I wasn't so dangerous, so I could wake him up just by covering him with kisses. I ignored Wendy Lee's voice in the back of my head, warning me not to
forget about his pretty, blond, extraterrestrial wife.

Back in school, in biology class, I'd learned that a rogue gene was
some chance strangeness that nobody could trace. That's how Touch
had meant it when he gave me my new name. Probably he had no way
of knowing the word could also mean just a plain bad person. Aunt
Carrie used to use it for horses that spooked easy. To my ears "Rogue"
sounded a whole lot more like what I'd become than Anna Marie,

that harmless and obedient country girl I'd left back in Caldecott County.

Touch had very long lashes, especially for a guy. I lay there looking at him for a while, until they finally fluttered open. He looked like I was about the best thing in the world anyone had ever seen.

"Hey," he said. He took his arm out from his sleeping bag and wrapped it around my waist. Pulled me close to him, but not before I had a chance to slip the balaclava up over my face.

"Hey yourself," I said. It sounded kind of muffled on account of the hat. This time Touch kissed me. On the other side of the wool I could feel his mouth open just the tiniest bit. I had never even French kissed before (Cody and I didn't exactly have time to get to that level), and I knew that if I was normal, that's what we would be doing right at this moment. But Touch was mostly getting a whole lot of wool on his tongue. He pulled away and picked off a strand or two.

"Sorry," I said.

"That's OK." He pulled me close again, but this time just kissed the top of my forehead in a brotherly kind of way. The way he pressed himself against me, though, through our many layers of sleeping bags and clothes, was decidedly not familial. I could feel the outline of his body against mine, and I knew he could feel me, and all I wanted to do was press against him, here in the tent. It felt amazing for about one full minute, before I thought I'd probably go crazy from wanting to feel his lips on my neck. Hell, wanting to feel his lips *everywhere* . . . I sat up. Touch said, "Are you OK?"

"Fine," I said. "Just hungry." I crawled out of my sleeping bag and out of the tent, then stood up in the crisp morning air. There was still a tiny chill left over from last night, but the sun was on the rise and I could tell the day was going to be hot.

The truth was Touch still didn't know what all could happen if he *did* touch my skin. It hardly seemed fair to keep letting him get so close when he didn't know the consequences of slipping up. Hadn't

I already taken two innocent people unawares? To say nothing of that poor little kitten.

I PUT THE NEW PLATES ON THE CAR, THEN LIT A FIRE. I THREW IN my driver's license and library card for good measure. If the FBI really were looking for me, it was better to have no identification than the real thing. And as for that Prius, I figured we should make it look like it had had a few years on the road, not so shiny and new, so Touch and I went to work, rubbing sand all over the car, trying to muck it up and make it look dingy and old. I dented it up with a rock and scraped the paint clear off in places. We worked on it about an hour, and it sure did look like a different vehicle than the one we'd stolen back in Napoleon.

After that we ate some of the granola bars we'd bought at Walmart and went off for a hike. I carried a little backpack for water, plus I figured we'd want to shed some clothes along the way when the day warmed up. Or I'd want to, anyway. We walked all through the dunes, till I worried we wouldn't be able to find our way back, everything looked so much the same.

Sure enough, it got hotter and hotter, and I found myself shedding clothes one piece at a time, till I was hiking in my leather jeans and tank top, everything else stuffed into the little backpack. I tried taking my shoes off, but the sand was too hot to go barefoot. Touch, of course, kept most everything on, even his hat.

"Where's the nearest ocean to here?" he asked me.

"Not for a thousand miles, at least," I said.

He shook his head like this was beyond belief. "Where I come from, there's no place that's a thousand miles from the ocean."

"Really?" I said. "Would you believe I've never seen it? The ocean, I mean."

Touch looked over at me and smiled, and though he didn't say anything, I could tell he couldn't wait to show me the sea. Kind of funny, if you think about it, that he could show me something in my very own world that I'd never seen before. I wondered if that's why he wanted to head west, then had to remind myself that he didn't know which coast was which, or where.

Around lunchtime we came to a very pretty stream, kind of flowing through the dunes. There was only an inch or so of water, but after we followed it awhile, we came to a spot where it kind of spread out into a little pond. The water rippled across it, almost like waves.

BY THE TIME TOUCH AND I HEADED BACK TOWARD OUR CAMP-ground, I was starting to feel like Colorado — the Sand Dunes in particular — might just be paradise. Staying here forever and ever seemed like a perfectly grand idea. It wasn't like we had any place to go, anyway.

"Sounds good to me," Touch said, when I told him this plan. Then I thought of something I didn't have the heart to share: how cold it would get here, at this high altitude, once wintertime rolled in. But for now it was summertime, and everything felt just perfect. Hot enough for Touch, at least with his extra layers, and dry enough that I didn't feel like I was about to melt into a puddle at his feet. For the first time in my life, I didn't feel anywhere even close to lonesome. And all of our various pursuers seemed worlds away — some of them literally.

What in the world could ever go wrong?

And dang if I didn't know better than to ask a question like that. If it had been dark, we would've seen them sooner. As it was we barely had time to dive behind a juniper bush and crouch down low. Spinning, whirling police lights, parked in our campground, one officer giving that car a careful inspection and the other one on his hands and knees, getting a good old eyeful of everything that was in our tent.

• • •

TOUCH DIDN'T UNDERSTAND WHY I'D PULLED HIM BEHIND THAT bush. I put my finger to my lips, then turned in the opposite direction. Luckily we were camped close enough to woodlands that I could drag him back into the cover of pine trees before he said anything. The only thing I took a chance on saying, in a real hiss of a whisper, was "Those are the people who're after me."

We crept through the woods awhile, till clearly we were walking up on hard ground, away from the sand — the dunes lay behind us, far enough that we couldn't see them. The police hadn't heard us, judging from the lack of footsteps behind us, but it would be nice to get to a point high enough that we could maybe see our campground, and whether they were still there. We walked around toward the eastern side of the mountain, hoping that if the police set off looking for us they wouldn't think we'd go *up*.

Toward evening, we sat down to rest a bit. I pulled a package of turkey jerky out of my backpack and we each had a piece. Here's what we had with us: one outfit each, which in Touch's case meant leather pants, a sweater, a hat, and his long leather coat, plus gloves. Touch had his little blue ball and his golden time travel ring. We had one quart bottle of water, three-quarters already drunk. And we had the package of jerky, plus a map of the park.

Back at the camp we had a fuel-efficient vehicle. We had a tent and two sleeping bags, plus all the warm clothing we'd bought for Touch at REI. We had a cooler full of food, several gallons of water, and our atlas. Most importantly we had the big wad of bills we'd got from the ATM in Napoleon, Ohio.

"Tell me about the people chasing you," Touch said.

I sighed. "They're called police. They're in charge of law and order. You got police where you come from?"

"We used to. Hasn't been a need for them in more than two hundred years."

"Well, there's plenty need for them here. They round up people who steal cars and set up phony bank accounts, and put them in jail where they can't hurt anyone."

"Jail?"

"Trust me. It's a place you want to avoid."

Even though Touch already knew about Wendy Lee, at least in a general sense, I didn't want to tell him that might be why the police were checking out our campsite. Truthfully, they could be looking for the stolen car, or they could just be there because we'd forgotten to pay the campsite fee. But I knew in my heart that even if it were just the campsite fee, the discovery of one thing would lead to another like a row of dominoes, and I would end up hauled in for the assault — or for all I knew murder — of Wendy Lee.

I asked Touch what he thought about using the golden ring. We could go back a few hours and clear everything out of the campsite. He shook his head.

"Maybe if they were right on top of us," he said. "But using the golden ring to escape your police could summon the people who are after me. And that would be like jumping into a snake pit to escape a bumblebee."

A shiver went up my spine. Then Touch elbowed me. "Look," he said.

By now the sky had grown dark. Through the trees, down toward the dunes, we could see flashlights trundling along, searching. For us, no doubt. None of them seemed to be going close to the right direction. But that didn't give me a whole lot of relief, since it still meant we'd have to leave everything we'd accumulated — not to mention the carefree days we'd imagined in paradise — behind.

• • •

GOING UP FARTHER IN ALTITUDE, WHERE IT WOULD JUST GET colder and colder, was not a possibility. As it was, I couldn't be sure Touch would make it through the night, once the temperature dropped. Luckily I could see in the dark well enough to read the little park map. The mountain where we were hiding was called Crestone Peak. If we stuck to the base, heading west, there were a bunch of little towns where we could possibly wrangle a car and some food. Maybe even find an ATM and get more cash if Touch didn't think it was too risky.

We walked for hours and hours. The old me might have been scared of all the nocturnal critters that surrounded us. The sign at the Sand Dunes Welcome Center said that mountain lion footprints were often spotted, and no doubt there were bears around, too, working on bulking up for hibernation. I never had seen a real live bear, and wasn't keen on the idea in this particular situation. But I didn't let any rustling in the trees bother me. The rustling that concerned me most was Touch, his teeth clattering as we walked along.

"Here," I said. "Take my jacket."

"It's not going to fit."

I took it off anyway. Then I pulled my sweater over my head, seriously mourning that whole pile of them left back in the tent.

"But you'll be cold," he protested.

"Not as cold as you. And I don't think I can carry you all the way . . ."

I paused. All the way to where? It would be easier to make a plan if we had some kind of destination other than just *west*. So far we both knew what we were running *from*, but lack of knowing where we were running *to* made all our moves just kind of willy-nilly. Which didn't seem to be working out very well.

Touch took off his leather coat and put my sweater on over his — it pulled real tight but for sure would warm him up at least a little — then put his coat back on and buttoned it all the way up to his chin. I gave him my hat, too, figuring it wouldn't hurt to double up. I cursed the loss of my balaclava, not to mention everything I had in that green duffel bag, including my map of the United States.

Clearly Touch was still powerfully cold, but he said the extra clothes helped a little bit. Up ahead I could hear a running stream; probably it wasn't safe to drink the water (Cody's Boy Scout training, coming in handy again, told me that I needed iodine tablets if I didn't want to get us sick), but I thought it might be a good idea to follow its direction. Before we got to a stream, we came upon this little pool. I knelt beside it, took off my gloves, and dipped my hands in so I could splash my face with water.

Fast as possible, I drew the hand out. The water was downright scalding. Right at that moment, I heard Touch stumble behind me, shivering something fierce. Somewhere in my head, one of us — me, Cody, or Wendy Lee — had heard about these natural hot springs in the West. Now I squinted through the dark, watching steam rise off the top of the water.

"Touch," I called. He looked to be on the brink of hypothermia. Something would have to be done about this temperature situation.

I marched on over to him and slipped my arm through his elbow. "Look," I said, pointing to the pool. It was just big enough so that he'd be able to submerge right up to his neck.

I don't think I ever heard a sigh so grateful as when Touch slid into that scalding hot water. The only piece of clothing he kept on was my hat, pulled down over his ears. And then he just lay there in the water, parboiling himself, with this crazy, happy grin on his face, like it was the first time he'd been warm since he left home. I tried not to look too hard at him, the nice, muscular lines of his body.

By now I'd started in to shiver myself. I gathered up all his discarded clothes and piled them on, folding up his pants to use as my pillow and pulling his long leather jacket over me as a blanket. I could feel his two treasures — the gold ring and the tiny blue ball of light — pulsing against me from his inside pocket. This arrangement sure didn't make me as comfortable as Touch, but at least it got me through till the morning sunshine.

TOUCH SLEPT ON BLISSFULLY THROUGH THE FIRST PATCH OF daylight, whereas I woke up at dawn with a little gasp in my throat, super-aware that someone was chasing me. If I'd had a pen and paper, I would have made a list, trying to figure out what we had going against us as well as what we might have in our favor. Certainly one problem was what clothes we had left — all the leather stuff, instead of the normal flannel and fleece back in the tent. It would be damn difficult to slink through a crowd unnoticed anytime in the immediate future. The thing we had to do, I decided, was find a car to steal, and then stick to remote country roads. The other thing we needed was a particular destination.

Touch's eyes fluttered open. He looked groggy, and surprised to find himself submerged in water. Then he closed his eyes again, taking a moment to luxuriate. "This," he said, "is the first time I've been warm in weeks."

"Sorry to tell you," I said, "but we'd better be moving on. Who knows where all they're looking for us."

Luckily the sun got strong real fast; by the time we got to a tiny little town called Alcove, I'd taken off my jacket and sweater, and Touch said he didn't need them. It seemed like the hot springs had warmed him up from the inside, and I hoped that would last him a good long while.

The town didn't have much to it — in fact it reminded me of the outskirts of Caldecott, the part that was county instead of town, with dusty roads and large tracts of land with modest little farmhouses. Touch and I veered off the road and walked through the fields until we came to a log cabin with a couple of junked trucks parked on the lawn. One of them was an old blue Chevy that looked just like Aunt Carrie's. I patted the hood.

"I can keep this one running," I told Touch.

We tiptoed over to the house, trying to get a feel for whether anyone was inside. It looked pretty well deserted — no lights on, no sign of movement, and the spot in the driveway where they probably kept the cars that ran was empty. I had a feeling this was a summer place, and the people who owned it had gone on home for the winter. I told Touch to fill up our water bottles from their outdoor spigot. Then I went back to the truck and opened the door. Touch came around and peered in the passenger-side window. Before I had a chance to lament losing my screwdriver, I saw that they'd left the keys right under the front seat.

A sadness washed over me. The house was nice enough, in a modest kind of way. And the fact that it was a summer house should've been comforting. But still you could tell the people who owned it weren't rich, and maybe even struggled to hold on to it. And they'd figured this was a place without any crime, where a person could just leave their keys right in the truck.

Unfortunately now was no time for a conscience. Now was the time to go on living. Not to mention the moment of truth. I turned the key in the ignition. It gave a little sputter, coughed, and died. So I pumped the gas a time or two, then tried again. This time it turned over. Not without complaint, but it did turn over. Touch opened the door and climbed up next to me.

"Let's put some distance between us and this place," he said. "We can get to a bank machine."

"Steal from the crooks," I said. That felt a whole lot better than stealing from normal folks. I steered the truck over the grass and onto the driveway, noting the address on the rusty old mailbox. Maybe we could stuff some cash into an envelope and mail it to them as payment.

For now we needed to put a whole lot of space between us and a town where people were sure to recognize this car. We took the back roads onto a small, rural highway. Luckily the gas tank was three-quarters full. Touch found a map in the glove box and sat next to me trying to puzzle it out. I watched him from the corner of my eye and got to thinking on what kind of father he might be. I pictured him on his hot planet, teaching his kid to sail and swim and do whatever passed for throwing a ball around in their world.

"He must be real cute," I said, because I realized I'd been so busy being jealous the other night I hadn't even asked about him. "Your son, I mean."

Touch looked troubled for a second, then he smiled. "He's beautiful. The most beautiful thing in the world. Sweet and funny, too. And an excellent swimmer."

"You must miss him something fierce."

He put the map down and turned his gaze out the window, at the passing sandstone and pine trees. If Touch didn't get so cold we could've rolled the windows down. I was starting to fall pretty well in love just with the scent of the West, which was like a lungful of sage, juniper, and pine every time you breathed in.

"There aren't words for it," Touch finally said.

I reached out and patted his knee, then let my hand rest there a minute. "One thing you never really said," I told him, "is whether or not you plan on going back."

His face got a hard look I hadn't seen before. "Right at this moment," Touch said, "my only plans are for you to keep driving."

"West?" I said.

"West," he agreed, though he still didn't say why.

And as for me, I quelled that impulse to ask questions. I just drove. I drove and didn't stop till the truck was almost on empty. Then we stopped at a little town just on the other side of the Continental Divide and went on into the gas station to look for an ATM.

Touch and I stood side by side, blocking the screen from anyone who might take a peek at us. He floated the little blue ball in front of the card slot. I looked down, waiting for twenties to start spitting out. This time, I thought, I wouldn't stop him quite so soon. But just our luck, not even one twenty sputtered out of that ATM. The screen blinked a minute, then kind of sputtered, then flashed the words, "Insufficient Funds."

"Dang," I said.

SO THERE WE WERE. A TANK OF GAS GOING ON EMPTY. NOT A penny — and I do mean not one single penny — in our pockets. Nothing to eat but a couple granola bars and half a package of turkey jerky.

We walked back to the truck, our shoulders slumped, neither of us knowing what the hell we'd do next. For a moment when we'd stood by the ATM I was terrified that the machine had swallowed the little blue ball, but then it came floating on back to us. Touch put it in the inside pocket of his coat. What we needed was a library or some such place where we could use a computer so he could figure out what the problem was. Maybe he needed to add more money to his fake bank account, or else make a new one.

For a minute we just sat in the truck, staring at the dashboard. I wanted to suggest using the golden ring again — what was the point of having such a handy device when you couldn't even use it? — but I knew he would say no.

All of a sudden something came to me — one of those memories that belonged to somebody else. I had been here, in this town, at this very gas station, before. Back then it had looked different, the gas pumps all old-fashioned, without the credit card swipes and whatnot. And it hadn't been a Gas n' Go, but just a little convenience store called Merle's Groceries. Of course it hadn't actually been *me* who came here, but Wendy Lee, when she was eighteen years old. Back when she barely knew how to bake a chocolate chip cookie. All she cared about was her boyfriend; his name was Joe, and he was just as Southern as she was but his daddy's family owned this ranch in Colorado. She'd heard him talk about it a million times — they'd dated all through high school, and she always hated kissing him good-bye when he headed out here for summer holidays. And now here she was, on vacation with him, about to see the famous ranch for the first time! Little did she know the heartache that lay ahead of her. On this very trip she'd get pregnant. Then the shotgun wedding, and the baby she'd lose, followed by the no-good husband running out on her and becoming an ex.

But guess what? That ranch was in Ferdinand, Colorado. Not ten miles down the road.

TOUCH AND I PARKED ABOUT A MILE FROM THE WHEELER PLACE. I felt a little rush of pride for Wendy Lee not keeping his name even though she didn't stop loving him. It was funny how I'd never felt particularly warm toward her back when I worked for her, but now after nearly killing her I felt almost like she was family. I guess it went back to what I'd learned from my English teacher, Miss Eloise Fitzsimmons: how you never could understand a person till you'd walked around in her shoes. I don't expect Miss Fitzsimmons could have imagined the extent to which I was now walking in Wendy Lee's shoes.

At this point some twenty years had passed since Wendy Lee's last visit to Colorado, and it didn't occur to me until Touch and I were walking down the dusty road that the family might not even own the place anymore. So I felt powerful relief when the sign at the end of the driveway, hanging above the rusty old mailbox and swaying in the wind, still read WHEELER in faded red letters.

"C'mon," I said to Touch, and grabbed his arms to duck into the pine trees. I figured we could follow the road from the safety of the forest that lined it on either side.

"I thought you'd never been out west before," Touch said, as we headed on up toward the house. On the drive over I'd told him a little white lie, about how this kid I knew from home, Joe Wheeler, had a ranch out here. I didn't like lying to Touch, but I couldn't bring myself to tell him I was a bloodsucking creature who drained people of all their memories and experiences.

"I haven't," I said. "But Joe talked about it so much I feel I know the place myself."

Back when Wendy Lee visited the Wheeler ranch, it had been rustic but with all the modern conveniences, like a TV and a big old PC sitting in a study off the main room. I figured twenty years later it would likely have WiFi and a MAC, too. When we got to the house, it looked pretty well deserted. A tractor and a pickup truck were parked in front of a detached garage, but something told me those vehicles were always there, whether the family was visiting or not. Just like the other house, where we'd stolen the truck from, the place had kind of a deserted look — no lights on, the curtains drawn. There were cows grazing on the hill ("Cattle," I heard Joe's know-it-all voice in my head. "You don't call 'em *cows*.") and a big barn a ways down another dirt road, probably full of horses. I guessed someone had to be around to take care of the animals, but for a moment I felt — I hoped — we would have the place to ourselves.

"Look," I said to Touch, walking him around to the other side of the shed. On the inside of a slanted eave hung a little nail where an extra house key dangled.

"Wow," Touch said. "Your friend Joe went into a lot of detail."

"He's a talker," I said, ignoring the fact that Touch clearly knew there was something fishy about this whole setup.

Turned out we didn't need the key at all — just as I'd suspected, the front door swung right open. "We don't have much time," I said to Touch. No matter how low-crime the area, if you were closing up a house for the season, you'd lock it. Whoever'd left the house, they planned on coming back sometime today. My heart set straight to reminding me I wasn't a natural criminal.

Luckily my stomach had some noise to make, too, reminding me how hungry I was, while Wendy Lee's memories kept chattering on about how he'd left her high and dry. I guess if we had to steal anything from anybody, it might as well be from someone I knew to be a scoundrel.

"You go in there and work on the computer," I said to Touch. "I'll get food and supplies."

"It's probably best if I don't use the same bank again," Touch said. "Any others you have a grudge against?"

"Sure. And it's not my grudge, Touch, it's the whole damn country's."

That made me think of something. I followed Touch into the little office, and as he was logging on to the computer I said, "Hey. If I give you the name of a bank, can you get into their system?"

Sure enough Touch could. I stood watching while he hacked into the system, bringing up Aunt Carrie's mortgage account. He asked a lot of questions while he worked. Apparently they didn't have mortgages in Arcadia.

"Look," I said. "All you really need to know about this world? The rich people own everything. Which leaves pretty much nothing for the rest of us."

Touch stopped typing for a minute and looked at me long and hard. "That's why we got attacked by those men at the barbeque place," he said quietly. "And that's why all those people were living in Smith Park."

"Yeah," I said, and patted him on the shoulder, not wanting him to get too wrought up over life here on planet Earth. The important thing was that in about two minutes' time, Aunt Carrie's mortgage was in their system as "PAID IN FULL." When I headed out of the office, I was humming a happy little tune under my breath. It's nice to throw in a good deed in the midst of criminal activity. I pictured Aunt Carrie and the look on her face when she found out. Maybe part of her would know, somehow, that I was the one who did it.

In the hall closet I found two bags, a framed backpack for hiking and a green army duffel like the one I used to have, only bigger. I ducked into the bedroom Joe used to use, but clearly it now belonged to a little kid, with stuffed animals and little plastic toys all about. Joe must have moved on over to the master bedroom, and in there I found, sitting on top of the dresser, a bunch of framed photos. He had lost a bunch of hair, but he hadn't grown much of a belly. Handsomer, I had to admit, than the sort of man Wendy Lee tended to date now. In fact it hurt my heart a little, how handsome he still looked to me. The pictures also showed his wife, who I thought looked a whole lot like Wendy Lee, maybe not quite as bleached and plucked and made up. I bet she couldn't cook as well, though. I wondered if she called him Jo Jo.

Luckily old Joe was nice and tall, so I threw a bunch of his blue jeans and long johns into the green duffel bag. Bunch of flannel shirts, too, and sweaters, and a nice puffy parka hanging in the closet. Not much that belonged to his wife would fit me — she was shorter and wider — but I did grab a denim jacket that would make me look less noticeable, plus a couple wool hats to pull over my freaky hair, plus a long flowery skirt with an elastic waist that looked pretty one-size-fits-all.

By the time I got back to Touch in the computer room, I'd filled the green duffel to brimming with stuff for him, but put only a garment or two in the frame pack. I figured we could use the rest of the space for groceries. When he saw me, he got up from the chair, looking like he was pretty well finished.

"You do what you need with the bank account?"

"Should be all set," he said, but he didn't sound that confident. Clearly the failure of the blue ball had shaken him up good.

"You head on back to the truck while I tie up some loose ends here."

He hesitated. "I don't think it's a good idea for us to split up," he said.

"I'll be right behind you," I promised. "Just a couple minutes, I swear."

Touch glanced over at the computer like he knew I had business on it that I didn't want him to know about. Then he looked back at me, directly into my face, real searching. I stared back at him hard, in a way that I hoped let him know that he seemed to be hiding plenty from me, too.

"Look," I finally said, when he hadn't budged. "Your vigilance is becoming a mite oppressive. Do I really need to spend every single second of my life from here on in with you looking over my shoulder?"

"Yes," he said. "As a matter of fact, given who's chasing us, yes. You do."

"Chasing us?" I said. "I thought they were chasing you."

Now I know for a fact it wasn't my imagination or Wendy Lee's paranoia. Touch's face went just a little bit pink. He recovered quick, though. "Look," he said. "You want some privacy? That's fine. I'll wait for you in the hall."

I thought about making a snide comment on how he hadn't been much of a bodyguard back in Kentucky. Then I remembered the dramatic fashion in which he'd saved us in Napoleon. So I handed him the empty pack. "Here," I said. "Why don't you make yourself useful instead of standing guard? Go fill this up with groceries."

As I handed him the pack, I noticed a flashlight sitting on the windowsill, so I tossed it in. Never knew when one of those would come in handy.

After he left, I sat down in front of the computer. The leather seat was still warm from Touch sitting there. I had to be quick. Who knew when Joe Wheeler and his family would be back from their trip to town, or their morning ride, or whatever? But I just had to look and see if there was any news about Wendy Lee. While I waited for the *Clarion-Ledger* page to load, I opened the desk drawer to see if there was anything I could use. And there sure was. A big silver money clip, holding together a nice-sized wad of bills. Too easy, particularly when I recalled how he'd never given Wendy Lee a single dime. I smiled to myself, taking the money out and throwing the clip back in the drawer in case it was a family heirloom. The clip made a little ping as I returned it, like metal hitting metal, and I pulled the drawer out farther. There, sitting right in front of me, was a .365 Magnum. It wasn't on account of Cody's memory, or Wendy Lee's, that I knew what kind of gun it was. Aunt Carrie kept the exact same one in a tin jar on the kitchen counter marked FLOUR.

I sat staring at that gun a full minute, thinking on all the various ways it might come in handy. But in the end I just slid that drawer shut. Considering what all my skin could do, lack of weaponry was not exactly my biggest problem. I went ahead and set to typing "Wendy Lee Beauchamp" in the search line.

And there it was, an article with a big old picture of her sitting up in her hospital bed, smiling at the camera. A woman that must have been her mama — bleached and gussied as she was, but about twenty years older — sat next to her smiling even wider. The caption under the picture read, "Bakery owner defies the odds, wakes up out of coma."

I sure would've liked to read the rest of that article. Even more than that, Wendy Lee waking up gave me hope for Cody. I wanted to check around for articles about him, too. But just at that moment I heard the front door open, and three or four laughing voices chattering away. The loudest one — my heart, infected by Wendy Lee's, skipped a beat — belonged to Joe. The voice was older for sure, but I would've recognized it anywhere.

Dang. Not only did I need to get out of there, I needed to get out with everything I'd taken. Touch, I figured, would be smart enough to hightail out of the back door off the kitchen instead of coming through the house to get me.

I shoved the bills into the pocket of my pants and took the time to exit out of the newspaper (no telling what dots Joe Wheeler would connect with one look at *that*), wishing I had time to clear the browsing history. I also took the time to pull one of Mrs. Wheeler's hats down over my head — might as well do what I could to make myself less recognizable. Then I zipped the bag closed and pulled it up over my shoulders. If I opened the window quiet as I could, maybe I could jump out to the ground and make a break for it without the Wheelers ever knowing I'd been here, and Touch would meet me on the lawn.

That's when I heard the dog barking.

Crap, I damn near said aloud. Forgetting about being quiet, I pulled at the window hard as I could, but it seemed painted shut. Finally I noticed that the little lock was pulled closed, but I'd barely set my fingers on it before that dog came barreling into the room, barking like a hellhound, with Joe Wheeler himself right behind him. I put my hands up in the air. The dog itself wasn't so threatening — a little mottled creature with pointy ears.

"What the hell?" Joe Wheeler yelled. He sounded indignant and very angry. I'd heard him use these very words in Wendy Lee's memories. But I wasn't near prepared for the sight of him. Just a regular, middle-aged man with faded red hair and faded freckles, but I stopped breathing for what felt like a full minute. I knew it wasn't logical, but it got my feelings hurt that his only reaction to seeing me there was being mad. He didn't even seem a bit scared, just kept on yelling, "What on earth do you think you're doing, girlie?"

His wife and a pair of kids — one a teenaged girl, the other a boy of ten or so — crowded into the room behind him. Joe raised his arm, backing the two kids out of the room, and I felt sort of touched by his protectiveness. Then I stopped feeling touched, because I saw his eyes flit on over to the desk drawer that I knew contained that .365 Magnum, and it was awful plain that he'd gladly shoot me over a wad of cash and an Indian skirt. No doubt Colorado was a "Make My Day" state just like Mississippi.

Before I could stop myself, I said, "Don't even think about it, Jo Jo. You always were a piss-poor shot."

The confused look on his face gave me just the opening I needed to reach on into the drawer and pull out that gun. My eyes flitted down to make sure the safety was fastened. I sure didn't want to shoot anyone, least of all a couple of kids.

Joe held his arms out wide while his wife started to back the kids out of the room. I would have let them go if it hadn't been for Touch. Who knew where he had got himself to by now?

"Hold on there," I said, enjoying the fear in Joe's eyes, not to mention the confusion (I was pretty sure from the look in his eye, nobody'd called him Jo Jo since Wendy Lee). I moved my finger back, trying to make it look like I had released the safety. "I need everybody to just stay put for right now. Nobody needs to get hurt. What's going to happen is, I'm just going to ease right on out this window and y'all are going to forget you ever saw me."

I backed up a couple steps, toward the window. The dog didn't know not to be scared of guns, and he ran up closer to me, barking his little head off.

"Call your dog, Jo Jo," I yelled. I sure didn't want to shoot anybody's dog, not even Joe Wheeler's. I could see his daughter's face get all teary and panicked, like she was way more scared of me shooting her dog than of me shooting her daddy. At the same time it struck me that there was nothing particularly terrible about Joe Wheeler to the naked eye.

"Radar," Joe called. "Come back here, boy."

I let out a little snort of a laugh. "God damn, Jo Jo," I said. "Can't you think of any other name for a dog?"

Joe's face got so red you couldn't even see them freckles he used to have. His wife gave him a funny look.

"Have we met?" Joe said, real confused, and I couldn't help laughing. By now my own damn heart was taking over Wendy Lee's. Maybe he wasn't too terribly terrible, but on the other hand I couldn't see anything particularly special about him. Now that Wendy Lee'd woken up from her coma, I hoped she'd be able to put her heartache behind her and find some unmarried fellow who loved her right back. But I had barely got to finish that thought in my head when . . .

Bam! Crackle! Boom!

Crap. By now I knew that noise, and what it meant — people from Touch's planet coming after him — and now me — with their scary weapons. I guess it had just been a matter of time before Touch and I encountered our different worlds' troubles at the very same time.

"Run," I yelled, loud as I could, to Joe Wheeler and his family. "Run for your lives!"

For once in his life old Jo Jo listened when somebody spoke to him. He and his family ran out of that house with their dog at their heels, about as fast as I'd ever seen four people and a dog run. Let me tell you I would have been right behind them if it weren't for Touch. I couldn't go anywhere till I knew where he'd gone to.

From the driveway I heard the sound of a car starting and then peeling away. Sure enough they'd be driving straight to a police station, but that was a problem I'd have to sort out later.

"Touch!" I yelled.

The bam-and-crackle sound had come from over in the kitchen, so I headed that way. Sure enough, a light was emanating from that direction, bright but not blinding. And I could hear whistling voices, talking — by now I recognized Touch's voice when he spoke in his own language. Neither voice sounded so angry or urgent as it had back at the Chevy dealership, but I didn't get a chance to ponder this at all, because the next thing I knew some kind of snarling beast burst through the kitchen door and headed straight toward me.

Now "beast" might not sound like the most specific word to you, but let me tell you that what I found myself running from did not fall into any other category I'd ever seen before. All I saw was a whole lot of hair and teeth attached to a creature that was at least the size of me, headed in my direction making decidedly unfriendly noises. And it was headed in my direction *fast*. I'd been half the length of the house away when I turned to run from it, and in seconds it was right on my heels. I slammed myself into Joe's bedroom and headed for the closet. As I struggled with the safety on Joe's gun, I could hear the thing scratching and tearing at the bedroom door. It took about two minutes for that sound to be followed by the whole thing crashing down. Of course if it could break down the bedroom door, it could break down the closet door, but damn if I couldn't figure out the safety with the way my hands were trembling.

Those terrible claws raked the outside of the closet door. I pressed my back against the wall, all Mrs. Wheeler's dress hems tickling my face. It felt like the whole house shook as that thing tried to claw its way in to get me. As I finally figured out the gun, a giant claw came ripping through a panel in the door. It raked right through my leather pants, the claws and pads of its paws pressing themselves against my suddenly bare skin.

Here we go, I thought. The gun skittered out of my hand and hit the door, going off with a deafening retort. It may have hit that beast, but at this point that seemed a little redundant, because I'd already heard it flop to the floor. While my body sucked in the greatest surge I'd ever felt, of strength and power.

I picked up the gun and got to my feet. The creature had fallen against the door, and I thought I would have to give it a mighty heave, but the door swept the body aside as if it weighed no more than a pile of maple leaves. I stood there looking at what I'd just absorbed. A big, furry brown creature that looked like a cross between a grizzly bear and a wolf. Its rib cage rose and fell, so I knew it wasn't dead. Chances were slim it would ever wake up out of its coma, but I couldn't risk the Wheelers coming home to face it. I closed my eyes and pointed the gun, my whole body jerking back as it went off. When I opened my eyes, the thing had stopped breathing. Now I could get back down to business.

"Touch!" I yelled.

The house had gone eerily quiet. Where the hell could he be? And where the hell were the people or where the hell was the person who'd come after him? I held the gun close to my chest and tiptoed back into the hallway. Nothing. But from down the road, I could hear the sound of distant sirens. I had to get out of this house. I went back through the kitchen, but there was no sign of anyone or anything, except cupboard and pantry doors left open. The back door also stood wide open, and I headed on through it.

No sooner had my feet stepped onto the grass than the sounds started echoing all around me, and I don't mean the sounds of the Ferdinand PD. It was like a great big lightning storm erupting: flashing lights and violent wind — no, not wind exactly, it was more like the grass and trees were bending close as they could toward the ground, like the plants themselves were scared of what was coming. I couldn't help but duck down, too, worrying that Touch had already been swept back to his home planet, leaving me all alone, never to see him again. I could almost stand the thought of getting killed right here and now by whatever was chasing Touch. What I couldn't stand would be never seeing him again, and finding myself all alone.

My eyes fought to stay open against whatever force buzzed all around me. And then, coming toward me, I saw her. Even though Touch had only said a few words about her, I knew right away who she was. She looked like an oversized Tinker Bell floating in my direction, all flaxen blond and wispy limbs, and eyes the pale blue of the most gentle summer day. About ten times more beautiful than I ever could have imagined.

Alabaster. Touch's wife. Walking directly toward me, with a look on her face that I didn't quite buy: serene and well-meaning, like she wanted me to think she was here to help. She opened her mouth to speak, and out came that same kind of whistling sound Touch had made when he'd told me his name. Was this her way of demanding to know where he was? Or did everything in their language sound this way and she wasn't saying his name at all?

Alabaster pointed at me as the air kept crackling all around us. She was dressed in some kind of light, lacy clothing that didn't cover much more than your average bathing suit. She had a cape tied around her neck, also light and lacy, that flew back luxuriously amid all the electric crackling. But I could tell the temperature took her by surprise. These people really needed to start communicating with each other a little better. She was shivering, and her lips had started to turn blue.

She spoke to me again in that unearthly language. It sent shivers up my spine, the sound was so beautiful. Of course I had no idea what she was saying. It could have been *Hand over my husband, you shameless hussy!* Or something even worse, like *Kneel, lowly Earth creature, and prepare to meet your doom.*

Just thinking on my doom gave me a little rush of adrenaline. Alabaster was so clearly miserable, shivering in the cold despite all the power she'd conjured up around her, that maybe I could make a break for it. I got to my feet and aimed for the woods. Behind me, I could hear her cry out, and from out of nowhere appeared two more of those beasts. I lifted up the gun and shot the first one straight in the heart — it dropped with a tragic yelp. But that second one looped around and slammed me from behind, tackling me to the ground and sending the gun flying.

I honked desperately, the wind knocked out of me, while the creature kind of straddled me, duffel bag and all. Maybe it was aware I'd killed its two friends because it sure seemed furious. Its rancid breath wafted over my face, and it bit into my shoulder — I felt it rip through layers of leather and wool, all the way through, so its teeth scraped my skin, a wound that opened and bled.

I tried to roll over on my back, but the damn bag prevented me getting enough leverage to get my feet under the beast's stomach — I hoped maybe a good kick would do it. At the same time I hardly had any hope at all, was really just going through the motions, fighting the creature because I couldn't stand the thought of going quietly. My shoulder hurt like hell. Now I could see the thing alive — not only half-bear, half-wolf, but plus something that didn't grow on this earth, with red eyes, long fangs, and claws to match. The only thought my head could form was *I guess this is how it all ends.*

Probably rolling over was the worst thing I could have done, because the beast liked the look of my neck, the one part of my body that was all exposed and waiting to be torn open. The thing was, when he bit my shoulder, all my layers of clothing had protected his nose and gums — letting just his teeth scrape through. But heading in to relieve me of my jugular, he made skin-on-skin contact, his nose pressing into my neck before he got the chance to sink his teeth in.

All around us, the electricity quieted. The grass and trees stood back up to full attention. From where I lay, looking past the dog-bear-beast, I could see Alabaster, turning even whiter as the beast shuddered and fell back, like it had turned to stone and was on its way to cracking, before collapsing lifeless on the ground.

Alabaster looked at me like I was the devil himself. The gun lay at her feet and she looked down at it. I held my breath, but I guess she didn't know what it was, because she just left it there. She grabbed the hem of her cape and kind of snapped it, and she and the creatures — the dead one and the stunned one — disappeared.

And now I had two of these creatures, pulsing through me.

I didn't have time to gather myself and recover. The sirens were getting closer. My only chance was to head for the truck and hope that somehow Touch had made it there. Since I didn't want anything more to do with that gun, I left it where it was and set off through the woods, out toward the truck, running not with Cody's speed but something new, something even faster, something not human.

I ran the mile through the woods in just under two minutes, the trees a blur as I flew by. And there to my great joy and relief sat Touch, drumming his fingers on the dashboard, looking like any impatient man waiting on a woman, except maybe a damn sight handsomer.

"What the hell happened to you?" he said, through the open window. If I hadn't been in such a hurry, I would've laughed at the sound of his elegant, almost-foreign voice cussing.

Instead I said, "What the hell do you mean, what the hell happened to me? You were there!"

"There?" he said, like he had no idea what I was talking about. "You told me to get food and then wait for you at the truck, so that's what I did."

The adrenaline from my run started to wear off in a sudden burst. I almost thought I would fall on the ground. "But you didn't," I said. "You said you wouldn't and then I heard you in the kitchen talking to someone."

"No," he said. "I grabbed what I could from the kitchen and then I came out here to wait for you. Just like you told me." He said it real firm. Almost too firm. Then I guess I looked like I might be about to keel over, because he reached out through the window to steady me. "Rogue," he said again, softer this time. "What happened to you?"

"Your wife happened to me," I said. "As if you didn't know."

I shrugged away from him, threw the bag in the bed of the truck, and climbed on into the passenger seat. Touch said, "I knew I shouldn't have left you alone."

"You didn't. I know you didn't. I heard you."

"You're hurt," he said. "You're confused."

That first part was certainly true. Maybe the second was, too. I sure did feel dizzy, and not at all like arguing. "Just drive," I said. "Fast as you can in any direction. Just get the hell out of here."

Touch did as he was told. As the tires kicked up dirt and gravel, I wondered if it were true, if he'd really left the house before Alabaster arrived. What reason would he possibly have to lie to me? I lifted up my leg to examine where the creature had scratched me. It looked superficial, the worst damage done to my pants. My shoulder, on the other hand, throbbed something fierce, and I could feel the blood seeping through my sweater. There was nothing I could do for it right then, though. First we had to get away from everything that was chasing us.

I had told Touch to just go. But of course he went in the direction he always went. West.

"YOU'RE BADLY HURT," TOUCH SAID, ONCE WE'D PUT A FAIR BIT of distance between us and the Wheeler ranch, and the sirens. I pushed my shoulder forward — the gash looked to be right above the shoulder blade, so I could just sort of see it if I pushed my chin down toward my back. On top of everything else that damn beast had ripped my only clothes, and stained them, too, since blood was still seeping through at a good rate.

"We've got to put something on that," he said. "To stop the bleeding. And get you to a doctor."

"A doctor?" I said. "Are you crazy?"

I pulled off my jacket, then pulled my sweater over my head. It was black but would have to do. I bunched it up, pushed the strap of my tank top aside, and pressed it to the wound to try and stop the blood. The cut hurt something fierce, burning and aching.

"You know what a doctor would do?" I said to Touch. "Call the police and stitch me up, in that order." It scarcely seemed worth mentioning that I probably wouldn't even get as far as the doctor, since the admitting nurse would likely die attempting to take my blood pressure.

"Stitch you up?" he said, with that quizzical look he got. The familiarity of that look flooded me with warmth toward him. Plus, I appreciated that he hadn't yet said a word about his wife on account of being too preoccupied with *my* well-being.

"Yeah." I did my best to explain needles and thread to him.

"I guess I can see it, for clothing," he said. "But are you saying doctors do this, insert needles into your body? Sew skin together?"

"Well, yeah," I said. "How do they fix up cuts where you're from?"

He sighed. "I'm not a doctor," he said. "So I can't tell you exactly how the elixir works. I can only tell you it *does* work. You go to the doctor, you take a swig, you go to sleep. Wake up good as new."

"No kidding. What if you're sick?"

"Same thing."

"Any kind of sickness?"

"Yes, any kind."

"Even cancer?"

His brow furrowed.

"So you're telling me that where you come from, there's no poverty, no needles, no incurable sickness. Remind me again why you left?"

A look came over his face that was so sad I felt sorry I'd said anything. "I left," he said, "for all the wrong reasons."

There wasn't time to ask him what he meant by that. The gas gauge had sunk to the very bottom of the E, I didn't know when we might have a chance to fill up, and my shoulder was on fire. "We need to pull over at the next gas station," I told Touch. Then I pulled out the bills I'd taken from Joe Wheeler's money clip and started in to counting them, trying not to wince or pass out from the pain as I did.

• • •

FOR SOME TIME NOW, I'D BEEN TAKING CARE OF MYSELF. NOT always doing a very good job of it, but at the very least I'd kept myself alive and sheltered. Before that, like with most kids, I guess, I'd just kind of been a passenger on a moving train. Plenty of days I didn't even know what I was eating for dinner till the plate got plopped in front of me. And I guess there'd been a part of my brain, from the moment I'd hopped into the first stolen car of our journey — no, I corrected myself, Touch had bought that car — I'd expected to be a passenger. I knew now that I'd mistaken Touch's otherworldliness for worldliness. Sure he could keep me company. But something about the way he'd reacted to the gash on my shoulder, and the news that it needed stitches, reminded me that whatever super gadgets he might have in his possession, he was about as new to this planet as an eight-week-old baby. If there were any plans to be made, it was going to be up to me to make them.

While Touch filled up the truck with gas, I marched right on into the convenience store wearing nothing but my jeans and tank top, my hair down to cover up the injury and Mrs. Wheeler's black wool cap over my hair. I bought gauze bandages, a traveling sewing kit, a hand mirror, a bottle of ibuprofen, a new road atlas, and some hydrogen peroxide.

"Lady," a man said to me, as I stood in line waiting to pay. "You're bleeding."

I shot him the evil glare that had started to come naturally. "No kidding," I said, holding up my purchases so he'd see he wasn't telling me anything I didn't already know.

"That some sort of dog bite?" Mr. Busybody said, hovering dangerously close, like he wanted to take a look. "Dog bites you, you need to report it. You need to make sure it's got all its shots."

I stepped forward and put my purchases on the counter. "Wasn't a dog," I said, hoping my tone made it clear this was none of his business. "I scraped it on an old barn nail."

The clerk handed me my first aid kit in a bag. I snatched it and started heading out the door.

"Make sure your tetanus shot's up to date," the busybody hollered after me, guaranteeing that every last one of the ten people in the store would remember I'd been there, if ever they were questioned by the police.

SITTING IN A MOTEL SIX JUST OUTSIDE OF DOVE CREEK, COLOrado, I squinted my eyes to thread the needle. Joe Wheeler'd had five hundred and fourteen dollars. Touch and I figured it was best to postpone using that blue ball as long as possible, so we wouldn't be staying in hotels much more, not even cheapos like this one.

Finally I got the needle threaded and ripped off the bandage I'd slapped on in the car — it was soaked through with blood, as was my tank top. The only light garment in my possession, and now I'd have to toss it. Joe Wheeler's money might buy a few days' worth of food and gas, but it didn't exactly leave room for a shopping spree.

I thought again how I should have let Touch go in and buy the first aid supplies. Noticeable as he was, he wouldn't have drawn nearly as much attention as a girl in ripped-up leather pants with blood running down her back. And he'd gone in anyway, right after me, while I bandaged myself up as best I could. "What'd you buy, anyway?" I said. "When you went into the store."

"Whiskey," he said.

"Whiskey! Don't tell me you have alcohol in that perfect world of yours."

"I was introduced to it back in Jackson, by my friends in Smith Park. Made the cold a little more bearable. Thought it might help you with the pain."

I'd already taken about five ibuprofen, which had done something to cut through the bloody pain of the creature's bite. But I knew that as soon as I started sewing myself closed, the pain would get a whole lot worse. It's not as if I'd ever plunged a needle in and out of my own body before. I'd only had stitches once in my life, when I tore the back of my leg open on a staple in some old upholstery. I was only about ten at the time, and it took two nurses to hold me down for Dr. Sparks to get the stitches done. Now here I was, all grown up, with nobody stitching me up or holding me down because nobody could do it and survive.

"Hand it over," I said to Touch, meaning the whiskey. He pulled the little bottle out of the inside pocket of his leather jacket (one of these days I'd have to take a look myself into that inside pocket) and handed it to me. I put down the needle and thread. The bottle unscrewed with a click as the tamper-free seal broke. I took a swig, enough for the warmth to start flowing from my throat to my stomach. Then another, and I stopped myself. I'd only drunk whiskey a time or two before; I needed just enough to dull the pain, but not so much to make my hands unsteady.

"OK," I said, letting out a long string of breath. "Hold up the mirror."

Luckily the damn beast had gored my left shoulder. Right shoulder and I never would have got it done. As it was, I had to scrunch up my face, plunge the needle, stop a moment working real hard not to scream, and then pull the thread through. Each time I could see Touch's face contort in sympathy, and the real effort not to reach out and hold me. He wanted to comfort me so bad, but my arms were bare. So he restrained himself, occasionally reaching over to give my leather-panted thighs a squeeze.

"Hold it up," I said, for the sixth time. "Hold it up real good and let me see."

The cut looked terrible. Before threading the needle, I'd burned the end of it, then doused the whole thing in hydrogen peroxide, so it was as sterile as I could get it in these conditions. The five stitches I'd managed looked wide and uneven — holding the skin together sloppily, with little blue bruises and a pinprick where each stitch had gone in and out. It was going to leave one hell of a crazy scar.

"One more stitch," I said, like I was cheering myself on. I thought of the slug of whiskey I'd take — washing down at least one more ibuprofen. I knew what I really needed was antibiotics, and a tetanus shot like Mr. Busybody'd said. Not to mention a rabies shot — I had to remember to ask Touch if they had rabies where he came from. Because rabies was just what I needed to make my untouchability complete!

I forced my eyes to stay open, plunged the needle in, then out, pulled it to suture the skin together. Touch cut the thread with the little traveling sewing kit scissors, and I tied the two ends together, double and then triple knotting. Then I lay down on my stomach while Touch poured some more hydrogen peroxide over the whole mess. I had to put my hands over my mouth to keep from screaming.

Touch put his hand out, like he wanted to stroke my head, but stopped himself. He said, "I know what did this to you."

I wondered when he would come around to talking about it. "Oh yeah?" I said.

He made a low noise that sounded less like a whistle and more like growling. If I hadn't been in so much pain, I might've laughed. "That'd be a perfect name for that thing, if it didn't sound so pretty," I said.

"They're not generally vicious," Touch said. "I've never met a vicious one, anyway, though I've heard stories about what they used to be like, in the old days. Before Arcadia, they were used as guards at the palace. Now the palace belongs to the people, and those creatures — wildebears, that's the best translation I can come up with — they roam free in the outskirts, the forest land. I haven't heard of one attacking a human during my lifetime."

I pushed myself up to a sitting position and reached for the box of big square bandages. "How'd you know that's what they were, then?" After I spoke, I ripped the package open with my teeth, then pulled off the protective layer and slapped the bandage on my shoulder. I leaned forward so Touch could take a look at it. "Is it completely covered?" I asked.

"Yes," he said. "It is. I've heard rumors over the past year. That certain factions were rounding up the wildebears. Training them as guards and worse." He said this with a very concerned look on his face, and I figured he was thinking on his son, hoping he wasn't being exposed to the wildebears.

"Listen," I said. "Whoever trained this one did a damn good job. It went after me like a coyote after a rabbit."

"But you got away," he said. "I'm very impressed by that. From the stories I've heard, it's almost impossible to survive a wildebear attack. And you survived two."

He handed me the whiskey. I took another swig. When I handed the bottle back to Touch, he took a swig himself.

"Are you worried," I said, "about your son?"

Touch frowned. "I'm always worried about him," he said. "But not that Alabaster would hurt him. Hurt him physically, that is. There are other ways to hurt a person. And if Arcadia falls, if there's a war, nobody will be safe for a long time."

I nodded, and Touch said, with a little crack in his voice I'd never heard before, "But it's not only that. I don't want him fed those ideas, about what he deserves, and what's right for others. And if the wrong side wins . . . I don't want him living in a world like this one."

A *world like this one*. I almost wanted to tell him it wasn't so bad, that despite everything that was screwed up about my world there was still plenty of joy to be found between the cracks. The pain in my shoulder started to subside a bit, though the cut still throbbed in a hot and distant manner. And I just couldn't engage too hard in such philosophical conversation. Touch must have realized this, because he stopped talking. I could tell it still weighed heavy on his mind as I plopped down onto the scratchy motel comforter, my head landing on thin pillows. Touch sat on the opposite bed, taking an occasional sip of whiskey and watching me. He still hadn't said a word about his ex-wife (I decided in that moment that's how I was going to think on her, not his wife but his ex-wife).

"Touch," I said. My voice came out in this husky little whimper. "I gotta tell you about that. How I survived, I mean. It's time you knew the whole truth."

He held up his hand. "Let me tell you what I think it is," he said. "There's some kind of power in your skin. If it touches somebody else's, you absorb everything about them — their memories, their abilities, their very essence. Their life force. Losing all that, they collapse, sometimes never to get up again."

For one full minute the pain went away. Hell, I think *I* might have gone away. Disappeared right on the spot. How could a person just come up with that explanation? And describe it way better than I could've myself?

"I knew a man once, who had that same ability," Touch explained.

"*Ability*," I said, a hard edge of anger sculpting the word. "Affliction is more like it."

"Of course," he said. He had a funny kind of look on his face, like he was troubled but not by what we were talking about. Like there was something in the world even more worrisome than my skin meaning instant lifelessness. "Of course it feels like an affliction. But it's a power, too, there's no denying it. Did you feel like you gained anything? Special powers? From the wildebears, I mean."

I told him about how fast I'd been able to run from the ranch to the truck. Touch nodded.

"That makes sense," he said. "They're known for their speed. It's one of the things that makes them so dangerous. And useful. I bet you'll find you're a lot stronger, too. Probably it's one of the reasons you were able to endure all this." He motioned with his hand at the wreckage left behind, the needle and bloodied bandages and various wrappers.

A man like you. What a strange thought. An amazing thought. "What became of him?" I asked Touch. "The man like me."

"Well," Touch said, like he was choosing his words very carefully, "where I come from, most people are like me. Plain old humans, with varying abilities and talents. But there are other people. They're larger than life. They have powers. Special powers. Like yours."

"All of them?" I said. Between the whiskey and this news I could barely form a full sentence.

"All of them are special in some way," Touch said. "Sometimes minor, sometimes major — like being able to fly, or shift shape. Sometimes dangerous, like being able to create fire. Or rain."

"How? I mean, how do they get that way?"

"The same way anybody gets attributes. How do I have blue eyes? How are you tall? It's genetics, Rogue. Most are the result of inheritance. But some are the result of changes. Mutations."

That didn't seem like much of an answer but I decided to let it go for now. "And what do you do?" I asked. "With the dangerous ones. The ones like me."

"There are centers," he said. "Like schools. To help them get their abilities under control. Like this man I knew. Gordium is what you'd call him here. He learned how to control the effect of his skin."

This information made me do the impossible. I sat up straight. The throb in my shoulder became still more distant. "What do you mean, control it?"

"I mean, he learned how to keep his skin from having that effect, unless he wanted it to."

"So he could touch people?"

"Yes. He could touch people. If he wanted. He could touch them and have no effect at all. Or he could touch them and take just a little bit of something he needed. He could control it."

"Do you think," I said, afraid to even put the sentence together. "Do you think you could take me back there with you, once all this is all worked out? And I could go to that center, that school, and learn how to . . . touch people?"

Touch's face contorted. "No," he said, and he sounded real firm. Like he'd made up his mind before I even asked. "I can never take you back there."

"But . . ."

He held up his hand. "They're close," he said. "I've already said too much. You need to rest, and recover. We don't want to risk another showdown."

I nodded. But still that old word — "hope" — it had risen in my heart. Nothing Touch said could squelch the fantasy, of going back to his planet with him and learning how to control my affliction — no, my ability! — and coming out able to join the world. Able to hold hands and pick eyelashes off people's cheeks and wear summer dresses without worrying about brushing against someone else's elbow. And best of all, be able to touch him, Touch, wherever and whenever and however I wanted.

I didn't hear what he said next. The pain and exhaustion and liquor overtook me. I slept twelve straight hours, what might've been my longest uninterrupted sleep since we started this whole journey. When I woke up, Touch had wrapped me up in a sheet, like a little mummy, and his arms were tight around me, so that I hardly minded the dull, throbbing pain in my shoulder.

We gathered our things together, got into the blue truck, and headed out for Utah.

TO ME UTAH LOOKED LIKE ANOTHER PLANET, WITH HOODOOS
and red clay, and towering rock formations everywhere. Even more
than in Colorado, I felt like finally I was not just driving but *traveling*.
Seeing the world. I'd never even imagined anything like this place in
my whole life.

Touch had got very quiet. He just sat staring out the passenger
window, his chin in his palm. I kept pointing out different rocks and
colors and mountains in the distance, saying how pretty everything
was. But he would just say, "Hmm," or nod, like he wasn't impressed
at all. Or else like he had too much on his mind to appreciate even
this scenery.

As for myself, I felt strangely cheerful. My shoulder didn't hurt
near as much as I expected it to, and it had stopped bleeding. That
morning, Touch and I had both dug into Joe Wheeler's clothing, so
we looked a damn sight more normal than usual. Touch wore blue
jeans and a plaid shirt under a thick wool sweater, plus a down vest. I
had to stick to my leather jeans, but I wore one of Joe's T-shirts and
the jean jacket I'd taken, along with my white tea gloves, and a wool

cap over a ponytail, making my hair a whole lot less conspicuous. As I drove and Touch stayed quiet, I thought on two different plans that fell into two different categories: Immediate and Planet Earth was one category; Future and Planet Touch was the other.

As for Immediate and Planet Earth, there were two big concerns: get me away from the law and get Touch to a place where he wouldn't freeze to death come winter. So I was thinking Mexico. We were pretty much headed in that direction anyhow. I figured we didn't need particular identification, because as far as I was concerned, we wouldn't be coming back. Not ever. Of course this meant leaving behind everything in the world I'd ever known. Come to find out, this did not trouble me in the slightest.

When I thought about Future and Planet Touch, I found myself getting downright giddy. Because what news he'd given me last night! Not only was there a person *just like me* where he came from, there was a whole host of freakazoids that weren't treated like freakazoids at all! They got to be part of the general population and work for Arcadia. They even had a special school! I loved that there was a world where such a thing existed — peace and simplicity and enough of everything for everyone — and that I could maybe be a part of it, not wicked and evil, like Aunt Carrie always said I'd turn out.

Touch hadn't said it outright, what he planned on doing. Sometimes, when he talked about his son for instance, I'd get the impression that Touch planned on going home eventually. Other times it seemed like he wouldn't go back, not ever. But now that I knew about what I'd be on his planet, "larger than life," all I wanted to do was go. There at that school they'd teach me how to control my affliction — no, my power! — and Touch and I would become like a regular couple, able to do all the regular couple things in the world. So what if he had to fight off his ex-wife, and those ponytailed men? Maybe it was just dumb beast courage, but I felt like I could take on anyone, anywhere. And even if he didn't want to go back home for me, eventually he'd want to go home for his son. I had a feeling that was why he'd got so quiet today. He was thinking on his son, Cotton, and worrying about him all alone with that crazy wife and her wildebears.

Of course I couldn't push him just yet, about my Planet Touch plan. That one would take some finessing and some time. So when we stopped for lunch in a place called Escalante, after I slathered peanut butter onto bread with my fingers, I opened up the atlas and showed Touch what all I was thinking of. To my surprise, before I could say a word, he pointed at the exact route I was going to suggest.

"This way," he said, like it wasn't a point for argument.

I looked down at the map, and at the roads winding through Utah and Arizona to Mexico. I pictured Touch and me together in a tropical paradise, nobody chasing us at all.

Touch held on to his sandwich, examining the map. We sat overlooking this wide lake in the middle of a place that was kind of how I pictured the Grand Canyon — towering rocks, and more of those crazy, spirally pillars — but with the water all huge and placid running through it. Touch had already collected some pamphlets from the visitors center, and we'd read all about how this lake, Lake Powell, had been formed by the Glen Canyon Dam. Touch handed me one of his pamphlets, this one about the Anasazi ruins. "What can you tell me about this?" he said.

I pushed it away, gentle as I could. "Nothing," I said. "Never heard of them."

Touch said, "Let's get a boat and go out on the water."

I stared at him like he was crazy. "A boat?" I said. "Aren't you listening? We got to make some ground, head on down to Mexico. Then at least we'll only have your people chasing us."

Touch looked out at the water. He drummed his fingers on the picnic table. I'd already devoured my sandwich and he hadn't yet taken a bite. Something knotted in my stomach, seeing the look on his face.

"Touch," I said. "What's got you in such a faraway mood today? It's not on account of *her* is it?"

He looked at me a minute, like he wasn't sure what I was talking about. Then he said, "Oh. Alabaster. Well, in a way it is. I mean, she's part of it. But not the way you mean."

"What do you mean, the way I mean?" I could hear my voice get defensive, and that made me even more defensive. You see, I'd never even had a real boyfriend before. And here I was with a grown man who had a wife, and the only experience in my head belonged to Wendy Lee, who was more inclined to throw a vase or get her shotgun. In fact at this very moment, remembering Alabaster's very beautiful if clearly evil face, and seeing the conflicted and preoccupied look on Touch's very beautiful and clearly not-evil face, I could hear Wendy Lee's voice inside my head: *Sugar,* she said. *Nine times out of ten when you think a man might be lying you're right. And I don't care how it might look to you right now. But I'm here to tell you that a man don't leave his wife. Not for the likes of you, anyway.*

He already left his wife, I thought. Even before I showed up. That must count for something, right?

"I mean," Touch said, "that I'm not thinking about her in a romantic way. I haven't thought about her like that in a while . . ." His voice trailed off. After a bit, he said, "I just hope my son is safe. I wish I'd gotten him away from her before I came here. I wish . . . I wish a lot of things."

This may have been very bad of me. But I could tell he was having second thoughts. Regrets. Which could mean that he'd head back to Planet Touch, and take me with him, all of his own accord!

Still I did feel bad, him looking so worried and guilty, like he had more thoughts than a person could bear rolling through his head. So I said, "Sure, Touch. Let's get a boat."

He smiled a little, and then he finally took a bite of his sandwich.

This look came over his face like he'd just been poisoned. He put his hand to his throat as he swallowed.

"What the hell is that?" he said, his tongue sticking out, the first gesture I'd seen from him that I would not describe as elegant.

"Why it's peanut butter," I said. "You don't have that where you come from?"

"No." He picked up a bottle of water and took a deep swig. "We don't."

And even though I never in my life met a person who didn't like peanut butter, I figured every little thing he didn't like about Planet Earth couldn't help but work out in my favor.

THERE WERE A LOT OF VERY COOL THINGS AROUND ESCALANTE. On the way to rent a boat, Touch and I stood in a dinosaur footprint. I tried to explain to Touch about the dinosaurs and evolution.

"Someday I'll show you a picture in a book," I said. "They were like lizards only bigger. Much, much bigger. And some of them could fly."

He looked at me like I was maybe a little bit crazy, then knelt and touched the hard rock that formed the footprint. "Pretty fascinating," he said. The way he said it made me remember how, back where he came from, he'd been a scientist. "Remember when you asked me, how the people with powers — the people like you — came to be that way? It's just what you're talking about. Evolution. Gradual changes, mostly, but sometimes sudden ones that set a single member of a species apart from the others."

"You mean one day everyone will be like me?"

He looked at me and smiled. Then he said, "One can only hope." I didn't point out that this would mean pretty much the whole world in a coma.

At the little marina we found a Navajo man who was selling hand-made jewelry and renting boats. We hired what Cody would've called a jon boat — just a simple little fishing boat with an outboard motor attached. Even though Touch was the one who came from a place that was mostly water, I drove. Cody'd had one just like it that he used to travel through the bayous, and on the Mississippi when it was calm enough. Touch finally started talking, prattling on about how transportation was different on his planet, none of this messy gasoline to spill and wreck the water. He was pretty horrified by the slick our little boat was leaving behind us.

"It makes sense you wouldn't have gas if you didn't have dinosaurs," I said. And I explained what little I knew about fossil fuel. "They say it's wrecking the planet," I said. "Making it hotter. On account of . . . the ozone layer and such." I expected Touch to be a whole lot more interested in this, but he just clammed up again. I wished I knew more about it, to impress him with my knowledge. I'd been pretty good in school, but our science class hadn't spent a whole lot of time on climate change since the Mississippi legislature didn't put much stock in the theory. Probably it was becoming clearer and clearer to Touch that I was no kind of scientist. I wondered if Alabaster had been one.

"What does Alabaster do, anyway?" I said. "For a living I mean."

"A living?" That look again, and then he turned away, looking back out at the landscape. "I don't know," he said. "It's hard to explain. It all works so differently here, some things just don't translate."

"Well," I said, "is she an inventor, a scientist, like you?"

"No," he said. But he didn't get into it further than that.

I puttered the little boat along in the water, the great canyon walls rising all around us. It was stupid to feel jealous of an evil woman from another planet. But I couldn't help it. I wondered what would happen if next time I saw her, I took off my gloves and just grabbed her. Maybe I'd absorb some of her beauty, plus I'd know everything she knew about Touch. But then of course she'd be comatose or dead, and no matter how Touch felt about her now, he likely wouldn't take kindly to that, her being the mother of his child and all.

My mind went to thinking on everything Touch had told me about his home. "Utopia," I found myself saying.

Touch turned his head toward me. "What did you say?"

"Just this word we learned in social studies, a word for an ideal society. Utopia. Sounds like Utopia, where you're from. I guess it's just another word for Arcadia. A perfect world."

Touch thought on the word. I could see him turning it over in his head, thinking on it, comparing it to whatever bells and whistles his language would use to say it. Then he nodded, agreeing with me, but he looked powerfully sad. "Yes," he said. "I guess it is. Or at least, it used to be."

WE PUTTERED ON THROUGH THE CANYON. AS A MISSISSIPPI GIRL I'd spent a good bit of time in church. But I want to say that never did I feel such a sense of spirits — of God — as I did floating down that waterway, with the towering walls of rocks — some of them meeting in arches, some of them rising up in crazy shapes. You could watch those rocks the way you watched clouds, thinking on all the things they looked like. A bull's head there, a sneaker over yonder. A lady with long, flowing hair. But unlike clouds, they didn't wisp up and fly away. They stood firm, looking back at you. It was like the soul of whatever shape you saw lived on inside them.

We pulled the boat over on a little island, dragged it up on the sand, and went for a walk. Touch had figured out maps by now, and he followed the directions in his little Anasazi booklet. He read aloud to me as we walked, and I learned how the Anasazi were these ancient people who lived in huts and cave dwellings all through New Mexico, Arizona, Colorado, and Utah. You could find remains of their villages all over the Four Corners region, and before I knew it Touch and I were standing in the middle of one — this little village, with paths carved out and caves built into the rocks, big enough for us to crawl into and hunker down.

More than ever I felt the spirits all around me. When I closed my eyes I saw the whole place full of life, little kids scampering about, women carrying baskets and jugs full of water. There was so much to admire about the way this tiny village was built, into the rocks, like a crazy high-rise apartment that blended in perfectly with the landscape. You could see which parts of the structure belonged to the natural wall of rock, and which parts they had made with mud and rock from the riverbank.

Touch didn't seem to want to go inside. He stood on the perimeter, walking up and down, examining it so close, like this was what he'd come here to see in the first place. "Hey," I said. "Don't you want to come look close up?"

"No," he told me. "I want to get a sense of the construction."

I shrugged and ducked through a little archway. Snug in a little canyon cave, I crossed my legs and then held up my hands, putting my thumb and forefinger together. The kind of position I remember my mama sitting in, concentrating with all her might. *Hush, Anna Marie. Mama's concentrating.*

I opened my eyes and saw Touch, his hands on his hips, looking at me. I smiled at him, and he smiled back, but it wasn't quite as twinkly as his smiles used to be.

"You got places like this?" I asked him.

He got another of those troubled looks across his face, then he jutted his chin toward the wall behind me. "Look," he said. "Art."

I stood up and took a good look at the wall. The cave that I'd crawled into was shaped differently than the other rooms, kind of round, and all of a sudden I had this strong realization. The reason I hadn't seen the drawings straight off was that the walls were charred, different layers of black, and somehow I knew that this room had been a place of worship. The word "kiva" came into my head, a word I'd never heard before. If there ever had been a ceiling it was long gone. The sun warmed the top of my head.

The drawings on the wall looked primitive. Lines and circles and squares. I could make out different kinds of animals — bears and deer and wolves — plus people of different sizes, some of them with animal heads, some of them *holding* what looked like human heads. Staring at those, I had this feeling they were meant to stand as a warning. Like maybe I shouldn't be in this little round room, staring at this art.

"Touch," I said. "I feel a little bit afraid."

"It's OK." His voice sounded very different to me just then. It sounded firm, no devil in it, with a certainty I hadn't heard before. For a moment I felt like he knew exactly where he was and what he was doing. Like he had some sort of purpose beyond escaping from capture.

The world started to pulse around me. I couldn't stop myself. I reached out toward one of the drawings, the tallest character. His head was surrounded by what looked like a sun, and he didn't have any human head dangling from his hands. Still I could tell he was a warrior, or maybe even a god, with a crisscross shield drawn on his chest.

"Rogue," Touch called out, and whether he meant to stop me or encourage me I couldn't say. All I knew was that as soon as my fingers made contact with the drawing, my body shot through with something terrifying and powerful. Something warm and bright as the sun itself. It shook me to the core, the way even absorbing Cody, Wendy Lee, and the wildebears had not. I could see the very earth in all its newness surrounding me. My veins felt flooded with the red clay beneath my feet. A sort of knowledge that didn't have any words attached to it took over, filling me to the rim of my head, having to do with the inconsequential nature of anything human, anything manmade.

Tawa. The word, a name, pulsed in my ears. In front of me, on the wall, the picture came to life. He lifted his shield and shook his fist at me, as if I'd done something very wrong. And then he knelt, right off the wall, and peered into my face.

"Touch," I whispered. The whole world had gone blurry. My face was hot from the sun burning inside me. Touch's voice came from very far away, and slow, so slow, like a recording on the wrong speed. I couldn't understand what he was saying. But I did recognize something in the face of the picture — the moving, living petroglyph — in front of me. *Tawa.* That was his name, and I saw that he was searching my face, deciding whether or not I was worthy of what I'd just taken from him.

And then a whole world exploded inside me. It burst. It crackled so I thought my eyes would pop straight out of my head. I wanted to scream, but something else battled those cries down.

"Warriors don't scream," Tawa said. "Warriors stand firm and fight."

"And gods?" I said, maybe out loud, or maybe in my head. "What do they do?"

"They don't give away their powers," Tawa said. "You cannot drain them of theirs."

"That's not what I mean . . . I didn't mean . . ."

"Hush," Tawa said. "Hush, little girl."

I realized with both horror and comfort that I was still touching him. Beneath my fingers, the cave drawing trembled. It faded and grew bigger, then diminished, then disappeared altogether. Suddenly the red earth rushed up to meet my face. I felt a great surge, like a river current covering me, only it wasn't water, but sun.

"Take what you need," Tawa whispered, "and nothing more."

• • •

WHEN I OPENED MY EYES, THE SKY STOOD BLUE AND PEACEFUL
above me. The cave drawing of Tawa had returned to its spot, untouched and unchanged. Unmoving. My whole body felt wrecked and
ravaged, like it had been though something enormous, something it
needed recovering from. I sat up and blinked against the sunlight. My
shoulder didn't hurt. I pushed my shirt aside to examine the wound. It
had disappeared, healed up, only an odd zigzag scar in place of the
thread and blood. Almost as startling, the skin on my forearm and
across my back had changed color, darkened, to a ruddy complexion,
mirroring the landscape all around me.

"Touch," I said, my throat hoarse, my insides drier than the semi-
desert all around us. "Did you see that? Did you hear?"

But he didn't answer me. Not exactly. He just said, "There. Just
let them try to take you now."

TIME PASSED. I LAY ON THE FLOOR OF THE KIVA, NOT READY OR
able to get up quite yet. My limbs felt immobile, my body drained, like
I'd just run a marathon, or recovered from a killing fever. This would
have worried me if Touch hadn't seemed so calm. He just stood in his
same spot, arms crossed, watching me, like this had been his plan all
along.

And something else. What I'd touched had been too huge, too
powerful, to take whole. Maybe even to take at all. At the same time, I
knew that a piece had been given willingly, added to my growing col-
lection of life forces. Tawa. The tiniest piece of him was larger than a
whole person, or two wildebears. However much the absorption had
weakened me, I knew that when I recovered I'd be stronger than ever.

Finally I crawled out of there on my hands and knees. Then I
stood up and walked over to Touch. The sense of *recovering* had

started to lift, and I felt damn near *recovered*. In fact I felt better than fine. The canyon buzzed all around me, speaking to me, infusing me with more and more strength.

You would think Touch might say something, about what had just happened — me convulsing and hitting the ground, then standing up with skin a shade darker. But he just said, "There's a canyon deeper than this, south of here." Somehow I knew exactly what he meant.

"Sure," I said. "It's right on the way to Mexico."

"We'll head there in the morning."

"Fine with me." Of course I'd always wanted to see the Grand Canyon. I just wasn't quite ready to ask Touch how the hell he knew about it. My body still felt strange and tingly, too crowded and at the same time strong and invincible.

The two of us made our way back to the boat. Maybe what I'd just been through, what he'd just witnessed, went too far beyond words to talk about. On the water, we puttered past all the rising rocks and ruins, both of us feeling a thousand ancient faces watching us. And we knew, somehow, that they wished us well.

WHEN WE GOT BACK TO THE BOAT RENTAL PIER, THE NAVAJO guy returned the fake license Touch had given him; I guessed he'd kept a few from his friend in Smith Park. Of course I'd only ever had one form of identification, the real driver's license that I'd burned back at the sand dunes. I wondered if I should think on how to get another one over the next few days. It wouldn't take us much longer than that to get into Mexico.

Touch put the fake ID back into his inside pocket. The Navajo peered very carefully into my face. "Are you OK?" he asked.

"Sure." I tried to sound casual. Like, *Why wouldn't I be* OK?

"You look different," he said. "Different than when you first came."

"I got a lot of sun," I said.

He nodded, real solemn. "More sun than you'd bargained for, I'd say."

There was no good answer to this. My shoulders went a little soft. I let myself lean into Touch.

"Here," the Navajo said. He picked up a little silver chain with a sun pendant. In the center of the silver sun was a round piece of turquoise. "You take this. You keep it."

"Will it keep me safe?"

"Listen," he said. "When I was a boy, my grandparents told me never to go inside the ruins. 'Look at them from a small distance,' they always said. Because when you go inside, you never know what spirits might jump inside you. Good or bad."

The foggy, fuzzy sense of fever came back to me, but pulsing far away, like a memory.

"What I'm saying is," the Navajo told me, "you don't need jewelry to keep you safe. Not anymore." But he dropped the necklace into my hands all the same.

TOUCH AND I FOUND OUR WAY BACK TO THE TRUCK AND DROVE just a little ways, till we found a campground. This time we were very careful to fill out the envelope with cash slipped inside, and the model and make and license of our truck. I felt a little nervous with the truck's original license plate, but at the same time I had this hopeful feeling that whoever owned that truck had left it behind for the season and wouldn't discover it missing till summer rolled around again. On the whole, I'd recovered from the incident at the ruins. My skin, though, stayed dark and ruddy, and my brain wouldn't stop tingling. What's more, I couldn't shake the feeling that Touch had known exactly what he was doing when he walked me into those ruins. When I asked him about it, he just said, "How could I?" And since I didn't have an answer, I left it at that.

We didn't have a tent to pitch, so we just climbed into the bed of the truck and wrapped ourselves up in Joe Wheeler's blankets. I pulled his big green duffel bag right in between us.

"What's that for?" Touch said.

"You know what. You don't want to end up like those wildebears, do you?"

"I can think of worse ways to go."

At last that playfulness had come back into his voice. I sat up on one elbow and looked over at him. He had on about every piece of clothing we'd stolen, though to me the night felt pretty warm — warmer than it had been in Colorado.

"Touch?" I said.

"Rogue?"

"What happened back there? In the ruins?"

"I think," he said, "that those cave paintings were more alive than we realized."

"Did you know that was going to happen?" I couldn't help but ask again. He didn't say anything, and too quickly I added, "What did you mean when you said they couldn't take me now?"

I wished right away that I hadn't added the second question, because he chose to answer that one instead of the first. "It seemed like you became more powerful," he said. "Now you've got the wildebears in you, plus the Anasazi. I'd say that makes you a very strong woman."

Touch smiled at me, and I smiled back, even though smiling felt like changing the subject. It was dark, the sun had set, but above our head shone about a million stars. He looked from my face back up at the sky. Then back at me.

"Hi," he said, like he'd just noticed I was here.

Then he did something I hadn't expected. He took his top blanket off (he'd taken two versus my one) and threw it over me. It covered my whole self — my head, my face, everything. I felt an instinctive rush of fear, like he meant to kidnap me. Then I remembered I'd already been kidnapped. And that was just fine with me. I didn't push the blanket away, though that was my natural reflex. Instead I just lay down, my head still under the blanket, the stars taken away from my view. And in the instant I knew what Touch would do next, he went ahead and did it: he climbed on top of the blanket, which meant he climbed on top of me.

The weight of a man, on top of me, his body fitted to mine — I'd never felt that before. It could have been a frightening thing, I guess, except for the fact that I trusted Touch. Even though I was confused by all that had gone on that day, deep inside I trusted him. And I loved him. There. I'd said it — or at least thought it. Part of me was afraid that if I said the word aloud he would get that confused look I'd come to know so well, like when I first said "air conditioner."

But my whole heart told me no. He wouldn't get that look at all. The blanket was made of cotton flannel, soft and warm, but thin enough that I could feel the heat of him, and smell the scent of him. He clasped his arms around me, and pressed his cheek against mine, and through the blanket I could feel his lips moving against my ear, whispering something in his own odd and beautiful language. And even though I couldn't understand it, I liked hearing it. It made me feel close to him, a little less like there was a blanket between us. I concentrated on the weight of his body on mine.

Touch knew what love meant.

I didn't care about seeing the stars, or if Touch had brought me to those ruins on purpose. I didn't even care about breathing. I just pressed myself back up against him, relishing the feel of his stomach breathing against mine, and his lips by my ear, saying things I couldn't understand but loved the sound of. I could've gone on like that all night long and forever, but finally Touch fell asleep, and very carefully I rolled him off myself, and put the duffel bag between us, because you never could be too safe. Not with someone you loved.

• • •

IN MY LIFE, I'D KNOWN PLENTY ABOUT GUILT EVEN BEFORE what happened with Cody. I guess it's an emotion everyone has, and with me it sure didn't help having Aunt Carrie harping on the evil that lived inside me. When I started heading toward the teen years, she warned me about men, and the parts of my body that nobody was ever supposed to touch. Including me. Maybe if she hadn't warned me against touching myself, it never would've occurred to me to do it. But all her yammering got me curious, and there I was one night — in the dark with nobody looking — so I gave it a try, and what do you know if it didn't feel kind of good. So it became my new way of falling asleep, touching the places I wasn't supposed to, and not long afterward breasts started sprouting up on my chest, and then hair in places where there hadn't been any. I felt sure I'd brought it on myself, that if I'd listened to Aunt Carrie my body would've stayed the way it used to be. So I stopped cold, but the damage was done. I kept growing up, into a woman. And even after I figured out that of course it wasn't my fault, and my body would've changed anyway, I never could start in on that habit again. Something in my mind made it wrong, dirty. Even the feelings I had for Cody sometimes made me feel like I was doing something wrong. Impure.

Maybe by the time Touch came along, I felt catapulted so far out of my own world that those thoughts never entered into my mind at all. I never felt a bit guilty. Or maybe it was because the pull toward him was so strong that it obliterated everything else. Love. Yes. There was no other word for it. I'd loved Cody, too, but this was different. It was bigger. More grown-up. More permanent.

And that's what did it: brought the guilt back. Because of my little spasm of puppy love, Cody lay in a hospital bed, drained of his past and his future. And me, I'd just decided to move on to the next guy.

Probably these thoughts were why I had a dream about Cody that night, sleeping in the back of the blue pickup truck. Cody would've loved that truck, and in the dream he and I were sitting in its bed on either side of a little campfire, roasting marshmallows. Cody was patient with his marshmallow, turning it round and round real slow, letting it get just the right shade of pale, bubbly brown. Whereas I would just light mine on fire, blow it out, and peel off the charred layer. It burned my tongue a little every single time.

"You have to slow down," Cody said, turning that marshmallow carefully as could be. "There's no hurry, Rogue."

It sounded very funny to my ears, hearing him call me Rogue instead of Anna Marie. "How'd you know my name?" I asked him.

"I've known you since the beginning." I saw his eyes fall on my hands, the ring he'd given me.

The dream felt so real. Not in the way my other dreams had. It lacked the dreamlike quality, but felt just like normal life, except somehow *deeper* than real life, like I had to be carefully on the watch for hidden meaning. Cody looked just like he always had, very young and alive, but he spoke much more precisely. I remembered all the times when he'd been the only person I could talk to. He took the marshmallow out of the fire and held the stick out to me.

I said, "No. You have it, Cody. You worked so hard on it."

"It's yours now," he said. "It's important that you have it."

It felt rude to say no when he held it out to me that way. Like a gift. So I took the stick from him and pulled the marshmallow off real careful, remembering what he'd told me — I had all the time in the world. The marshmallow tasted wonderful, crispy on the outside, meltingly sweet on the inside, and I closed my eyes for a minute to savor it. When I opened my eyes, Cody still sat across from me, but the fire was gone, and he had pulled his knees up to his chest. His arms were around his legs, hugging them, and his face was buried in his knees, and he was crying, shaking, sobbing.

"Cody," I said. "Please don't cry."

Before I could stop myself, I reached out to touch him, not re-membering until the last second that I shouldn't. But Cody remem-bered, and he pulled away just in time, like he'd never done in any of the other dreams.

"Careful, Rogue," he said. "That's the most important thing. Care-ful while you're here. Careful while you're there."

The tears were gone. He was standing up, looking down at me. He looked very serious, but not angry, and not scared.

"While I'm there?" I said. "Where's there?"

Cody said, "Listen. There's only one world for you."

This made me kind of mad, considering all the plans I had in my head. So I opened my mouth to ask him how he knew that, and why he'd said it, and just then the scene changed, and I was Cody, a tiny little toddler, setting in a baby swing, and his mama was pushing me. Every time I came toward her, she'd grab my feet, and rub her nose against mine, and I would laugh and laugh, loud peals of baby laughter ringing in my ears.

All of a sudden I was myself again, grown-up, sitting on one end of a seesaw. Cody sat on the other end, way up in the air.

"It's time, Rogue," he said. "It's time."

I woke up with a gasp, sitting up in the bed of the blue truck, Touch sleeping soundly right beside me. A million, trillion, billion stars above my head. Everything quiet and still.

The letters. I'd forgotten all about writing the letters to Cody's folks. And what with the law on my tail, I couldn't see any possible way to start writing them again. Which may actually have been a re-lief to them. Either way, it left me feeling the same, which was guilty. I lay back down, pulled my blanket over me, and stared up at all those stars for a long time, listening to Touch's slow, steady breath and won-dering which faraway ball of light might be his home. One thing I knew for sure, what had just happened had been no ordinary dream. That had been Cody, come to see me from another place. Being with him, seeing him whole, comforted me as much as it confused me. And I hoped against hope that he was dead wrong about how many worlds there were for me.

FINALLY I GOT BACK TO SLEEP, AND BY THE TIME I OPENED MY eyes Touch was already up, bustling around the campground, making a little fire even though we had nothing to cook. It was September now, and should've been cool in the morning, but the sun had already risen pretty high in the sky and beat down with ferocious warmth. Still Touch was all bundled into his padded flannel, rubbing gloved hands together like he needed to warm up. I wondered if I'd adapt to the temperature on his planet once I'd talked him into taking me there.

"Just how hot are we talking about?" By now I'd brushed my teeth and joined him by the fire, wearing a T-shirt and the flowery skirt I'd stolen from Joe Wheeler's wife. I had my sweater, the one with the built-in gloves, over my knee and was stitching up the hole made by the wildebear. The sweater was so dark that the blood-stain wasn't too noticeable, and it was too useful a garment to just throw away.

"By your temperature system? Probably an average of one hundred and twenty-five degrees Farenheit. One hundred twenty-five to one hundred fifty, I'd say."

"Good lord." I couldn't imagine being in a place that hot, what it would feel like. "Everyone must move very slow."

Touch laughed. "It's what we're used to. I'll say one thing, we don't have to bother with so much clothing, the way you do."

"What about sunburns?"

"We've gotten pretty advanced with protection."

I pictured Alabaster's pure, untouched skin. Pretty advanced was right, maintaining that look under a 125-degree sun!

We ate some beef jerky — Touch could stomach that only marginally better than the peanut butter — while I looked at the map. "It won't take long to get to the Grand Canyon from here," I said. "Just about seven hours, I'd guess, with stops and so forth. Do you want to go down into it once we get there?" I was hoping he'd say yes. I'd always wanted to take one of those mules down into the canyon.

"Definitely go down into it," he said. With the daylight, the thoughtful look had come back over him. But he smiled at me, then tossed his jerky into the fire. "How much money do we have left?" he said. "Let's get some real breakfast before we set out. Then maybe we should try an ATM."

I counted out the last of Joe Wheeler's money. Back in Caldecott County five hundred dollars would've been a fortune. I'd run away from home with not much more than that. But life on the road was proving expensive. Between the motel, the boat rental, the campground fee, and the few supplies we'd bought, we only had about a hundred and fifty left.

"Probably better to get more money here," Touch said. "Then put some distance between us and the machine."

I nodded and handed the money to Touch. It would be safest in that inside pocket of his. He stood up and came over to sit beside me. "Let me see the wound," he said.

I hesitated a minute, then figured what the hell. Nobody else was around to see me. And he was wearing his gloves. So I just pulled the T-shirt up over my head, sat there in my bra and skirt, and turned my back to him.

He pressed his gloved fingertips very gently around where the wound had been. It didn't feel tender at all, just completely healed.

"Amazing," he said.

I drew in my breath. Touch moved his finger from my scar to my spine. He ran it down very careful, almost all the way down to my backside. It sent shivers right through me, that gentle touch, and I concentrated on being grateful for it — even luxuriating in it — instead of wishing I could feel his real fingertips and not just leather. He let his other hand get into the act, touching my back in very gentle swirls, until I was a quivering mess there on the log. I couldn't help it. I turned around to face him.

As I turned, his hands kind of slipped off my back onto his knees. And then he lifted those hands and put them right on my breasts. It nearly startled me out of my skin. Then the startledness went away, and it felt not only amazing, but right. The shivers turned into a warmth that started at the very core of me. I closed my eyes, concentrating on his hands, and the warmth pulsing through them, from me and into me, and it was like the world's strongest magnet was pulling me in, toward his lips, to kiss him. And he started leaning in toward me, too.

I stopped us just in time, standing up so abruptly he nearly fell off the log. He righted himself, then shook his head real sharp, like waking himself up out of a trance.

"I'm sorry," he said. "It's just that I want to so badly."

"Tell me about it," I said. And headed over to the truck so I could drape and cover myself in all the clothing possible.

BY THE TIME WE SAT EATING EGGS, TOAST, AND COFFEE AT HARvey's Diner, I was sweating, back in my leather pants and flannel shirt and jean jacket. I guessed if I wanted to live on a 125-degree planet I'd better start getting used to it. Touch sopped up egg with toast, polishing the meal off in about two minutes flat, then ordered another plate with an extra side of bacon. He was a very big guy and had hardly been eating enough to keep a mouse alive these past few days. Between what had happened between us last night and this morning, not to mention all our days on the run together, I was feeling awful close to him. So I went ahead and told him my dream about Cody.

Touch listened carefully. "Interesting," he said. "It's almost like he knows what's going on with you, like he's watching you from his hospital room."

"Yeah," I said. "But it's a dream. So he knows what's going on with me because *I* know what's going on with me. It's happening in my head."

"Maybe. Or maybe he's communicating with you across an astral plane."

"An astral plane!"

Touch said, "The Anasazi were very mystical people. They weren't tethered to just one world, like the people who live here now. Maybe now that you've absorbed some of that warrior's power, you're not tethered here either."

Despite all the food, my stomach suddenly felt very hollow. All these things Touch was saying about the Anasazi, he hadn't got them from any park service pamphlet. I put my toast down and stared at him. "That something you do on your planet?" I said. "Communicate with ancient Anasazi from Planet Earth?"

He said, "I don't know about that. But I do know about astral planes. Only very advanced mystics can get there. I've never done it. But if you have two people, both capable? They can visit each other. In dreams. Or elsewhere."

Elsewhere. Touch always talked so perfect and fancy. I loved the thought of elsewhere.

"Maybe," I said, "you and I could meet on one of them astral planes one day. And you could really touch me. No gloves. No clothes."

He put down his coffee and looked at me, long and deep. When I first saw Touch, I'd been impressed by his eyes on account of their color. Their shape. Their prettiness. Now when I looked at his eyes,

I saw all those qualities, but I also saw something more. Sorrow, and kindness, and the weight of the whole world. Plus maybe — and it might've been wishful thinking — love. Maybe I saw love, too.

He reached across the table and put his gloved hand over mine. "Just don't let Cody touch you on an astral plane," he said, and my heart leaped straight to my lips in the biggest smile ever. He loved me! He did. Why else would he say that? Touch loved me.

I saw it as I held his hand and smiled right into his devilish eyes. Love. Plain as day.

WHILE TOUCH PAID THE BREAKFAST BILL, I WENT TO USE THE bathroom. Soon as I closed myself into the stall, I saw it — a big, fat, brown leather wallet, sitting on the back of the toilet.

Inside my chest, a *thump thump thump*ing started. It was a sign! Someone up there wanted us to continue. I scooped up the wallet and sat down on the toilet. It belonged to Mary Ginsberg from Flagstaff, Arizona. She was twenty-two years old, and nothing about the wallet said she was rich — it was old and battered — except for the fact that she had three hundred dollars cash in there.

I sat there long after I'd finished peeing, staring at her picture on the license. She looked like a nice enough person. Part of me just wanted to wait awhile, to make sure she wouldn't come in looking for the wallet.

By the time I came out of the bathroom, Touch already stood outside in the parking lot, waiting on me. I took a deep breath and marched that wallet right up to the front counter. "Someone left this in the bathroom," I told the clerk, sliding it across to him, and hoping he wouldn't pocket the cash himself.

As I walked out into the bright sunlight, the fact that Mary Ginsberg's driver's license sat in my back pocket made me feel only slightly less virtuous. I'd done the right thing. Arcadia, here I come.

• • •

UNFORTUNATELY, NO GOOD DEED EVER GOES UNPUNISHED.
Touch and I moseyed on into the convenience store that adjoined the
diner, so we could use the ATM. We floated the blue ball into it. This
time the screen didn't say "Insufficient Funds." It didn't say anything
at all. And it didn't spit out any bills. Almost worst of all, when Touch
tapped on the slot, the blue ball didn't come back to him.

I reached out and shook the machine as hard as I could.

"Hey," yelled the man behind the counter. "You there! What do
you think you're doing?"

Just great. And me without my hat, too, just wild loose hair with
white streaks. Couldn't be more recognizable if I tried. Damn virtue,
I thought, thinking on that three hundred dollars. Damn.

Out on the sidewalk, Touch and I stood together in front of the
blue truck. "Well," he said. "We'll just have to manage without it."

"Well crap," I said. "What if someone else gets ahold of it?"

"No one from your time would know how to use it."

"My *time*?"

"Your planet." He said this in kind of a rushed, distracted way,
then added, "It might be a good thing, actually. Leaving it there. It
might confuse the tracking devices."

Which was great news, but didn't solve the issue of how the hell
we were going to get by with no source of money. But still I tossed
Touch the keys. I knew a hell-bent man when I saw one. It was Grand
Canyon or bust.

WE MADE IT TO THE GRAND CANYON LATER THAT AFTERNOON.
That old blue Chevy truck, it was a gas guzzler. By the time Touch
and I stood at the rim, looking down into a vastness I never could have
dreamed, the truck was near on empty, and we had twenty-two dol-

lars left, tucked into the back pocket of Touch's blue jeans. How the hell would we get from the Grand Canyon to Mexico on twenty-two dollars? All my life I'd dreamed of a moment like this, looking out onto a natural wonder of the world, standing beside a man I loved. And all I could think on was how that pimply clerk had probably pocketed Mary's cash so he could buy a new iPod, and here we were, dead broke.

Touch looked like he had more lofty thoughts on his mind. He looked pale and shaky and filled with awe. I slipped my arm into his and tried to divert my thoughts from the practical and selfish to the larger wonder of the world, like a good girl from a perfect society would do.

"I've never seen anything like this in my whole life," I said, my voice full of honest reverence. When I looked into the canyon, I knew I wasn't putting on the wonder, but felt it absolutely, in my gut. I felt it more than I'd ever felt any kind of nature, all the rocks and trees and water breathed in perfect concert with my new, darker skin.

"I have," Touch said. "I've seen something like this."

His voice sounded different than I'd ever heard it, it sounded shaken and gruff. I realized his arm was trembling against mine.

"Rogue," he said.

I knew exactly what Touch was going to say before he said it. Part of me had known it for days. I just hadn't been ready to say it. I squeezed my elbow tighter against his. He looked straight ahead, out into the greens and browns and blues, the endless width and descent of a crater that went on forever.

"Touch," I finally said. "You're not from another planet. Are you?"

"No," he said. "I'm not."

"That time travel ring. It works better than just a few hours here and there. Don't it?"

"Yes," he said. "Yes, Rogue. It does."

I took a deep breath. Anything he had to say next seemed way more important than the fact he'd been lying to me all this time.

"How far?" I said, impressed by how calm my voice sounded. "How far in the future do you come from?"

"Ten thousand years," he said, his voice real quiet, but still seeming like it echoed, on account of the wide world spread beneath us.

"Ten thousand years," I said, echoing the echo.

I didn't look at him. I couldn't, just then. But I could feel him nod, staring way down into the void. And when he spoke, it wasn't so much to tell me something new, but more like he just wanted to hear himself speak the truth after all these days of lying. A few feet below, a golden eagle swooped, graceful circles, making it seem like the two of us were standing right smack in the middle of the sky.

"I'm home," Touch said.

· *9* ·

IN THE SPACE OF A FEW MINUTES, FUTURE AND PLANET TOUCH
had become just Future. Touch and I stood there, staring over the rim
into the canyon.

"Ten thousand years from now," he said, "this canyon is half-filled
with water. You can hike down a long ways, and there's a mesa that
kind of juts out into the lake. I've gone diving there with . . . I've been
there on vacation."

"Why did you lie to me?"

"I didn't mean to," Touch said. "I mean, I wasn't planning on it.
You asked me, remember? You asked if I was from another planet. And
it seemed like you'd have fewer questions that way. I felt like the less
you knew — the more oblique your information was — the safer you'd
be. And honestly it didn't seem too much like a lie. Ten thousand
years from now, this really is like another planet in many ways."

I drew in a deep breath. My mind went into a kind of frenzy, trying to piece together the truth from what he'd told me. I guess Touch
could tell this, because he said, "I haven't been lying to you about

where I come from, Rogue. Not really. Just think of everything I've told you and substitute the word 'time' for 'planet.'"

"So that means in ten thousand years, the earth will be ninety-five percent salt water?"

Touch nodded. I tried to imagine it. All the pieces of the world that would drown. Mississippi, for example. Can't say why, but the idea made my throat fill up with tears. Home, sunken.

Maybe I should have been mad at him. Maybe I *would* have been mad at him if I hadn't been keeping a secret of my own — what all my skin could do — till right about yesterday. As it was, I could hear Tawa inside me, telling me to pipe down with all my girlish feelings. There were more important issues at hand.

"So what do you want to do now?" I finally asked Touch. It seemed we had been standing here half the afternoon, just staring, letting me absorb this new revelation.

"I want to go down there," Touch said, pointing into the canyon.

AT THE VISITORS CENTER WE FOUND OUT THAT THE SPIT OF land Touch remembered — what in ten thousand years would be the bottom of the canyon, at least as far as land — was called Horseshoe Mesa. It would take about three hours for us to hike down there, by which time it would be dark. We gathered everything from the truck that could fit into the frame pack, which Touch carried. Even though we'd filled that pack with blankets and clothes, when I picked it up to put it on his back, it felt like it weighed about two ounces. I guess on account of my new strength from the wildebears and Tawa.

The walk was very steep downhill, with loads of switchbacks, so you had to watch your footing every step of the way. Still, Touch and I talked as we went. It was true that knowing he was from the future, instead of thinking he was from another planet, inspired about a million more questions. You can guess the first one I had for him.

"So," I said, "why did you travel back ten thousand years?"

He was quiet for a few paces. Then he said, "There are a lot of gaps in our history. The history of our people. Archaeologically it's complicated, because almost everything's submerged. We don't know much about what came before. The only thing we've ever been able to find are places like the one you and I saw yesterday, the Anasazi ruins, and so many of them are under water."

"Wait a minute," I said. "When you say places like the one we saw yesterday, you mean buildings. Cities. Right? I mean, even if most of the world is under water . . ."

Touch said, "I never saw a single piece of your world until I came here."

"You mean to tell me there's nothing left from after the Anasazi? No cities or towns or buildings or *anything*?"

"No," Touch said simply. "I didn't know what I'd find, as far as civilization, until I got here."

Something inside me stopped cold. In ten thousand years' time, all traces of the life that currently existed on Planet Earth would be gone. Wiped away. What in the world had happened between my time and his? What had we done, my branch of humanity, to destroy everything we'd spent millennia building, so much that future civilizations wouldn't even know we'd existed? *Leave nothing but your footsteps*, Cody's scout leader used to say, when they headed off into the wilderness with the troop. Somehow I knew in my heart it wasn't on account of being careful that we'd left nothing behind for Touch's generation to find.

"So you came here as some sort of anthropologist?"

"You might say that," Touch said.

"And those people who are chasing you . . ."

"I told you," he said. "They want to overthrow Arcadia."

That didn't exactly tell me how the two issues were connected. But Touch started walking faster, like what he'd said ended the whole matter. I knew that if I asked any more questions, he'd tell me I was about to make the whole anti-Arcadia army appear right in front of us. Which if you asked me was a little too convenient, so I piped up with something else that was on my mind.

"If that golden ring of yours is one of a kind, how come all your friends can travel through time to find you?"

"They need a target to do it," Touch said. "A specific DNA configuration. Even with that it's very complicated."

"But they're managing."

"Apparently." He sounded very grim.

Never mind how strong I'd become. On my shoulders I felt the whole weight of the world. Plus I felt worried. Worried about our various pursuers, and worried about money and how Touch and I would survive without a way of getting it. I worried about how hungry I felt — we hadn't eaten since breakfast, and the sun had started dipping in the sky. All we had for tomorrow was a package of cookies, some bread, and the peanut butter that Touch wouldn't eat. We'd filled up water bottles at the visitors center, but that wouldn't last us more than a day or two. And then what?

Here was the only thing I knew about the future, not Touch's future, but mine, ours, this civilization where I'd spent my whole life up till now: something would wipe us out, almost all of us, and not only that, every trace of the lives we'd lived. When would it happen? If I didn't go to the future with Touch, what would I live to see?

Ten thousand years from now the world would be mostly water. It would be very, very hot. And the people left behind — the great-great-great-great- (and on and on) grandchildren of the people here today — would manage, at least eventually, to create a far better world than the one we'd gone and destroyed.

But wouldn't you know it: the bad ones, the evil ones, still managed to rear their ugly heads. Their ugly and greedy wants, threatening to destroy it all again. Those people living in Arcadia wanted to turn it back into a world ruled by rich people, taking away everything that ought to be shared. Just like our own world, which would destroy itself without leaving anything behind to warn the future.

By the time Touch and I got to Horseshoe Mesa, it was dark. Both of us were too tired to eat. We just rolled out our blankets, pulled on our hats, and fell asleep under the stars — both of us dreaming about time, backward and forward, and on and on, till the first rays of sunlight woke us.

TOUCH GOT UP FIRST, BUT HE DIDN'T BUILD A FIRE LIKE USUAL. For some reason he seemed energized and twinkly again. "Good morning, Earthling," he said, when he saw me sitting up on my blanket.

"Good morning yourself," I said, and then added, "Earthling."

It almost managed to break me out of my funk, seeing him step so lightly as he knelt and dug through the pack, setting out food and water. My stomach rumbled greedily at the sight of stale bread and peanut butter.

"Did you bring that flashlight?" he asked, digging through the pack.

"Yeah," I said. "It's in the side pocket." What I wished I had was a toothbrush. I crawled out from under the blanket and swished some water around in my mouth. Next time we were near a convenience store, I didn't care if we only had two dollars left, I was going to spend it on toothpaste and a toothbrush.

"What are you thinking?" I said, spreading peanut butter on bread. Touch had found the flashlight and tucked it into the front of his pants.

He gestured toward the ground. "Caves," he said. "When I came here before, we went diving underneath, through caves. I collected crystals from the ceiling to use in my work. I want to explore a little, see what they look like without the water. And see if the crystals are there, if they have the same properties."

"Hey," I said. "You went traveling here, and in the sand dunes. Where all did you live?"

We had left the atlas in the truck, so I took a stick and drew him a map of North America. I didn't sketch out the countries or the individual states, which wouldn't mean much to him anyway. It was just the shape of the continent that mattered.

"I think here," Touch said. He pointed to a spot southeast of us, what would now be the middle of New Mexico. And he pointed out the perimeters, what the continent would come down to. In his world, North America only went so far west as Nevada. The East started somewhere in north Texas. Just one little chunk of land, mostly high ground, left of what had been North America. Touch knelt down and erased what would go missing with his hands. I fought the chills that crawled up my spine, seeing it all wiped away under his palm.

He ate the cookies, and we split up the last two pieces of beef jerky. Then we took careful sips of water — it would be important to conserve — and went off into the caves underneath the mesa, to search for what remained of the future.

I'D NEVER BEEN IN A CAVE BEFORE. TOUCH LED THE WAY, HOLDing on to the flashlight with one hand and my hand with the other — both of us with our gloves on. My hands were sweating, and I wanted to take off my jean jacket, but I also wanted to keep getting used to it — the heat, feeling hot, sweating. Because I still wanted to go to Touch's world, even if it wasn't a different world after all, but my own world way off in the future.

"It seems like you could fix an awful lot," I told him, "just by traveling back in time. All you'd have to do is find out where you went wrong — where the world went wrong — in the first place."

"Ah but that's where you have to be careful," he said. He stopped and shone the light up at the ceiling, which was just inches above our heads and lined with glimmering stones, quartz and crystal, just dazzling. "It looks different out of water," he said. "It's very beautiful." And then he said, "Changing history, changing the past, is a tricky business. You never know what else you'll change inadvertently. For example, if this civilization doesn't end, ours may never rise."

"But you went back in time," I said. "To come here, you went back in time."

"I didn't have a choice," he said.

"But then you told me you did it again, back in Jackson."

"Just an hour here and there," he said. "A few days or a week. And I was very careful not to do anything differently, not to travel back to days that had been personally significant for me. I promised myself that once I'd got the hang of it I'd only go forward in time, and only in an emergency. The only time I made an exception was with you."

We ducked through an archway — the caves were connected to each other, like rooms, one after another. As Touch talked, we walked deeper into the mesa, holding hands, stalactites dripping over our heads, little bits of moisture dropping down. Remembering our water shortage, I stuck out my tongue to catch the drops.

Touch said, "I knew the time was right to run from Jackson. I'd been there too long, I'd used too many materials. It was only a matter of time before the tracking found me. I knew I wanted to leave, but I didn't want to leave without you. So I went by your apartment, but you were gone."

"Gone?"

"Yes. Gone. I managed to get the door open, and there were a few things left behind, but most of it — most of your clothes, and the map you'd had on the wall — was gone. I couldn't continue on without you. I had to bring you with me. So I broke my own rule."

"You came back and got me."

"I turned back time."

I nodded, though he couldn't see me without shining the light on my face. It was so dark in the caves — by now we were so deep inside them, not even the barest bit of light could make its way in from the outside. I wondered where I'd gone when he came by my apartment, where I fled to without him to pick me up on the street after what happened with Wendy Lee. Where would I have headed? Where would I be now?

"You turned back time for me," I said. It would be hard to put into words, how much I wanted to kiss him at that moment.

Touch looked like he felt the very same way. The two of us stood dangerously close. Then he stepped back. He pointed the light toward the ceiling of the cave and all the dense crystals. I watched him reach out to touch them and I did the same, running my hands over their cold, damp bumpiness. But Touch wasn't just feeling the crystals. He was plucking them, digging his hands deep into the sediment and pulling out chunks of clear, sparkling rock.

"Hey," I said. "Are you supposed to do that?"

He didn't answer, and I figured at this point, whether I knew what he was up to or not, I was in this for good. With Touch. So I started collecting crystals, too, scooping them off the ceiling and handing them over. Touch stuffed them into a little pouch.

"That's probably enough," he said when it was full. He put the flashlight down by his side. It shone on the dirt floor of the cave, sending up a muted kind of light all around us. I don't know about my face, but his looked eerie and beautiful and full of emotion, as if emotion were a liquid, like water.

Then all of a sudden, the flashlight flickered. It died a moment, then came back on, then died again. I fumbled in the dark, grabbed it from his hand, and slapped it against my palm. It came on for one second, then it went out. Dead. The two of us were left standing in such complete darkness, not even my cat eyes could see so much as a moving shadow.

• • •

ALONG WITH THE DARKNESS THAT WAS TOTAL AND ABSOLUTE
came silence. Stillness. Me and Touch, standing together in the
caves, so deep in there, with walls and ceilings that we couldn't see
close around us. It was the quiet of a mistake of monumental propor-
tions. One of those things they don't teach you in school: When going
deep into a series of caves, make sure you have more than one flashlight. Or an extra set of batteries.

Finally Touch broke the silence. He said, "I don't understand
what happened."

The mistake hit me full force in that moment. It was all my fault.
Touch had no idea about batteries. In his perfect and waste-free society, light devices probably shone on forever. I fumbled through a lame
explanation of the short life of batteries, almost glad that I couldn't
see the expression on his face.

"Primitive," he finally said. That old growl sounded real angry.

The situation was clearly hopeless. We'd already traveled from
one cave to another, through archways, not a huge distance but a very
winding one. We'd brought ourselves to the center of the mesa, underneath, where not the tiniest bit of light shone through. Black. Too
black even for our eyes to adjust, too black even for shadows. We
couldn't see each other's faces. We couldn't see the crystals, glimmering all around us, or even the walls that they were embedded in. It
was darker than closing your eyes — because even then, you can see
colors, light from the other side of your eyelids. I tried to search the
store of people I had inside me. Not one of them knew how to navigate out of these caves in the pitch-black, except maybe Tawa. I tried
to summon the shreds of sun he'd left inside me, but no luck. The rays
wouldn't translate to the outside world.

"What about the crystals?" I asked. "Can you make something
with them?"

"Not without sunlight," he said.

Sunlight, steps away, or perhaps inside my skin: it might as well have been a million miles. I thought of the ring in the inside pocket of Touch's coat, and a spike of elation hit me. Surely this was a situation where we needed to grab at our last resort.

"No," Touch said. "It won't work. It only travels through time, not space. It would land us right here in the cave, in the dark, in another time." It amazed me, how calm he sounded.

"But that can't be," I said. "You're from New Mexico. You ended up in Jackson, Mississippi."

"Before I used the ring for the first time, I took a boat and sailed east."

"Why?" Inside my head, things had gone very loud. Even if Touch pulled that golden ring out of his inside pocket and used it, we would only land in the darkness of the cave, in another time. Ten thousand years back? Still here, inside these caves. Ten thousand years forward? Still here, inside these caves, only with the added bonus of being underwater.

Touch wasn't answering my question, and anyway, the most important thing was figuring a way out of this. "What if you brought us back like fifteen minutes, when the flashlight worked?"

In the blackness, I could feel him shake his head, inches away from me. "Doesn't work that way. Time for the flashlight, for the *batteries*," he said that last word in a completely disgusted tone, and I can't say as I blamed him, "is still moving forward at the same rate. We'd return to fifteen minutes ago with a dead flashlight."

I stepped in the direction of his scent, his breathing. His arms came around me. For a second I felt myself calm down a little, followed immediately by a new flutter of panic. What if in this darkness, this blackness, his face brushed against mine?

Touch didn't need light to read my mind. "Shhh," he whispered, like he could see the panic plain in front of him. "It doesn't matter now."

"It sure as hell does matter," I said. "You think I want to sit here and wait to die alongside a corpse? If this is gonna happen, I at least want some company." It chilled me to the bone saying that. Of course if he could manage not to touch my face — the only part of me that wasn't covered by clothing — I would die before him. I was smaller, leaner. Starvation and dehydration would get me first.

"Look," Touch said. "Let's not give up hope. There's always the chance other hikers will come along, exploring the caves."

I nodded, hoping he could feel and hear the movement of my head, because I couldn't rightly speak. "Or a forest ranger," I said. "A ranger could come upon our stuff up on the mesa, and come looking for us."

"So we'll wait," Touch said. "We'll wait and we'll listen. We'll sip water, we'll eat what food we have left."

"And if nobody comes along . . ."

"We'll die," he said simply.

We stood quiet a minute, both of us with our deep and sorrowful guilt. As for me, I felt like I'd been so careful not to touch him, to keep him safe, and then I'd managed to kill him in a different way, with a different sort of carelessness.

His arms were still firm around me. I pressed my face into his leather jacket. If I kept it there, pressed into him, it couldn't hurt him. It felt so hot inside these caves, despite the dampness coming off the walls, and I didn't dare take off a single layer of clothing. I tried to guess at what it would feel like, if everything I wished came true, and some other spelunker — a smart one, with two flashlights and extra batteries — came along to rescue us. We hadn't seen a single soul on our way down here, so I wasn't exactly holding my breath. But if that wish came true, maybe my other wish would, too, and Touch would bring me along home with him, to his time, my own planet. There, ten thousand years from now, I'd always feel this hot, this sweaty, even walking around stark naked. Who would've known, all that time wearing leather in the summer, I'd been in training for what would one day be my fondest wish.

Without saying anything, the two of us sank to the sandy floor. Like I said, your eyes can't adjust to total blackness — that's what it was, not just darkness, but blackness — in the sense that you can see anything. But part of me had started getting used to it. Isn't it amazing what a person can get used to! We managed to kind of scoot back until Touch's back rested against a cave wall, and I rested against him, keeping my head down low, pressing my face against him, breathing in his familiar smells.

"Hey," I said. "What's it like, anyway? Living on a hundred-and-twenty-five-degree planet?"

Touch sighed, and I pressed myself even closer into the movement of his chest. He gave a little shiver, like someone who'd been cold way too long. "It's wonderful," he said. "In fact I never really appreciated just how wonderful it was until I realized I could never go back."

So there in the darkness, not sure whether we would live or die but pretty sure it would be the second, Touch went ahead and told me everything.

THE STORY HE TOLD ME STARTED A LONG TIME FROM NOW. NOT ten thousand years, but almost. I hardly know whether to tell it in the past tense or the future. But since the past tense is how I heard it from Touch, I guess I'll stick to that.

Five hundred years before Touch was born, the world was kind of like our world, only maybe even worse. The water had long since washed away most of the earth. There was so little land, which meant very few resources. As you can imagine, once the world was mostly sea, the ocean was the place most of the food came from. People ate fish, and seaweed. Some crops were grown on land, but it was very arid, and rain only came seasonally. Somehow it got worked out that just a few families on each of the continents (there were three, at this point, as far as I could figure: smaller versions of North America, Africa, and Asia) were in control. They lived in giant estates, and all the luxuries to be had belonged to them.

And the rest of the people? They worked for the ruling families, spending most of their lives at sea, on boats and under the hot sun, fishing and cultivating seaweed and diving for shellfish. They only ever returned to land to deliver goods to the ruling families, who pretty much just sat on their butts and waited for the deliveries. The lucky commoners — I guess what you'd call the middle class — lived on land and worked for the ruling class in their houses, waiting on them and such. But most people were out on the ocean, where life was hard and short. Life on land was lazy and luxurious, at least for the people in charge, so it was all super-unfair, and I guess it went on like this for thousands of years.

Touch said he thought that was probably part of the reason that they didn't know much about us, the people who came before, and not only because we'd managed to somehow lay waste to all traces. The society was so corrupt, and so focused on bringing pleasure to a very few people, that there never was a whole lot of reflection on the past.

And then, about five hundred years before Touch was born, an idea started on this one fishing boat. All these people, they had shrimp nets put into their hands almost as soon as they could walk. They grew up under the hottest sun you can imagine, with very little space for anybody and no choice except to fish and sail until they died, usually very young. But on this one boat people started talking. Touch couldn't come up with a translation for the name of the boat — the word in his language sounded like the most ghostly whistle you ever heard, echoing through the caves at Horseshoe Mesa — so I decided to call it the *Lincoln*. All these people worked on the *Lincoln*, never wearing much clothes, living on the scraps left over after they made their deliveries to the rich folks on the three continents that remained. And they got to thinking — realizing — that the people in control couldn't do a damn thing for themselves. And so instead of making their deliveries, they started sailing around the sea, meeting up with other fishing boats, and convincing the people — who outnumbered the ruling families by thousands — that there was no need to continue living this way just because they always had.

The first revolts started. Over the next hundred years the ruling classes were overthrown. It was a long and bloody revolution, but when it was over a new government emerged, except it wasn't like the government we had at all. It was just a world where everyone worked together, and everyone had what they needed, and nobody had more of anything than anybody else. When people turned eighteen, they had to go work on the fishing boats for four years. After that, they could go home and pursue anything at all. The whole world worked in concert, with all people choosing the thing to do — the thing they did best — and using it toward what was best for everyone.

What Touch did best, what he liked to do, was build those devices that to me seemed like magic — like the translator, and the blue ball, and the golden ring — but in his world they counted as technology. When he came home from serving his time on the fishing boats, he set to work making new inventions, traveling in ways that had never been seen before.

"I know what happens next," I said, as Touch paused. "It's the families, isn't it? The original families. They want things back the way they used to be. They don't want everything shared. They want everything for themselves."

"Yes," Touch said in the blackness. "That's exactly right."

"So Alabaster," I said. "She must be descended from them, the original aristocrats?"

"Yes," he said again. "She is."

We sat quiet awhile, and I thought on how human nature never changed. Not even in Arcadia. A different picture of Planet Earth was forming in my head, and suddenly I wasn't thinking of it as many different seas and landmasses, but as one gigantic ocean. That's what the Earth was really, one rising sea, and all the land jutting up from under it was temporary. It didn't really matter what became of our world, even as I knew we were hurtling toward being buried under water. Even Touch's world — for them it was just a matter of time before the one sea rose and claimed them all. These may sound like depressing thoughts, but honestly they comforted me, because after all I was sitting there waiting to die, and if losing whole worlds didn't matter, what could be less significant than two people, trapped inside a series of caves?

"The thing is," Touch said, and I stopped him.

"I know what you're going to tell me," I said. "It's not just Alabaster who's descended from those families. It's you. Right?"

Touch didn't say anything. He just nodded. I felt his chin bumping against the top of my head, and I buried my face even closer against his chest to protect him.

And I couldn't help but smile a little, thinking on how elegant Touch had seemed to me, even when I first found him scamming for food stamps on the streets of Jackson, Mississippi. Those upper-crust types. It doesn't matter whether they come from the Bellhaven neighborhood in Jackson or from Arcadia ten thousand years from now. You can spot them a mile away.

TIME CONTINUED DOWN THERE IN THE CAVES, IMPOSSIBLE TO measure. Every once in a while we'd take a sip of water or eat a cracker. We slept, and woke up thinking we'd heard someone, but it always turned out to be our sleepy imagination. At one point I woke up and thought the cave was full of light, but it must have been an image left over from my dream, because the next second all the blackness had returned.

"Touch?" I said.

He didn't answer.

"Touch?" I shook him a little, wondering if I should just let him sleep. Who knew how long we'd been down there? Time had stopped moving. Even if we could've taken out the ring and gone forward and backward thousands or even millions of years. For us all of time existed without light, here in the caves, and there was no measuring it any longer.

Before, I'd figured I would die before Touch on account of my size. But I'd forgotten about the wildebear, and Tawa, and the extra strength they'd given me. I closed my eyes, and when I opened them they were full of water. Touch, dead in the cave, me not far behind him, and I never even got around to saying I loved him.

"Touch," I screamed, in the general direction of his ear.

I felt him bolt upright. "What?" he said. "Rogue, what?"

The relief I should have felt didn't get a chance to wash over me. Because exactly in that moment, the cave went from blackness to blinding white light — too bright even for the crystals to glitter.

Bam! Crackle! Boom!

He'd done it on purpose. I knew it. He'd talked and talked about his world, hoping the words and the stories would bring one of his hunters to us. Because it was our only chance. My only chance. He was willing to be captured to give me a chance to live. Because he loved me. I knew it. He did.

"Touch," I whispered. "You shouldn't have done it."

At least I got to see his face — pale and beautiful and full of dread — one last time. Because there in front of us, lighting up the cave, stood Alabaster. I never would've thought such a tiny person could look so fearsome and so formidable. But there she was, like an angel out of hell, this time all bundled up in white wool, her arms outstretched, her face a study in fury.

And she wasn't alone. A man stood beside her, with eyes as blue as Touch's, but with none of their kindness, and a craggy brow — that same deep line Touch got between his eyes, but in the other man's case etched there permanently. He looked, if it were possible, even madder than Alabaster, and when he spoke it was in a deep and frightening tone, a low and angry note, sustained too long.

As the man spoke to Touch, who was so weak he could barely raise his head, Alabaster turned toward me. The expression on her face softened. And when she spoke, it wasn't in that whistling language, but in English, and her voice sounded kind and even nurturing.

"Dear one," she said. "Step away from him. Let us keep you safe."

I looked over at Touch. He shook his head, just perceptibly enough that the man barked something very sharp at him.

"Don't listen to Touch," Alabaster said. "He's not who you think he is."

A very large piece of my insides melted away, a cool gust of fear that froze my organs solid. All the moments when I hadn't quite been sure of Touch — when I first hadn't trusted him, and then had decided instead to mistrust my own reactions — started playing on a frantic reel inside my head.

Which I guess is what Alabaster wanted, because she took the daintiest step toward me. I saw that she wore gloves, and one of her hands was cupped — no doubt hiding one of their bite-sized and all-powerful weapons. At the same time the man with her raised his hand. He didn't seem to be holding anything, he just spread his fingers wide, and from them emanated a loud, eerie, and piercing noise. At that moment I saw that both he and Alabaster were wearing tiny little plugs in their ears, no doubt to guard themselves from this particular weapon. Touch immediately sank to his knees, hands over his ears, in agony.

I waited for the same effect to take over me, but I must have been protected by the strength I'd gathered along the way. The noise sounded unpleasant and spooky — echoing through the caves — but not debilitating.

Now was no time for mistrusting Touch, or myself, or anyone except these two people from the future. I knew that if I didn't act fast, Touch would be whisked away, and I would be left here in these caves, alone, to die. So while Alabaster and her friend looked at me, amazed that I was still standing, in that split second I stepped forward and grabbed one plug out of each pair of their ears.

·10·

THE WILDEBEARS MUST'VE SUPPLIED ME WITH GOOD SURVIVAL instincts along with strength, because it came to me at exactly the right second. While Alabaster and her friend sank to their knees — the terrible noise still blasting through the caves — I grabbed Touch around the waist, scooted him onto me piggyback style, and went running for the archway. It may have seemed like I was using him as a shield, and I kind of was, but I knew that they wouldn't kill Touch. Because they needed him.

The noise stopped abruptly, which I knew meant they'd be right on our heels. Alabaster and her companion brought so much light with them that it spilled on into the next cave. As I rounded the second cor-ner, what felt like ropes curved around my ankles. I fell face-first to the ground, with Touch sprawled out on top of me. He rolled off my back, and when I looked down at my feet I saw tentacles of light winding around my legs, and reaching back into the cave behind us.

Touch knelt down and pulled at the light cords. They wouldn't budge. A second later Alabaster came around the corner, holding the other ends. She had lassoed me like she was a futuristic cowgirl and I

was a runaway steer. Except thanks to the wildebears I was more pred-
ator than prey. So I leaned down, picked up the slack of that glimmering rope, and bit right through it. Sparks of light erupted all around us,
flying out toward Alabaster, who stepped backward. The next thing I
knew Touch had thrust the golden ring into my hand. The whole world
whirled and whooshed. This time, since I knew what was happening, I
felt a wonderful rush of adrenaline along with it, plus the worry that he
and I would end up in just another piece of the bleak, black cave.

But when we arrived, the cords around my legs still shone, bright
ribbons of light. Touch and I knelt to unravel them, then held them
out in front of us to lead our way outside, where we were greeted by
morning sun, and the most fantastic quiet all around us.

Never in my life had I been so happy to see the wide blue sky over
my head. I breathed in a great lungful of dusty air, like someone dying
of thirst might gulp down a glass of water. Which is not to say I wasn't
thirsty, too. Hopefully our water still sat waiting for us at the campground. I had no idea how far ahead in time Touch had brought us.
Not to his time, certainly, because although it was hot, the temperature felt familiar, bearable. And the other half of the Grand Canyon
stretched out below and all around us, still a long way away from being filled with water. Touch stood there on the other side of the ring,
the two of us still holding onto it. He looked gaunt and dehydrated
and very pale, more like the man I'd seen in the SNAP office than the
man I'd come to know since we'd been on the run. And I could not for
one second think on believing what Alabaster had implied, that he
was anything but exactly who I thought he was: the man I loved.

Back in the caves I'd almost lost him without ever saying the
words. Who knew what these next few minutes would hold? I wasn't
going to let another opportunity go by.

"I love you," I said. "I love you, Touch."

His face changed. The twinkle came back into his eye, and his
mouth turned up at the corner. "Hey," he said. "I love you, too."

The natural thing to do then would've been to kiss. But of course we couldn't do that. So we just stood there, staring, drinking the sight of each other in, while the morning around us grew brighter.

AS WE WALKED UP THE RIDGE TO OUR CAMPGROUND, TOUCH told me he hadn't brought us far ahead, just to the next day. This seemed pretty risky to me, since what would stop them from just hanging around and waiting for us?

"I don't think they will," Touch said. "For one thing, they have no way of knowing which direction in time I went, or how far. For another thing, it's so cold here. These are not people who enjoy being uncomfortable. It makes much more sense for them to go home and try to track me from there."

His hope was that if he only went ahead a day, the stuff we'd left at the campground might still be there. But when we arrived, the ground was empty, no trace of the blankets or extra clothing or food. Alabaster must have taken everything before she returned to the future.

Touch reached out his gloved hand and took mine. Squeezed it real hard, almost until my bones crunched, as if that pressure could make up for the lack of skin on skin. We'd barely eaten or drank or seen the light in days. We had no money, no food, nothing but the clothes on our backs.

But we had each other. And just then, in that moment, it made us feel like the richest people in the whole damn world.

THAT FEELING DIDN'T LAST LONG. AS I'D OFTEN HEARD AUNT Carrie say, a person can't live on love. Touch and I, we didn't have a drop of water. We didn't have a scrap of food. We were dehydrated and starved. And to even get started on figuring out what to do, we had to get up to the rim of the canyon, which was a good four-hour hike.

That hike was the worst thing I ever had to do in my life. Worse than the days in the cave, and worse than being attacked by those wildebears. In fact I think having the wildebears in me was the only reason I made it at all. I don't know how Touch managed to do it — I couldn't even let him lean on me on account of the trail being so narrow. The whole trail was this series of very narrow switchbacks, so you never even knew how close you were to the top. I kept looking to the end of each section, hoping against hope this was the last bit, only to come to the top and find myself at the bottom of another. One after another, switchback after switchback, the two of us staggering from hunger and thirst and exhaustion, but careful not to stagger too much; otherwise we'd teeter over sideways and fall miles and miles, down into the canyon, to certain death.

And then, with no warning, Touch's footsteps slowing down behind me, we turned a corner and saw the rim of the canyon. What seemed like a hundred fat tourists in flowery shirts, with cameras dangling from their necks, stared down at us — two tall, starved, wild-looking people dressed in leather.

I kept walking, two, three, four, and then ten more steps, before I collapsed right at the feet of an old couple. The sky above looked perfectly blue, not a single scrap of a cloud, but Grandma and Grandpa's hair wisped white into the background. Grandpa had a bottle of water in his old, gnarled hand. He must've just bought it, because I could see how cold it was, the condensation sweating under his fingertips; I think one gorgeous little freezing drop might have even fallen on my bare cheek.

Don't ask me how Touch managed to still be standing. Maybe because for him it wasn't so hot? He reached out his hand toward the old man. "The girl is very dehydrated," he said. "May we take your water?"

It may not have been out of the goodness in his heart that the old man handed it over. He might've been just a teeny bit afraid of Touch.

Touch unscrewed the top and took a drink of water himself, a long, slow draw that half emptied the bottle. Now, I never had been on an airplane, but Wendy Lee had, and I remembered how they say in the safety rules that you've got to put on your own oxygen mask before you help anyone else. He knelt down beside me and very carefully lifted my shoulders till I was in a sitting position, sort of half lying against him. Then he brought the water to my lips. I drank and drank, the best stuff I'd ever tasted in the world, until it was empty.

"You need a doctor, honey?" Grandma asked. By now she was handing us her own water bottle, which made me feel real warm toward both of them.

"No," I croaked out, as Touch took the bottle and then handed it to me. "No doctor. I'm fine."

They looked at each other a little too quickly, Grandma and Grandpa. And I knew however kindly they might be — or maybe even because they were kindly — some authority or other would be hearing from them about us.

Life sure would've been easier with only one set of pursuers.

WE HAD TWO PIECES OF GOOD LUCK. ONE, THE BLUE TRUCK SAT waiting for us right in the parking lot where we'd left it. Two, we weren't penniless after all, because Touch still had that twenty-two dollars in the back pocket of his jeans. Twenty-two dollars may not be much, but since we'd thought we had nothing, it suddenly felt like a fortune. It felt like the difference between making it to the next minute or not.

"Let's put ten dollars of gas in the car," I said, "and spend twelve dollars on food." Ten dollars wouldn't get us far in that guzzler, but it would get us far enough that we could think on what to do next.

Touch and I drove to the nearest gas station and filled up the truck, the whole twenty-two dollars' worth. Then we stopped at a little café and ordered plenty of food, but light food. We didn't want to wreck our empty stomachs, so Touch had toast and tomato soup, and I had oatmeal with fresh fruit, and we drank lots of iced tea, not that rancid sweet tea like they serve in the South, but good black tea over ice with just slices of lemon. It was the best meal I ever ate in my life, and when the waitress went into the kitchen to pick up some other customer's food, Touch and I skedaddled on out of there. We climbed into our blue truck and drove and drove till the sky was dark and the tank was near on empty.

We had exactly one of Joe Wheeler's blankets left in the bed of the truck, and we snuggled up together underneath it, taking care to keep our skin from touching. The sky was just as clear as it had been when we hiked out of the Grand Canyon, and we could see a million stars, but now I wasn't looking for Touch's planet anymore. I was on Touch's planet and he was on mine, the two of us Earthlings who never should've met.

He closed his arms around me tightly and whispered, "I love you," into my hair. We were both exhausted. We had driven the truck way off the road, not into any kind of campground, just into a patch of rock and cactus, nobody around us for miles. Tired as we were, if we could've, we would've kissed. And kissed. And made love. My whole body ached to, and I knew his did, too. The thing is, we were too tired, with our brains not working well enough to get creative like we had in the past. If it weren't for my dangerous, dangerous skin, it wouldn't have mattered how tired we were, we could've just fallen on each other in all our sleepy, lovesick hunger.

But no. We had to use every ounce of strength we had left to restrain ourselves. And then we fell asleep, me risking my bare face near him, just so we could be together.

"Touch," I said, my voice so hoarse and strained I barely recognized it. "That man with Alabaster."

"Yes," he said, sparing me speaking any more.

"He looked kinda like you. Who was he?"

"That was my father," Touch said.

My body went real cold for a moment. Then I told myself it didn't matter how messed up the future was. The present was pretty damn messed up, too. Maybe that's what Cody had meant when he said there was only one world for me. Because this world now, and Touch's world later, it was all the very same place.

I WOKE UP BEFORE TOUCH AND CREPT INTO THE FRONT OF THE truck, where I went over the atlas — one of the few valuable possessions we had left, along with Mary Ginsberg's driver's license and the golden ring. Hopefully Touch still had one of his fake IDs tucked inside that bottomless pocket of his. If he did, we only had about a three-hour drive before we could cross the border into Mexico. At least then we could quit worrying about police. With Wendy Lee alive and well and icing wedding cakes, the FBI would have better things to do than mount an international search for little old me.

So the only thing we had to do this morning was figure out how to get enough cash to keep our gas tank and our bellies full. I looked in the rearview mirror to see Touch, sitting up in the bed of the truck and waving.

I crawled on back there and stretched my legs out over his lap. He put his hands on top of my pants. I had been wearing those pants through so much, for so many days straight. What I needed was a good long shower and a change of clothing. We both needed a makeover, Touch and I, if we were going to get through the border check without drawing attention to ourselves. And in my head Mexico was becoming more and more important. The place where Touch would show me the sea. The place where the two of us would be together. Like the song in that old movie Cody's mama used to like watching, "a place for us."

• • •

IN A LITTLE TOWN CALLED BUCKEYE, WE FOUND A SALVATION
Army store. Thanks to Joe Wheeler, Touch's clothes — apart from the
long leather jacket, which he didn't have to wear — looked pretty
close to normal. Except that those clothes had got beyond filthy in our
little stay under Horseshoe Mesa. So we went into the store and gathered up a new pair of blue jeans for him, and a couple T-shirts, and a
couple button-downs, plus a sweater. He changed into most of it in
the grungy fitting room and put the rest in a backpack that we'd found
in the school supply section. Then it was my turn. It was kind of pathetic how normal and pretty I felt wearing a pair of green cargo pants
and a long-sleeved T-shirt. I grabbed a big blue hoodie, too, which
would be perfect for both covering up my hair and protecting my face
(or other people from my face) when I needed to. I wound a filmy,
flowery scarf around my neck and left my leather jeans and my blood-
stained sweater right in the fitting room along with Touch's discarded
clothes. Then the two of us walked on out of the store without paying.
Nobody even gave us a second glance.

While I'd been in the fitting room, Touch had pocketed a screwdriver, I guess in case we needed to steal another car. We drove toward Tempe, and then into a little town on the outskirts. I knew that
plenty of people who spent the winter in Arizona wouldn't have
shown up yet. Our plan for the day was to find a little deserted house
where we could shower and rest and eat up whatever dry and canned
goods the owners had left behind. Then after a good night's sleep we
could figure out how to get gas for the truck and make our way
across the border.

WE FOLLOWED A MAIL TRUCK DOWN A LONG, DUSTY DRIVE. I
figured we'd be able to tell which people were away for the season

because the mailman wouldn't put anything in their boxes. Must have been a lot of houses on this road in that situation, because he only delivered mail to a few. We waited until the little white truck had trundled back onto the main road, then we headed down the driveway at the very end of the dirt road. There we found this little tan-colored house with a red tile roof and flowers wilting in the window boxes. Touch did something funky with his screwdriver at the back door and we let ourselves in. The house was made out of clay, I guess, this style of house we'd been seeing since we got to Arizona, and once we got inside I could see why it was good building material for the climate. Inside it felt nice and cool; Touch started shivering as soon as we walked through the door. He found a nice thick sweatshirt hanging in the hall closet and bundled it on under his leather jacket. Then he set about searching for tools. He didn't tell me what all he was up to, but I decided to just let him be while I explored the house.

Everything was so light and airy, with comfortable leather couches and pretty Indian rugs. The kitchen was huge, with a big stainless-steel stove and refrigerator, plus a walk-in pantry. In there I found all kinds of cans of soup and crackers and oatmeal and granola bars. I grabbed a package of cookies and walked on back through the house, so I could share them with Touch.

I found him in the sunroom. He had the little sack full of Grand Canyon crystals by his side, and he was kneeling by an electric socket holding the screwdriver. "Uh," I said, "don't put that in there."

He looked up at me and smiled. "Don't worry," he said. "I'm just trying to figure out ways to add properties to this." He held up the screwdriver and examined it like he'd never seen something so promising. "It's a primitive design," he said. "But it has potential."

"Yeah, that's us," I said, handing him the cookies. "Primitive." One thing I'd noticed about Touch on our travels, he had a sweet tooth.

I left him there to explore a little more. Something about the sun-filled house, all that light after the dark of the caves, made me feel safe and calm and happy. I liked knowing Touch was there without seeing him, working away on a project. "Hey," I called to him when I found a nice little bathroom. "Take off your clothes."

This got his attention. You would've thought he had a little wilde-bear in him, based on how fast he got to me. "What?"

I took a big, plush robe off its hook and threw it at him. "Take off your clothes," I said. "I'm going to find the laundry room."

IT FELT EASY TO FORGET WE WERE BOTH ON THE RUN AS I PUT-tered around, doing laundry, cobbling together lunch in that huge, comfortable kitchen. After we ate, we sat around wearing borrowed bathrobes while our clothes tumbled in the fanciest dryer I'd ever seen. I thought that the people who owned this house were crazy. Now, I am not a person who particularly enjoys the heat, but if *I* owned this house? You can bet I'd never leave it.

By now I was ready to get down to the thing I'd needed most when we first got to the house. A shower. I made my way into the big-gest bedroom, which had the most beautiful adjoining bathroom I'd ever seen, more cool red tile under my feet, and all along the walls, too. The shower had three different heads that you could fiddle with and make spray you from different directions at different speeds. It was as near to heaven as I'd come, and I think I stayed in there going on half an hour without the temperature dropping down even a nick.

But the best discovery came on my way out of the bathroom, off the big bedroom, this little stairway that led up to a lookout tower where you could see the mountains. The Superstition Mountains, they were called, I knew that from the atlas. I stood up there for a while, enjoying the view, and on the way back down the stairway I peeked behind a little cedar door on the first landing. I had never been in one before, but I knew what it was right off (Wendy Lee's memories again, that woman sure had been around). I ran fast as I could, which at this point was pretty damn fast, to the other side of the house, and the sunroom, to tell Touch to stop what he was doing and come on with me.

"WHAT IS IT, EXACTLY?" TOUCH SAID, POKING HIS HEAD IN through the little wooden door. It smelled like eucalyptus and cedar. The room was tiny, like maybe five by five, and I pointed to the little wooden bench attached to the wall.

"You'll see," I said. I cranked up the little dials on the wall, then sat as far as I could from Touch on the bench and took off my robe. His eyes kind of narrowed, suspicious but in an interested way, and I put my head back against the wall, waiting for the steam to start.

The steam got so thick that I couldn't actually see him as clear as I'd hoped. I tried to stare through it with my cat eyes, directly into his wide open face that was full of love and longing. And I hoped that if he could see me at all my look conveyed the picture in my mind, of his hands everywhere they wanted to go. No barriers at all, just the two of us, doing anything in the world we wanted. Because outside of my mind we could only sit naked on opposite sides, staring at each other, feeling the heat all around us.

I GUESS IT WAS GOOD THAT THE REFRIGERATOR WAS EMPTY EX-cept for a little box of baking soda. It at least comforted me that the owners of the house wouldn't pull a Joe Wheeler and come waltzing on in. Still it would've been nice to have something fresh, eggs or herbs. While Touch finished up his work in the sunroom, I found some chicken breasts in the freezer, along with a square of frozen spinach. I thawed the chicken breasts in the microwave, then slathered them with barbeque sauce from the pantry and popped them in the oven. Then I cooked the spinach in a saucepan on top of the stove.

By now I was back in my Salvation Army clothes, minus the hoodie. I hadn't bothered rummaging through any drawers here. I knew it was just survival, but I loved this house so much it sort of made me feel like I loved the people who lived here. There were a few framed pictures of a gray-haired couple, both wearing glasses and holding tennis rackets or golf clubs, plus family pictures of them with people who must've been their kids and grandkids. They all seemed nice and smiley, and why shouldn't they be? I'd be smiling every day of my life if I lived in this house.

Touch had to steal clothing from them, to keep himself warm. I had to steal food, and I guess whatever electricity we were using to run the sauna and lights and so forth. But beyond that I felt I'd rather leave their things alone. Everything I used, like the plates I set out for our dinner, I would wash and put back where I found it. The candlesticks on the table had already been lit, so what harm, I figured, was there in letting them burn down a little more. When Touch came into the dining room, I was lighting them. We could smell the chicken baking in the kitchen, and the sun had started to set. Tomorrow Touch and I would cross the border into Mexico. Tonight we'd have a candlelit dinner.

BUT FOR SOME REASON MY SENSE OF SAFETY WENT DOWN with the sun. I sat at the head of the table and Touch sat to my left. The sauna had warmed him up pretty good, so he just wore a knit hat, sweatshirt, and jeans. He sawed into his chicken and took a bite without saying it tasted good. Not that I'd worked hours to prepare it or anything, but still in all, I *had* cooked it. Would it have killed him to say it was delicious?

"That sauna," he said, "is my favorite thing about this time. I might even sleep in there."

And here I'd thought I was his favorite thing about this time!

Don't ask me what came over me. Earlier I'd felt so happy and so connected to him. Now, suddenly, I just felt . . . dark.

"So," I said, spearing a piece of chicken. I put it in my mouth and chewed. I thought it was delicious, even if he didn't. "What do you think Alabaster meant when she said that? About you not being who I thought?"

Touch stopped eating and stared at me. "She was trying to unnerve you," he said, and then added, like I might be the stupidest person in the world, "of course."

"Of course," I repeated. The words tasted sour in my mouth. "How'd you two meet, anyway?"

"Meet?"

"Yeah. How'd y'all meet? It's a pretty basic question."

"Well," Touch said. "Where I come from, in the future . . ."

"I know it's the future," I said. "We've established that pretty well by now. But it's also the past, your past, and I'm wondering how you managed to fall in love with someone so evil. Someone who says you're not who I think you are."

"Well," he said again. "She wasn't always evil. She didn't seem that way to me, at any rate. There was a sweetness about her. There still is, in ways. Especially when it comes to Cotton."

Dang. I didn't realize until he answered that I was hoping he'd tell me he'd never been in love with her.

But no. Apparently instead I'd set a little trap so he could wax all nostalgic for the beautiful innocent person Alabaster used to be, and in some ways still was.

"I knew her practically my whole life," Touch said. "She was always so fragile. And so beautiful. Not as beautiful as you." He added this last hastily enough to make it seem like a big fat lie. Anyway, I'd seen Alabaster and I'd seen myself. I knew who was winning in the beauty department, and it wasn't the one with granny stripes in her hair.

Touch took a bite of spinach but didn't find that any worthier of comment than the chicken, even though I'd sprinkled garlic salt on it. "The thing is," he said. "Sometimes I really don't think it's her fault. She had people, her family, filling her head with all the wrong ideas. If you're brought up on a notion from the time you're very young, it can be very difficult to escape."

"But your family felt the same way," I said. "Your daddy wants things back the way they used to be. Before the *Lincoln*. And that didn't rub off on you. You're strong enough to fight right against him."

Touch didn't say anything. He just speared another piece of spinach and put it in his mouth. Then he said, "Alabaster was raised on the wrong ideas. She never really had a chance."

"Right," I said, my voice dripping with sarcasm. "She sure is innocent. I can see that now."

"That's not what I meant at all."

"I suppose it doesn't bother you that she's probably raising your child on those same ideas?"

"It bothers me more than anything," he said. Touch looked pained, and downright misunderstood.

Suddenly I didn't feel hungry. "Never mind," I said, pushing my plate away. "I don't feel much like talking anyway. You go ahead and sleep in the sauna."

I marched out of the dining room and down the hall, and went on into one of the guest bedrooms. I didn't want to be in the main bedroom, which Touch would have to go through so he could go into the sauna. Even in the dark I could see the outlines of the mountains through the windows, but suddenly I understood. The people who lived in this house, they weren't smiley every day of their lives. No matter how perfect and wonderful and beautiful things seemed, it was always possible for sadness to come raining on down out of nowhere.

I got undressed and climbed under the covers. Part of me wanted to fall straight to sleep — maybe meet Cody on an astral plane as a little revenge — and part of me wanted, more than anything, for Touch to come looking for me.

He didn't though, not for a long time. From way on the other side of the house, it sounded like he must've finished his dinner. After a bit I could hear some clanking around in the kitchen, like maybe he was washing the dishes. I wondered if they had to wash dishes in Arcadia. Where I grew up, in Aunt Carrie's old farmhouse, we didn't even have a dishwasher. It seemed plenty enough like Arcadia just to pile the dinner dishes into that stainless-steel contraption, but Touch didn't likely know how to use it.

Finally I heard him wandering around the house, opening and closing doors. It seemed like an awful long time before he opened my door. The lights in the hall were off, too — we'd already decided it wouldn't do to light the place up, alerting any neighbors that the house was suddenly inhabited. In the dark, he padded across the tile and rug and then sat on my bed. He didn't perch or sit toward the edge. He thumped right down, exactly next to me, so that his butt melded into the curve of my body under the blankets. He put his hand on my shoulder and I noticed he was wearing gloves. Not the thick, fat gloves he usually wore, but a thin suede pair. They looked soft, like they belonged to someone very rich. He must've found them in a drawer around here.

"Hey, Earthling," he said.

"Hey yourself."

"I come to you across a lot of years," Touch said, in a low and very serious voice. "I'm older than you in several different ways, and I lived a life before I met you. But that doesn't mean I don't love you now. Because I do. I love you. Very much."

"OK," I said, real quiet, because suddenly I felt very silly for ruining our nice dinner for no particular reason.

"Rogue?" he said.

"Yeah."

"Now you say it."

"What?"

"You know." I liked the way his voice sounded, even though it sounded a little angry. It felt kind of fun — close — for him to be ordering me around.

"I love you, Earthling," I said.

He pulled back the covers, not a bit surprised to see me totally naked — all my clothes were tumbled, plain as day, right at his feet. I'd been lying on my side but now I rolled over onto my back.

Touch started at the crown of my head. With soft, sueded fingers — lambskin, I think those gloves must've been — he traced every bone in my face. I kept my eyes open, staring at him. He let his fingers travel down my neck, across my collarbone, and down to my breasts. At that point it wasn't just his fingers, his hands were completely involved, wide and spanning and touching me everywhere, just like I'd imagined in the sauna. Of course in my imagination it had been *his* skin, not some poor dead lamb's. Still and all. It felt amazing. My breathing went crazy. It felt like nothing I'd experienced before.

"Say it again," Touch ordered.

And I did. I said it over and over again. I said it loud like a scream and soft like a mantra. I said nothing else, just *I love you, I love you, I love you*. Finally I had to close my eyes. It felt so good, and at the same time I wanted so much more that I thought I might die.

Except I didn't die. Not at all. I lived through what seemed like lovely and excruciating hours of it, until I fell asleep with Touch on the other side of the covers, wrapped around me. It was the longest, deepest, best sleep of my entire life. When I opened my eyes Touch was still sleeping. I put on those lambskin gloves myself, pulled back the covers, and woke him up with the same treatment.

After that Touch took one last sauna while I got the house in order. Then we piled on into the truck and set off on our last stretch before crossing the border into Mexico.

TOUCH PULLED INTO THE FIRST GAS STATION WE SAW. I REMINDED him we were out of money, as in zero dollars, but he just looked over at me and smiled. Then he got out of the truck, walked around to the pump, and took that screwdriver out of his pocket. He had worked on it for hours, doing something with the sockets and the crystals and the sun coming through the windowpanes, but it looked just exactly the same as when he'd stolen it from the Salvation Army store. He slipped the screwdriver into the credit card slot, put the nozzle into the gas tank, flipped up the pump switch, and sure enough the numbers started to roll and the gas started flowing.

Now, that, I thought, is one useful device.

Touch went into the convenience store, then came back with a couple bottles of water. He threw his backpack into the backseat and handed me a granola bar. He also handed me two twenty-dollar bills, so I figured the screwdriver worked on ATMs, too. I stuffed the money in my pocket and decided to ask him about that later. For some reason while he was in the store I'd started thinking on Alabaster, and how she looked just like her name — every bit of her white and glowing, except her eyes, that soft blue. And Touch.

I realized that in his time people must get named according to their main qualities. My face got a little hot, thinking of last night. But that wasn't all, the only kind of touch he had. Look at the things he'd made, that little blue ball, and the translator, and the golden ring. Now he'd turned an ordinary screwdriver into something magical and useful. Talk about having a touch. He turned the key in the ignition. He was wearing a Red Sox baseball cap, with his hair in a ponytail. Anyone looking in the window of our car would see an ordinary man, on the young side, sure, and also way far on the handsome side. But I knew he wasn't ordinary at all, that he had this specialness, this brilliance, this touch. My heart swelled with love and pride.

I DIDN'T HAVE THE HEART TO TELL TOUCH THAT ALTHOUGH IT was warmer than most spots in North America, Mexico didn't tend to get all the way to a hundred twenty-five degrees. Still it seemed true what he kept saying, that he was starting to get used to the temperatures here. He still wore his leather jacket, but just a T-shirt and a flannel shirt underneath it.

Truth was, I felt pretty excited about Mexico myself. Maybe when we got there, it would be like the Perfect House of countries. I was ready for a little peace. Peace and safety. Like a family would have. Maybe after rejuvenating ourselves in Mexico, we could head on into the future, where they'd teach me how to control my powers so I could touch people, and then Touch and I would come back here, to the present, avoiding the nasty war. Maybe we could even bring Cotton along, and then have more kids together. We'd go back to Mexico circa now and have our own family, our own little world together.

Now there was only one U.S. highway left, 85, a straight shot down to the border crossing at Lukeville and Sonoyta. Mary Gins-

berg didn't look a whole lot like me, but she was tall with brown hair
and blue eyes. Close enough, I figured, for someone glancing at the
picture and then at me. And anyway, I figured they weren't as particular about people going into Mexico as they were about people coming
out, which I planned on doing never.

"I got a question," I said to Touch. "How come you didn't just tell
the people in charge of Arcadia about the rebels who want to take
over? Couldn't someone have helped you?"

"It doesn't work that way where I come from. Not anymore, anyway. There really isn't anyone in charge, the way you mean it."

"No police? No president? No jail?"

He shook his head, like he knew what these words meant but
found them sad and ridiculous. "So primitive," he said.

"Yeah, primitive, maybe, but they sure do come in handy as far as
foiling evil plots."

Touch said, "We're talking about a world where no crimes have
been committed for hundreds of years. There's no system in place to
prevent them, because essentially they don't exist. Probably what
we're headed toward is a world where jails and police will be needed
again. But first there'll be a war. And it's going to be bad. Very bad."

I sat quiet a minute, not thinking so much about that last part, but
about a place where no crimes had been committed for so long. It
sounded safe and very lovely. It also sounded like an excellent place to
commit a crime.

"Are you hungry?" Touch said, trying to change the subject. We
were approaching a little town called Gila Bend, and from the looks
of the landscape there wouldn't be a whole lot more options before
we hit the border. So we pulled on into the parking lot of a place
called Outer Limits Space Age Restaurant, this very nutty-looking
building that appeared to be constructed out of scrap metal, with a
little UFO kind of balanced on top of the whole thing. The sign said it
served Mexican and American food, and I figured this was the last

time in my life I'd have the chance to eat American food. As Touch and I slammed the doors of the truck, I decided I was going to order a big old chicken-fried steak with a side of fries and a Coca-Cola. Thinking on what Touch's reaction to the sight of that heaping plate would be made me laugh out loud, and I reached over to take his hand, the feel of that lambskin through my cotton tea gloves making me shiver just the barest little bit.

Crack! Boom! Boom! Crackle!

Shit.

Out of nowhere, all of a sudden, there he stood, Touch Sr., right smack-dab in front of us.

I felt afraid. I truly did. But I also have to say that not for a moment did I think this was the end. At this point, people from Touch's time had appeared and tried to capture us and they had failed. We got away. I sure did not want to deal with Touch's daddy, not one little bit. But nowhere inside me did I really think that he would succeed in catching us, in taking us away or hurting us.

And it truly might've worked out that way — us escaping — if only Touch hadn't let go of my hand. It must be hard to think straight is all I can say, when the people who are trying to run you down and ruin all you hold dear are members of your own family. It would make me mad enough if a police officer showed up to run me into jail. But if Aunt Carrie were trying to arrest me? I would have a thing or two to say to her, you can bet on that.

Touch reached into his coat, like he was maybe going to avoid all that — getting involved. But then his daddy said something in that musical language of theirs. And Touch let his hand fall to his side. He said something back, real furtive. I took the opportunity to look at his dad, not quite as tall as Touch, with the same long hair but tinged with silver. The same blue eyes but not kind at all, just fierce and greedy.

"Touch," I said. "Don't get into it with him. Let's just get out of here."

I thought maybe we could time travel, or just run for it like we'd done in the caves. But Touch's daddy reached out his arm toward me, with his fist closed tight and facing up. It must've been a gesture that meant something in his world, because Touch yelled out, not in English but his own language, although from the way he said it I understood perfectly.

"No!" Touch yelled.

Fear gripped me; it poured over me like a bucketful of water, on account of the terror in his voice. I expected Touch's father to make a move, to grab him or attack me, but he didn't have time. Because Touch ran at him. As he ran, he reached into his pocket. First he pulled out the golden ring, which didn't make sense because he was headed in the wrong direction. He was headed away from me. I heard something else clatter to the ground, but I scarcely noticed it, because Touch didn't hold that golden ring out toward me. He held it out toward his father.

"No!" I screamed. I started to run at wildebear speed, but it wasn't fast enough. Touch pulled the golden ring up over his father's hand. And before I even had a chance to blink, they vanished. Both of them. Gone. Completely gone.

Another crackle. Another boom. And I stood in the parking lot of the Outer Limits Space Age Restaurant, completely alone, the perfectly ordinary looking screwdriver resting quietly at my feet.

THIS HAD HAPPENED TO ME ONCE BEFORE, THE WHOLE WORLD changed forever in a split second. But you never do get used to that sort of thing. Standing in the parking lot, one slow car making its way around me, I felt emptied out, hollowed. Like a pumpkin getting ready to be a jack-o'-lantern, like someone had just reached in and scooped out all my seeds and innards. Somehow I managed to kneel down and pick up the screwdriver. In that moment I didn't care about what all it could do. I only cared that he'd made it, Touch; it was magic he'd created. With my teeth I pulled off one filthy glove, then closed my hand around the flat end of the screwdriver. Was it my imagination, or was it warm? Could I feel his intelligence, his talent, his *touch* radiating from the metal onto my skin? I only knew that no matter what happened, he wanted to keep on taking care of me.

Touch was gone. He'd left in order to protect me, that was the only explanation. I knew deep down in my bones that the only thing that could have ever made him leave me here all alone was the desire to keep me safe. And what would he find, when he went back home? What had he risked to save me? Something as small as his whole world, or as large as his own child.

Maybe now — no, not now, ten thousand years from now — Touch regretted that impulse, that moment of weakness.

Another car pulled into the lot, this one not so patient. The red-faced man had a tired-looking wife and a car full of toddlers. He laid on his horn so that I jumped over to one side. The screwdriver pulsed, warm and comforting, next to my skin.

No, that pulse said to me. *He doesn't regret it. He never could. And another thing: he's going to find his way back to you.*

There had to be a place for Touch and me. A place and time. So you better bet I would stick to that plan, the one we'd made together, and get on in the truck and drive in the direction I'd told him I was going.

It was the least I could do, after he'd risked his life — his whole life and world — to save mine.

NEEDLESS TO SAY I DIDN'T FEEL LIKE EATING A CHICKEN-FRIED steak. In fact I didn't feel like eating anything at all, ever again. I walked over to the blue Chevy truck, still feeling like a jack-o'-lantern ready to be carved. It was like someone had programmed me and now

I could go through the motions like a robot. Walk across pavement. Open truck door. Climb behind wheel. Insert key in ignition.

But then when I closed the door, something came over me. For one thing, the whole cab, it smelled like cedar and eucalyptus, like cinnamon and ginger. It smelled like Touch, and not just him but the two of us, this whole journey we'd taken together.

I knew I needed to turn the key in the ignition. I needed to point my car south, toward Mexico, and get over the border and wait on Touch. He said electricity made it easier to track people, so I'd get to the biggest town I could find. Hell, I had a screwdriver that made gas pumps pump and ATMs part with cash. So maybe when I got to Mexico I'd treat myself to a big resort. I'd lie out by the pool drinking piña coladas, and suddenly Touch would appear, way overdressed, standing at the foot of my beach chair.

But what if he didn't? Who knew what all they were doing to him, ten thousand years from now?

I couldn't help it. Something rose in my throat that I hadn't felt, not fully, in such a long time. And I did what I hadn't done when Cody fell into his coma, or when Wendy Lee fired me from the bakery. I put my head on the steering wheel and cried and cried and cried.

Finally I heard a little tapping. I lifted my head. My eyes were so puffy I could barely see. I wiped them dry, took a big snuffly breath, and rolled down the window.

It was a lady, a mom-aged lady, with short dyed blond hair and crinkles around her eyes, the kind that come from lots of laughing. But right now she wasn't laughing. She looked real sad. For a second I wondered what was wrong, and then I realized it was me — she was sad for me.

"You OK, honey?" she asked, real careful, and real concerned.

"Yes, ma'am," I said. "Thank you. I'm fine."

She tilted her head to one side and smiled a little. "You sure now? I'm happy to buy you a cup of coffee if you need someone to talk to."

I took a deep shuddery breath. Probably she was just some kind of Jesus freak, wanting to bring me over to God. Or else she was a sex trader, luring vulnerable young girls into a life of misery. She stood there, in her mom jeans and pink T-shirt, waiting on some kind of answer. And I knew she wasn't either of those things, just a nice lady, probably with a daughter about my age.

"That's real nice," I said. "Honest, just the offer makes me feel better."

"I'm glad, honey," she said. "But the offer is sincere. Let me buy you a cup of coffee."

"Thanks," I said. "I appreciate your kindness. But I have to go."

"You sure?"

I nodded, and she said, real reluctant, "OK, honey. You drive carefully. OK?"

"I will," I promised. And I drove out of the restaurant's parking lot, but not out of Gila Bend. Because that nice lady, she'd reminded me. I still had one last thing to do before I left the States.

Dear Mr. and Mrs. Robbins,

I sat in the Gila Bend Public Library, staring at the cursor. There were only five computers in the low, cool building. I thought how Touch should be here, shivering next to me. Before I started the letter to his parents, I searched on the Internet for news of Cody. And the truth was I didn't need to search, because I knew in my heart that he still lay sleeping in his coma. I could feel it in my bones, like they were filled with Cody's marrow along with his memories. It had been the Internet that told me Wendy Lee had woken up, not any special sense inside me. But Cody and I had been so much closer — and our contact had lasted so much longer. I felt sure I would know, right away, if ever he opened his eyes. No matter where I was.

Dear Mr. and Mrs. Robbins,

It was a dangerous letter to write. By now probably some connection had been made, back in Mississippi, between what happened to Cody and what happened to Wendy Lee. I wondered what they said about me, back in Caldecott County. What kind of gossip went on, about what all I had done to him, and did Aunt Carrie believe it? Did she hang her head in church now, over her failure at beating the evil out of me? Had she ever gone looking for me? I remembered how she used to sneak into my room at night and brush the hair off my forehead when she thought I was sleeping. Maybe she still went in there some evenings, just to sit on my bed and look at the big, square spot — whiter than the rest of the wall — where my map used to hang. But then, why should I think she'd leave the room the way it was? It could be she'd set up a little sewing room for herself, or some such thing.

Somehow, just like I knew Cody slept on in his hospital bed, I knew that my room sat waiting for me, exactly like I'd left it, if ever I chose to return. Which I didn't. I couldn't. After everything I'd become, everything I'd seen and done and been through, I knew there was no going back, not ever.

Dear Mr. and Mrs. Robbins,

Cody sure was a good boy, but y'all know that already. He wasn't much of a talker, though, so he might never have told you how much he liked those fishing trips he used to take with his daddy. He loved sitting in a boat with you on a sunny day, just all silent, knowing that it didn't matter if any fish got caught. He just liked knowing you were close by, and that he had you all to himself.

Honest, though, the person who pops into his mind most

often is his mama. He used to love sitting on the counter while you baked. He thinks you make the world's best lemon squares. One thing he remembers real clear, and real fondly, is the time you two went to the zoo in Jackson on a class trip. The parents weren't supposed to buy anything at the gift shop, but while the kids headed on back to the bus you snuck in and got him the stuffed giraffe he wanted. Do you know he still has that giraffe? Look on the shelf in his closet, underneath his base-ball glove. Sometimes when he was feeling blue he'd take it out and hold it awhile. He might like it at the hospital, come to think of it.

This is the last of these letters. I hope they brought you comfort. If they didn't, if they made you sad and sorry instead, I sure apologize. Mostly I just think it's important that you know, Cody thought you were real good parents. He sure did have a happy childhood, and was real grateful for it.

With Love from Cody

I didn't know how else to sign it. At this point it wouldn't do any harm to write Anna Marie, too, but I'd left that girl so far behind that writing her name felt like a lie. And I sure couldn't write Rogue. So I just left it at that, "With Love from Cody." Then I printed out the let-ter, and bought an envelope and stamp at a grocery store. This time it didn't matter where all it was mailed from. If ever anybody bothered to track this spot down, by the time they sent anyone for me, I'd be long gone. Given the location, they'd likely figure I'd disappeared into Mexico. But none of them would ever find me there, because none of them knew how to go looking ten thousand years in the future.

TRUTH IS, BACK IN THAT PARKING LOT, I'D CRIED SO HARD I didn't think my face would ever go back to normal. By the time I'd finished with my last errands, when I looked in the rearview mirror, the puffiness had mostly gone down, but my eyes were still a little red, my skin a little blotchy. I put on my Salvation Army hoodie. Touch had left his Red Sox cap on the seat of the truck, and I pulled it onto my head and stuffed my hair underneath. Staring back at me now was a girl, a regular American girl. A little sad, that's all. So long as he didn't look at my eyes too close, the border patrol officer wouldn't need to notice anything peculiar at all.

I pulled my truck back onto 85. That's how I'd come to think of it, my truck, even though I'd only had it a few days. Time had pretty much lost meaning, just as a result of going forward a few hours those two times. I had no sense what had happened when, or how long I'd been on the road. Hell, I didn't even know the day of the week. All I knew was that I was traveling south, heading toward Mexico, heading toward the future. Generally that's the only way possible to travel, toward the future, unless you know someone very brilliant, someone with a golden ring and an angel's touch.

Sun slanted through my windshield, warming up my face. I zipped my hoodie till it wouldn't zip anymore, and cranked up the heat. No part of me at all wanted to roll down the windows and enjoy the cooling air flowing in. The heat reminded me of Touch. The trickle of sweat on the back of my neck made me feel like he was right beside me. And anyhow: I had to get used to it, didn't I, being hot, if I was to go join him in his time?

That's how I had to think of it. That I was going to join him in his time. If I'd thought of it any other way, like Touch being gone for good, I would have cracked wide open, my innards exploding in the cab of my beloved blue Chevy truck.

And still I felt the damn tears spring up in my eyes again. Even if I'd been a normal girl, it would have been unlikely that I'd ever find anyone even close to him again.

The highway disappeared and reappeared under my wheels in

stretch after identical stretch. The plants around me were like nothing I ever saw in Mississippi — cactus and yucca, everything sharp and low and thorny, except for these real tall cactus that looked like prickly people, standing guard at the side of the road. The rocks and dirt were red and dark gray. Even the sky looked different, so much bigger, gaping over my head like a window looking out on the whole universe.

I wondered when it would happen, the doom Planet Earth was headed toward, the one that would wipe all traces of us away. If Touch never came back for me, would I live to see it happen? I shook my head, like I could shake that thought right out of it. Touch was coming back for me. There couldn't be any question about that, no sir, because I just wasn't willing to go on living without him.

By now this part of the atlas had implanted itself in my brain. The truck rumbled along, getting closer and closer to Lukeville, where I'd cross the border to Sonoyta, Mexico. After that I could head west, to Puerto Peñasco. Only a two-hour drive there, to the Gulf of California, and I'd soak my feet in the ocean for the very first time. Maybe by then Touch would've found me, and he could show me the sea himself, just like he'd wanted to.

I REACHED THE BORDER CROSSING SOMETIME AFTER LUNCH, not that I'd managed to eat anything. Lately it had started to amaze me how a person could keep going on so little food. Part of me wanted to make some declaration in my head, like I wasn't going to eat till Touch found me. But I knew that would be stupid. I could hear Touch's voice in my head telling me I had to eat, I had to take care of myself, I had to stay strong. Up ahead a long line of cars waited to cross into Mexico. I did a little calculating in my head and figured it must be the start of Labor Day weekend.

There was a little hot dog stand on the side of the road, so I pulled over and bought myself two hot dogs, a bag of potato chips, and the Coca-Cola I'd wanted back in Gila Bend. Once I got back into the car and took my first bite, I realized how hungry I was. I practically swallowed that first hot dog whole, then I went ahead and eased the truck into the line of waiting cars and munched down the rest of the food.

It kind of surprised me, how long this was taking. A couple of border patrol officers stood up at the front of the line of cars waiting to pass through what looked to me like a tollbooth. From what I could see so far, you either got a green arrow or a red arrow. If you got a green arrow, like most people, you got to just drive on into Mexico. If you got a red arrow, you had to pull over just past the booth — almost in Mexico. I couldn't see what all happened once you got there, but I pulled the baseball cap down close to my eyes. I'd put on Touch's lambskin gloves and tucked my T-shirt sleeves into them, just on the off chance someone tried to grab me by the wrist.

My heart beat hard inside my chest, *thump, thump, thump*ing away. There goes one car on through, then another and another, and whoops — stopping that one. It looked to me pretty random when they stopped people, and I prayed that I wouldn't be one of the unlucky ones. The good news was those officers didn't look super-official, like law enforcement, they just looked like tollbooth people. It didn't seem like they'd recognize me as a fugitive is what I mean by that.

Finally it was my turn. Mexico, just inches away. Leaving the United States behind me forever. I hardly had time to wish my Spanish was better, or to pray for a green arrow, before I pulled up to the booth. The patrol officer in his yellow neon vest looked over at me. I smiled and waved, trying to look innocent. Up over my head: red arrow.

Dang.

• • •

I PULLED THE TRUCK OVER BEHIND THE OTHERS THAT WERE waiting to be inspected. Talk about so close yet so far! I could see the little road that led on into Mexico; I could see the little stores, and even a couple scrawny dogs rooting in the garbage. I tapped my fingers on the steering wheel, wondering if I should just throw the backpack over my shoulders and make a run for it with my new wildebear speed. But then I'd have the Mexican officials after me, which would pretty much destroy the whole point of coming to Mexico in the first place. So all I could do was sit there, waiting for my fate to be decided.

Finally the agent stuck his head in the window. I rolled it down and tried to smile real friendly — not that that had done me much good before.

"*Hola*," he said. He had a nice bright smile himself, and I felt a little comforted. "You going on vacation?"

His accent was thick enough that it took me a second to understand him. "Yeah," I said. "You bet. I'm going on vacation. Down to see the Baja Peninsula. Do you know I've never in my whole life seen the ocean?"

He nodded. "You got any weapons in the car?"

"Weapons! No sir, I sure don't."

He waved his little clipboard, like I was supposed to get out of the truck. My whole body started to shake. The guard stepped back so I could push the heavy door open, and I climbed down to stand next to him. He came up to my earlobe. And damned if my knees didn't start knocking together. Seriously shaking and rattling together. The guard's eyes got kind of wide.

"Sorry," I said. "It's just I'm so excited to see your beautiful country."

He climbed on into the truck with a flashlight and peered into the air-conditioning vents, then shone the flashlight behind the seat. He leaned over to look under the seat. Touch's backpack had gotten kind of wedged under there. The guard gave a little tug to pull it out, and when he did, a couple twenty-dollar bills spilled out the top where it hadn't quite zipped shut. He got the backpack all the way out and stood by the car, letting it dangle from his fingertips for a minute before he pulled at the zipper. I could see from where I stood — and from the other bills that fluttered off the top — that the whole thing was stuffed with cash. Touch must've got it when he went into the gas station without me.

In other words: I should have thought to look in his backpack.

And I should have let Touch know, just in case, that crossing the Mexican-American border with a backpack full of money was a piss-poor idea, there being pretty much only two reasons a person in that situation would have that kind of cash: buying drugs or buying weapons. Oh, yeah, and a third one: starting a new life for yourself because you were wanted on criminal charges in the U.S.

Meanwhile the guard stood there, the backpack open, staring over at me. Then he pulled a little walkie-talkie off his belt and spoke into it. I could hear the words in Spanish, and the crackle from the static. There was only one thing left for me to do. I turned on my heels and started running, fast as I could, down the road toward Mexico.

Who knows if all those border patrol agents had time to admire my speed? The problem was there were plenty of them stationed in the direction I started running, and wouldn't you know they all had weapons of their own. The next thing I knew I had border patrol guards on all sides of me, Mexican and American alike, all pointing rifles in my direction.

The truth is a girl can have skin that brings men down with the slightest touch. She can have the strength and speed of two wilde-bears. But none of that matters much when she's faced with the barrels of ten good old American assault rifles.

I put my hands up in the air, not knowing what on Earth I was going to do next.

· *12* ·

STUPID OR UNLUCKY. STUPID OR UNLUCKY. THOSE TWO WORDS kept bouncing back and forth in my brain. Trying to think which one applied to me seemed a whole lot easier than figuring out how the hell I'd get out of this predicament.

The border patrol officers had managed to handcuff me without doing any harm to themselves on account of my sleeves being tucked into Touch's gloves. Now I sat by my lonesome in a holding cell, waiting for them to find out that I was not in fact Mary Ginsberg and that the blue Chevy pickup truck was stolen.

"Where'd you get that money?" three different border patrol guards had already asked me.

"My boyfriend gave it to me," I said each time. They could hook me up to a lie detector for that one!

"And what's your boyfriend do for a living?"

"He's in electronics." Pretty sure I'd pass with that answer, too.

"Where is he now?"

"I don't know."

They went ahead and tossed me in the cell, waiting on processing me, I guess, so they could deal with the less complicated arrests — the ones who had come quietly without trying to flee. When someone finally came to get me, I would have to make some decisions. But what decisions those would be I couldn't have told you. I didn't know much about being arrested. They had already taken away my personal effects, including Touch's magic screwdriver, leaving me with nothing but the clothes on my back. But I suspected that when an officer came to collect me, and process my arrest, he'd want me to take off my gloves to fingerprint me. And then who knows what all damage I'd end up doing, and what they'd do to me — remembering those guns — when officers started hitting the floor.

I sat down on a hard metal bench and closed my eyes. *Touch*, I thought. *If you are planning to ever come fetch me back to your world, now sure would be a good time.*

My eyes fluttered open, and I half expected to see him standing right there in front of me, his blue eyes twinkling, his lips pulled into that little half smile of his. Instead I just saw an empty cell, and heard heavy booted footsteps coming down the corridor.

"Mary?" the officer said. It was a woman, not much older than me, with her hair pulled back in a tight ponytail. She looked like she had a pretty nice shape under that uniform she wore, and I wondered what had made her ever want to go into law enforcement. Border patrol seemed to me like a particularly mean branch of law enforcement. Truth be told, the way she said *Mary* sounded real sarcastic, like she knew that wasn't really my name. Plus I didn't approve of her line of work. That didn't mean I wanted to send her into a permanent coma, so I kept my distance as best I could.

"You want to tell me what your real name is, honey?" Despite the term of endearment, she did not say this in a nice tone.

"Not particularly," I said, wishing some kind of plan would pop into my head. Honestly, the best chance I had seemed like running. If I could get to a place upstairs where I had a clear shot of the door, I'd not only have my super-speed, but an element of surprise, on my side. This time I bet I could make it before anybody drew a gun.

And what the hell would I do after that?

"Turn around," said the snotty officer. I did as I was told, offering her my wrists so she could cuff me. "A little chilly, are you?" she said, talking about the sleeves tucked into my gloves.

"I got a skin condition." This shut her up. She put her hand on the middle of my back and pushed me forward with her fingertips, out of the cell.

"Come on," she said. "We're going to get you fingerprinted then bring you on into interrogation."

We walked past the other cells, with forlorn and anxious-looking people — all of them men — crammed in there, waiting to be deported or incarcerated. My brain was working as fast as it could but coming up with nothing. This girl next to me — Officer Jeanne Sincero, according to her nametag — she looked so calm and unafraid, business as usual. But I felt like I was marching her to her death. What would happen when I took off those gloves and she reached over to press my finger into the ink?

There it was. I stood there looking down at it, a regular old ink blotter. Officer Sincero took out a form and put it on the surface beside it. Then she uncuffed me. Her face looked pretty, in a hard, regular kind of way. I wondered what special abilities she might transfer to me, what memories.

"Well," she said. "You gonna take off those gloves so we can get this done? Mary?"

"Sure," I said. I pulled off my right glove real careful, and Officer Sincero reached out to grab my wrist. I pulled it back from her. "Better let me do it," I said. "It's real contagious."

This made her snap her own hand back pretty fast. I pressed my finger into the blotter, and she pointed to the little spot for me to make the mark. "Press down hard but not too hard," she said. She handed me a paper towel, and I took it with the hand that was still gloved. "Don't look to me like anything's wrong," she said.

"You got a degree in dermatology?"

She snorted a little at this as I pulled the glove back over my hand and tucked my sleeve into it. From where I stood, I could see people coming in and out the door, but I couldn't bring myself to make a break for it. At some point I would have to figure something out, though, because not every officer I came into contact with would be as easy to manipulate as Officer Sincero was proving to be (a pretty girl hears the words "skin condition" and you can be sure she won't touch you anytime soon).

"If I were you," she said, snapping the cuffs back on me, "I'd be a whole lot less of a smart-aleck with the detectives. *Mary.*"

This sure as hell reminded me: It wasn't only the officers that needed protecting. Because once they figured out who I was, there were a whole lot of charges that would be leveled against me, including but not limited to car theft, assault and battery, bank robbery, and maybe even attempted murder.

Officer Sincero led me to a little room. There was a table and a couple chairs, and a long mirror that I figured was one of those two-way deals. She uncuffed me and told me to have a seat. "You want coffee or water or anything?" she said. You could tell this was the part of her job she hated most, offering lowlifes like me refreshments. For this reason only, I told her I wanted a cup of coffee, and she went off to get it with a scowl on her face.

I tapped my feet on the floor while I waited for her. Stupid. That was the answer. I was a moron for not checking Touch's backpack, a moron for trying to go to Mexico in the first place. Hadn't Touch told me that where he came from you could track a person across space and time? Too late it occurred to me that he'd be able to find me no matter where I was. Unless — and this was the thing I couldn't bear thinking about — something had happened that would prevent him from searching for me in the first place.

I looked down at my hands, encased in his gloves and resting on my knees. Was it just last night that these gloves had held his hands? I closed my eyes and whispered out loud: "I'm right here, Touch. Right here in Lukeville, Arizona. Come find me. Come get me." And then for good measure I added, "I love you."

When I opened my eyes I saw a man in a white button-down shirt, with a Styrofoam cup of coffee in one hand and a big fat file in the other. No doubt about it, that file was mine. Suddenly I was very aware they hadn't let me use the bathroom since they'd brought me in.

Sure enough that man kept walking straight toward my door, and when he opened it he gave me this knowing little smile and placed the coffee cup in front of me. I wanted to drink that coffee about as much as I wanted to give the person who gave it to me a big wet kiss. Which is to say, not one bit.

He took the seat across from me. Then he said, "Hello, Anna Marie."

Shit.

"You want to tell me what you're doing so far from home?"

"I don't know what you mean," I told him.

"I mean that you don't belong here in Arizona. You belong way back east in Caldecott County, Mississippi. There are some folks back there who are real frantic to find you."

"I don't know what you mean," I said again. "I'm not from Mississippi. I'm from Flagstaff, Arizona." I waited for him to ask me the address, which I'd memorized real careful, but he didn't.

Instead he smiled. Of course all I had to do to prove I was from Mississippi instead of Arizona was open my mouth, and I'd already done that. I couldn't rightly not do it again. Then it occurred to me: I *could* rightly not open my mouth. I'd seen *Law & Order*. I had the right to remain silent!

"Hey," I said. "Am I under arrest or what?"

"You bet you're under arrest, little girl," he said, tapping my file with his fat finger. I didn't much appreciate him calling me little girl, especially when he wouldn't be much taller than me if we stood toe-to-toe. "Under arrest for two counts attempted murder, plus larceny, plus resisting arrest. For starters."

"In that case," I said, "I want a lawyer."

He got this dark, squinty look on his face. Then he slammed his hand on my file, picked it up off the table, and walked out of the room. I heard him call to the next office, "Lawyered up!"

At least I'd gone and bought myself a little time. I crossed my arms on the top of the table and let my head fall into them. If I hadn't cried all the tears in my body out that morning, after Touch disappeared, I might've cried again out of sheer frustration. Never in my life had I been locked inside a room with no way of escaping. It was a very particular, very dreadful, very *primitive* kind of feeling, one I never wanted to experience again.

I didn't want to raise my eyes and face that room, so I just stayed with my face buried in my arms. They kept the room warm, probably on purpose, and I could feel sweat pooling at the base of my neck. Time clicked on by, and I thought of the ways it could move forward or backward — an hour here, a thousand years there. What happened when something changed in time? For example, when Touch came to find me at my apartment and I wasn't there, I must have been someplace else. Did that me disappear when he went back in time to find me? Or was she off somewhere, living the life I would've led if that Camaro hadn't pulled up beside me? What if Touch decided to go back in time, like half an hour before his father found us at the Outer Limits Space Age Restaurant? Would that be a different me that he'd rescue, and I'd have to go on by myself in this continuum, or would the present suddenly change? The thought of a whole bunch of different me's, all continuing according to when time had been interrupted or not, gave me a powerful headache. It also made me feel exhausted. But I refused to look up, just shut my eyes tighter against my arms.

And I didn't exactly fall asleep, but something happened — like a little lapse of some sort, my own kind of little coma — because for almost a full minute I wasn't in the interrogation room at all.

I was standing on a wide, white beach. The cleanest, purest, most sparkling sand you can imagine underneath my bare feet. The sun shone down, ultra bright. But the water lapped over my feet — the ocean! — and that felt wonderfully good.

"It won't be long now," Touch said. Because he was standing right there beside me, not bundled up at all, just wearing a pair of loose khaki shorts and nothing else.

"I'm not a strong swimmer," I told him. Even as I said the words, they sounded like a lie, because I'd spent my whole childhood splashing in the currents of the Mississippi River, and before that, when I was a little girl, I'd splashed in the bayou with the water moccasins and the gators.

"You don't need to be," Touch said. "I've got you."

When he said that, I realized that I wasn't wearing much more than he was, just denim shorts and a bikini top. And Touch's bare hand was reaching out toward me, getting ready to grab me around the waist and hold me close to him . . .

Fssszzt. Above my head a fluorescent light buzzed and flickered. My head jerked up out of my arms. I could see through the glass in the room that officers were packing up, getting ready to go home. And here came old Jeanne Sincero, marching down the hall toward me. She opened the door.

"Come on with me," she said. "We can't find a lawyer for you till morning. We're going to have to keep you here in a cell till then."

OFFICER SINCERO DELIVERED ME TO A CELL WITH A TOILET IN the corner and a little cot. "Someone'll be by with dinner soon," she said, then went off home, to her boyfriend, or her cat, or maybe even her family. Maybe in Lukeville, Arizona, people married young, just like in Caldecott County.

I guess they had me in the women's section of the jail, and I guess I was the only woman to get arrested trying to cross the border that day. It was ghostly, spooky quiet. All I could think about was that hot, hot beach. It had seemed so real. Was it really Touch, standing beside me, talking to me? Did he have my coordinates, or my DNA, or whatever it was he needed? Would he be here soon?

I knelt beside the cot and tried to duplicate the exact position I'd been in when the vision came. Of course I didn't have any window in my cell, and my eyes were closed, but still I had a sense of the night growing dark outside, while I waited behind bars to find out my fate. At some point someone slid a tray with greasy green beans and some chicken slices slopped in gravy under the bars. I could smell the food but didn't want it; the scent of chemicals rose from it, not any more appetizing than a can of lighter fluid. *Primitive*, a voice said in my head.

But Touch didn't come to me, so finally I crawled onto the cot, lay on top of the scratchy blanket and the cardboard pillow, and went to sleep.

BAM! CRACKLE! BOOM!

Even in my sleep, where I first heard the noise, I welcomed it. It filled my head like fireworks, even louder and brighter, happening behind my eyelids and sounding somewhere deep in the cushion of my brain. I leaped from the bed, hoping it would be Touch standing there in the cell with me. The light that filled the little cell was blinding, more difficult to see through, for me at least, than darkness would've been. I could see a man in the midst of it, tall, with broad shoulders, and a long leather coat. I took one eager step toward him.

That's when his face came into focus, a face not unlike Touch's, but twice his age, with arrogance in his eyes, and greed, in place of kindness.

"You," I said. The fear went away, replaced by hatred. For everything he'd taken away from me.

Touch's father spoke English. "It looks like I've found you in a spot of trouble." I hated to admit, he had a beautiful voice. It somehow kept the same flair of their language, a low and musical quality.

"What are you doing here?" I said.

"I'm here to rescue you."

He sounded so kind. For a second it flickered through my head: Maybe Touch was wrong about him. Or maybe Touch had convinced him to come over to his side. Of course there was only one person who could answer all that for sure. "Where's Touch?" I said.

"Touch is home, safe and sound. He sent me here to collect you."

It had to be a trap, of course. Touch wouldn't have sent his father. He would have come for me himself. But I didn't care, so long as I had a way to travel forward, to his time. To where he was. Funny. In this time — my own time — I had no idea what to do about being arrested and put in jail. But for the future, a plan formed in my head instantly. One way or another I would find Touch, and we would figure out how to save Arcadia together. I would do whatever it took to save the world he loved, including give my own life, and including time travel with his evil father.

"Well then," I said. "Let's go."

Touch's father opened up his coat. I stood there in the crackling, too-bright light, staring at him. "You'll have to come closer, my dear. If I'm to transport you."

I wriggled my fingers, still encased in Touch's gloves, and took a step toward him. What if his hand touched my face as we began our trip together? Much as I wanted to bring this man down, I didn't want his head inside of mine.

"Not to worry, my dear," Touch's father said. "I know all about your gifts. I'm prepared to protect myself."

He stepped toward me, that coat still open, and I realized with revulsion that I'd have to embrace him. I clenched my teeth. Whatever it took to get to Touch, that's what I was willing to do and more.

I closed my eyes and pressed my face against the older man's chest. He closed his coat around me and I felt a huge pull, a deep whoosh, and we were surrounded by colors, darkness, and noise — the sounds of centuries passing by.

When I traveled through time with Touch, we'd only gone a few hours. It happened so fast I barely got to notice the sensation; it was almost like a sneeze. But as his father and I went all the way to Touch's time, images swirled around us, staticky voices, the increasing heat of the sun, and finally water — rushing water, gallons upon gallons of it, rising and splashing and covering almost every inch of ground. It went on for ages — so much time that I lost my ability to measure its passing.

Finally the motion stopped. I opened my eyes and pushed away from him. He held on the barest second, maybe just for the pleasure of feeling me resist, then — like he remembered what all I could do — he let go.

"Well," he said. "Here we are."

I wanted to look around. Aware of the sound of waves, and light almost as bright as what had filled the caves under Horseshoe Mesa, I wanted to see what Touch's world, Arcadia, looked like. But I couldn't. I was surrounded by heat. Heat like I'd never felt before. Hot, dry air, closing in around me, filling up my lungs, making me long for water, not only to drink but to plunge into — cold, cold water up to my chin.

Sweat formed on my forehead, underneath my hair, in my armpits. I wanted to rip the clothes right off me, dangerous skin be damned. I couldn't stand it. Not for a single second.

"What's wrong with her?" a woman's voice said. Not in English, but in Touch's language, but still I understood it — maybe, I realized, because of the wildebears inside me. But that didn't make sense. Why would a wildebear understand that language any more than a grizzly bear would speak English? I couldn't think straight; it was like the temperature had seeped right into my brain.

"It's the heat," a man's musical voice answered. "She's not used to it."

I opened my mouth to say I was just fine, there was no problem at all, and what he needed to do was take me to Touch and pronto. Instead I staggered forward, my hands clutching my throat, and muttered something that sounded like "Water."

Then I fainted dead away, right at the feet of my enemies.

WHO KNOWS HOW MUCH TIME PASSED BEFORE MY EYES FLUT-tered open? Time had become very strange inside my head. I guess it would tend to when you found yourself on Planet Earth ten thousand and eighteen years after you were born. It took several minutes for my eyes to focus and take in the surroundings, which did not look futuristic at all.

The room was nice and cool. I don't know how they kept the temperature like this, because I didn't see any air-conditioning vents, or feel any cold air moving through the room. It just felt nice and crisp, maybe about seventy-two degrees, cool enough so that I was comfortable with the light comforter laid over me. I wondered how in the world they'd got me into bed without touching my skin, then realized I was still wearing my pants, gloves, and T-shirt. Across the room there was an oversized armchair with clothes neatly folded on the seat. I guess I was supposed to change into them when I got up.

I pushed the covers aside and sat up. The floorboards were wood, a pale color, and there was a round, braided rug on the floor. The bed had an iron headboard that someone had painted a pretty sage green.

The walls were a very pale yellow, and the armchair that held my clothes looked like the perfect place to curl up with a book. There were two nice wide windows on opposite walls. Except for the ceiling, which was rounded instead of slanted, it looked like a room you'd find in any well-kept farmhouse: pretty, clean, comfortable.

What I wanted to see was outside that window: what the world looked like, the world Touch had always lived in. So I threw my legs over the side of the bed. When I stood, they felt shaky, like maybe I hadn't used them in a long, long time. I put my hand on the head-board to steady myself, then walked to the window. The view was beautiful. Acres of red dirt and sagebrush, and mountains in the distance. No snow on top of them, of course; the trees grew all the way up to the top, green pine trees. I couldn't see any other houses, not through this window, anyway. Even through the window I could see that the light here had a different quality. Like there was not only no ozone layer, but no pollution to block the sun. It shone down so fierce it created a kind of mist, like if I were standing outside I'd be able to cup my hands and catch sunlight like it was rainwater.

Before, when I'd imagined the future, it was out of some movie, I guess, with tall silver buildings and hovercrafts whooshing through the air. But what I saw instead was a pristine landscape, unpopulated and so bright you'd think any second God was going to part the rays of sunlight like they were curtains and step on through. I pressed my hand against the glass, and felt its heat trying to pulse through to the coolness of my room. Then the window went black, as if someone had suddenly painted every pane so I couldn't see through it. I pulled my hand back real abrupt, as if I'd been scalded. Then I pressed my hand against the window again, and all the black disappeared. It wasn't anything menacing. Just the future's version of window blinds.

There were two doors in the room, one opening into a white-tiled bathroom. I could see a deep tub with clawed feet. On the opposite side from where I stood there was a door like any other I'd ever seen, white wood, with a pretty crystal doorknob that kind of — but not too much — matched the headboard. Pretty, subtle details. I crossed the room and placed my hand on the knob. It wouldn't turn. So here in the future, at least in this room, the main similarity to the past was the fact that I was a prisoner.

I went over to the armchair and picked up the outfit they had left for me. It was a pale, shimmery green jumpsuit, made out of the softest, lightest material I'd ever felt. Zipped up on the side, from the hip to the arm. It had a collar that would go all the way up to my chin, and built-in gloves, even built-in socks, like a little kid's foot pajamas.

It didn't exactly make me giddy, the idea of putting on a prisoner's uniform, which was what this was, no matter how pretty it looked, and how suited to protecting others from me. In fact it was a little *too* suited to that. Wearing this outfit, if for any reason I needed to use my . . . gifts, as Touch's father had called it, I'd have to dance cheek to cheek with the person I needed to attack.

But on the other hand, the Salvation Army outfit felt like something that had been slept in for days. I put the jumpsuit back on the chair and went into the bathroom. The toilet was filled with dirt instead of water, and there was a rope overhead that must be what flushed it. The room had its own windows, and from these I could see another building. It was shaped like a long tunnel, the same reddish color as the earth, and I guessed that from far away it would blend into the landscape nicely.

I pressed my hand against each window, felt that pulsing warmth, and then the glass went black. There was a funny sort of shower, sunken into the floor with tiled steps leading down to it, and the shower nozzle up above. No shower curtain and no dial. I took off my clothes and stepped down into it. As soon as I stood under the shower, water started flowing and I braced myself a second, ready for the scalding temperatures Touch liked. But it wasn't too hot, only just right, and despite the uncertain situation, I couldn't help but sigh as the warm water hit my back. I could see a towel rack where someone had laid out big, fluffy white towels. So far this was a much more luxurious incarceration than the one I'd left behind in Lukeville, Arizona.

But it was still an incarceration. As the time ticked by I became more and more aware of that, zipped into my green jumpsuit and pacing the room until my hair was dry. What's more, I was starving. I remembered the tray of food back in my other cell. It almost made me smile, thinking of the border police looking through the bars to find me totally disappeared, that tray of food just sitting there untouched — unless of course some little mice came out of the cracks in the wall to nibble at it. Now my stomach rumbled away, reminding me that the last thing I'd eaten was those chips and hot dogs at the border. I'd barely even taken a sip of my soda, and my mouth felt powerfully dry.

From the other side of the door came a knock, gentle and discreet. I froze. Was I supposed to call "Come in"? I sure didn't feel like doing that, considering I had no idea who'd waltz on in there. On the other hand, maybe it was Touch. I put my hand over my heart.

Before I could think what to do the crystal green doorknob turned. I stood stock-still. It would be too much to hope for that Touch might come walking through the door, and I reminded myself not to do anything rash. What I wanted to do was go charging through the door, past whoever was opening it, and go find him. But the smart thing would be to bide my time, get my bearings, figure out what all I'd need to do in order to get to him.

The door opened. It wasn't Touch. Instead, in walked Alabaster, all bundled up in a white fur coat, gloves, and a white knit hat. She closed the door behind her and I heard a little click. We were locked in here together, but when she shivered — a real pretty little shiver — I knew it wasn't on account of being afraid of me. She gave me this little smile, like she felt sorry for me and hated me at the same time, and

I felt my own, less pretty shiver inside of me. Alabaster looked like a porcelain doll. She had a pretty little face, with huge blue eyes and red lips. Dimples. Her hair poked out of her hat in gentle blond waves, and I could tell she'd arranged it just so. She'd wanted to look beautiful when she came in to face me, and it had worked.

"And so we meet again," she said, in English, with the same sort of clipped and elegant accent that Touch had. It made me feel sick to my stomach, noticing this sameness between them, as if he belonged more to her than to me. Before I could ask her how she'd figured out how to talk to me, she reached into her pocket and held out a little red ball of energy, like the one Touch used to have. A translator. It floated just above her gloved palm for a few seconds, then she closed her hand around it and put it in her pocket.

"He makes the most wonderful things, doesn't he? Such a talented man. It's why I fell in love with him."

Knowing that she'd understand me perfectly, I couldn't think what to say. So I said the only thing I had to say to her, the only thing I wanted to know. "Where's Touch?"

"Ah," she said. "My husband."

"Your *ex*-husband," I said, a little louder than I meant to.

She cocked her head and smiled, like this was the funniest thing I could have said. Then she repeated, "My *husband*. This was our home, you know. Where we lived together."

"I notice you're using the past tense," I said.

"Ah," she said. "But not for the reason you think. We're moving on, Touch and I, to a grander station. The station we were born to have. Where our child was born to be raised. Would you like to see a picture?"

For a moment I thought she meant a picture of their new, fancier house, but of course she meant a picture of Cotton. Their son. Alabaster didn't have to fumble through her wallet to show me what he looked like. She just drew a square in the air next to her with the tip of her gloved fingertip, and a colored picture appeared, of a little boy with white-blond hair and Touch's kind blue eyes. He was laughing and holding some kind of shiny beach ball. I could see the ocean behind him. He had his mother's dimples. For some reason the picture made me feel deeply afraid, and not of anything that might happen to me. It scared me that Touch and Alabaster had something so important together, something so beautiful. Seeing the picture made it much more real than just knowing it.

"His name is Cotton," Alabaster said. "At least for right now. Here, in our time, we get our lifelong names at twelve years of age. Sometimes people keep their original names, if they suit them properly. Like me. I've always been Alabaster, since the day I was born."

I just stood there, blinking at her, suddenly terrified that she could read my mind. She laughed. "I can't read your mind," she said flatly. "Just your face. It gives away everything. That's something you might want to work on."

I cleared my throat and straightened my spine, pulling myself to my full height, which had me towering over her, even though I was still in my jumpsuit socks, and she wore boots with big thick heels. Again, I said the only thing I had to say to her. "Where's Touch?"

She sighed. "A simple girl from a simple time," she said. "One thing on your mind, I see, and it's my dear, handsome husband. Don't you know better than to demand to see another woman's husband in her own home?" She pointed to the bed behind me, the one where I'd slept for who knows how long. "We made love in that bed, you know. Not that this is our room; we keep it for guests. But we've made love in every room in this house, even the kitchen. Is that too personal, this information?" She cocked her head, and I tried to erase my thoughts along with my reactions. Alabaster went on. "He's a wonderful lover, Touch. But I suppose you know that." She smiled again. She had very white teeth, just a little too big for her mouth, so that they rested on her bottom lip. It was charming. Sexy. I wanted to ball my hand into a fist and punch those teeth right in.

"No," Alabaster said, rethinking what she'd just said. "I guess you wouldn't know. Would you?"

I knew. I knew full well, even if I couldn't make love to him in every room in the house, not the way she had. But still I knew all about him, and I would keep reminding myself of that, and not fall for this bait.

"We used to know a man," Alabaster said, "called Gordium. I believe Touch has mentioned him. He had the same gift as you. But he learned to control it and lead a very normal life."

I realized I was still standing, and sank down onto the bed. I wanted to ask her so badly what kind of normal life, but at the same time I didn't want to ask her for anything.

"Yes," she said, as if I'd spoken out loud. "He could have relationships. Shake hands. Kiss. Make love. All of it. Just like a normal person. Except better than normal, because he had this power. Can you see how your power might be very useful, if only you learned how to use it?"

My face wouldn't stop reacting to what she was saying, no matter how hard I tried.

"Gordium could grab hold of a person's shoulders," Alabaster said. "He could take out as little or as much as he wanted. A bit of knowledge here. A little ability there. He could leave enough for the person, if he liked. Or he could take it all. Just as he liked."

A shiver went through me at the thought of wielding this kind of power on purpose. It was bad enough to do it on accident! The only thing I knew for sure was I didn't want to be taking Alabaster's word for anything.

"Where's Touch?" I said again.

"Touch is where he's always been. In his workroom. Designing wondrous inventions."

"I don't believe you," I said.

"Inventions like the one that allowed him to send me messages when he was away, and summon me back to your time."

"That's a lie," I said. "He was trying to escape from you."

"He told me to come," she said flatly, "and to bring the wildebears."

"Why the hell would he want to do that?" But even as I asked, I felt uneasy, remembering the way he'd brought me to the Anasazi ruins, and Tawa.

"Why indeed. He summoned me a second time. To rescue you from the caves."

"*Rescue* us?" I said. "That's not exactly how I think on that incident."

"But you'd be dead," she said, "if we hadn't arrived."

I couldn't think of an answer to that. I couldn't think of much of anything. "Where's Touch?"

Alabaster stepped aside and opened the door. Beckoned to me with her hand. "Come, impatient girl," she said. "I'll take you to him. You can see for yourself."

I stepped out into the hall, expecting to get blasted with heat. Instead it felt only a little warmer than it had in the room. Meanwhile Alabaster started taking her clothes off and hanging them on a rack of hooks outside my room. There were several hooks, with bigger clothes, for men I guess, and at that sight fear finally started to settle in around me. It was bad enough for your boyfriend's ex-wife to be able to barge on into your room without knocking, any old time she wanted. But the thought of strange men having that same privilege? That didn't set well, in this time or any other.

Once she'd taken off all her cold weather gear, Alabaster stood there in front of me, wearing a white lace bikini and a light little short-sleeved shrug. She kept on her clunky boots, though. I hate to say she looked pretty fantastic. I put my hand to my forehead, testing the temperature.

"You're not going to feel the heat," Alabaster said. "It's the garment. Touch designed it. It regulates body temperature, keeps the air around you at the precise temperature where you'll be most comfortable."

She started walking down the hall. The roof over our head was low and round. If most buildings in our world were constructed around angles, the buildings here seemed to be constructed through curves. I followed Alabaster down the hall. The house looked like it had been sculpted from one big piece of clay rather than connecting walls and floors.

I let Alabaster walk a few steps, then hurried to catch up with her. "Touch made this suit?" I said. "He knows I'm coming?"

"He designed the material," she said, ignoring my second question. "It was I who made the suit for you. We're a team, the two of us. Touch and I."

"That's not true." As soon as the words were out of my mouth I regretted them.

She stopped and turned toward me. I tripped up short, then righted myself. "It *is* true," she said. "It's always been true. That's why he didn't go to get you himself, you know. Because I didn't approve. Knowing how you felt about him." All I could do was blink at her. She smiled a little. "Never underestimate the power of a wife," she said, and started walking again.

I had been afraid of plenty in the last thirty-six hours or so. But now I also felt afraid about Touch, whether everything between us would be the same when I saw him. *Never underestimate the power of a wife.* That was exactly the sort of thing Wendy Lee's memories had been trying to tell me.

My hand brushed the silky fine material of the suit. I wondered how Touch could have invented this material when they'd only taken him yesterday. How would Alabaster have had time to make the suit? Of course Touch could've designed it before he left, but then why wouldn't he have made himself a suit to bring back to our time? It sure would've come in handy for him there, keeping him from being so cold.

Walking behind Alabaster, I wondered if she was swaying her hips like that for my benefit or if that was how she always walked. She reminded me of something that would pop out of an ancient lamp; she didn't seem quite real. I tried to shut out the image of her and Touch and every room in their round house, concentrating instead on the fact that I was going to see him. That is, if Alabaster was telling the truth.

Once I saw him, he would explain. Better yet he would look at me, and I would look at him, and then no matter what happened, everything would be OK.

Downstairs, the house was like a nicer, cleaner, rounder version of Joe Wheeler's log cabin — not huge, but airy and comfortable and very, very pretty. Gleaming wood and tile everywhere, and high domed ceilings. I noticed there were no lamps or lightbulbs, just lots of windows, with that ultra-strong sun pouring in. The walls were empty of electrical outlets; nothing had wires. If Touch had been there, I might have teased him that it looked primitive, except I knew this world was running on energy that didn't cost anything, or take away from anything else.

We went downstairs, into an open, rustic area, with a comfortable-looking living room and what must have been the kitchen, although it didn't have any stove or refrigerator, just lots of cabinets of varying sizes. My stomach rumbled, and I wondered if they were ever going to feed me.

Outside, we walked across a dusty yard. When I turned to look at the house where I'd been staying, it looked like no building I'd ever seen, a small series of rising domes. The broad sun reflected off its walls so that it almost became invisible — a pale shimmer, like a mirage. I could feel that same sun's heat on the top of my head, but the suit Touch designed kept me nice and cool. There was no grass underfoot, but all around were lots of wildflowers and low little bushes. It was real pretty. Alabaster didn't seem worried about me running away, even though she knew firsthand how fast I could go. She just sauntered on ahead of me, confident that I would follow her anywhere as long as she told me Touch was waiting.

If I found out anything had happened to him, she wouldn't find me so easy to lead. Right then and there I would grab her by the shoulders and press my cheek against hers, using all my wildebear strength to hold her as long as possible. Then all her memories — all her everything — would belong to me. And she'd be gone.

As we approached the long, low outbuilding, a portion of the wall disappeared so we could step through. Inside it looked as industrial as the house had looked cozy, with cold, hard floors made from a material I didn't recognize. It seemed much bigger than I'd imagined it, with door after closed door, each with a tile and a little symbol on it. Finally Alabaster stopped at one door and waved her hand in front of it. When that door disappeared into thin air, she walked through the opening. After a second of uncertainty, I went ahead and followed her.

The room was huge, with a high, curved ceiling and the same cold, industrial floors. Light seeped in through slats near the floor, so it wasn't as bright as the house had been. From the outside I would've imagined the whole building was about the size of this room. It was divided in the middle by a glass wall that went all the way to the ceiling and spanned the entire length. On the other side of the glass it was a whole lot homier, with wood floors and a braided rug like the one up in my room. Also a little living area, with a couch and chairs and a coffee table. Sitting in the big comfy armchair was Touch's father. And on the couch, his hands clasped together like he had nothing to do but wait, was Touch.

He looked well. Rested and well fed. He was dressed like I'd never seen him before, in kind of loose, light long pants and a short-sleeved shirt. He wasn't shivering or bothered by the temperature. He looked perfectly comfortable.

I ran to the glass. I pressed my whole body against it and yelled as loud as I could. "Touch! Touch!"

Alabaster rolled her pretty eyes. "Very romantic. But he can't hear you."

I turned toward her. "I thought you didn't have any prisons in this world."

"This world has changed."

Just then Touch looked up. For a moment I felt afraid that he wouldn't be able to see through the glass, but right away he got to his feet and walked toward me. I waited to see that twinkle in his eye, the little bit of devil that couldn't help shining through at the sight of me. Instead he looked like he could hardly believe what he was seeing. He walked real slow, and somehow I knew — if I could've torn my eyes away from Touch's — that his father and his wife were both smirking as they watched him.

Touch stood there, right in front of the glass. He raised his hands and pressed them against mine, our palms separated by the layer of glass, truly no closer to touching than they'd ever come. I pressed my forehead against the glass, too. It felt hot. And somehow I knew in that instant, Touch hadn't designed the material of my suit before he came to Jackson, any more than he'd designed it for me, so I could live comfortably in his world. He'd designed it for himself. So that maybe he could come back to me.

But standing there on the other side of the glass, he didn't smile or look happy to see me. He didn't look much of anything, really. Just blank. And I couldn't hear him when he spoke, or even read his lips, since no doubt he was talking in his beautiful, whistling language.

I sure didn't want to ask Alabaster. But she was the only one there, and I wanted to know so badly. "What?" I said. "What is he saying?"

She said, "He says now that the last weapon is here, we can move to the castle for good."

"Last weapon!"

"Yes. The last weapon in the war against Arcadia."

"War against Arcadia," I repeated, real slow, hating the way the words sounded.

Alabaster smiled. She had a very sweet smile. A believable one. So that it gave me even bigger chills when she said, right on the tag end of that smile:

"And now that you're here. Once and for all, Arcadia will fall."

I turned back toward the glass, hoping that Touch's face might tell me something different. But he only stood there, beautiful as ever and — to my eyes at least — impossible to read.

WHAT DID I CARE, REALLY, ABOUT A WORLD THAT HAD NOTHING
to do with me? Arcadia. No more than a word. A concept. An unat-
tainable ideal.

Ten thousand years from now, all our country's edges — the edges
that it has today — will be under water. I'm not talking about California and Florida falling into the ocean. I'm talking nothing left but the
Rocky Mountains and the desert surrounding them, maybe three
states' worth of land remaining. Same situation on every other continent except for the ones — like Europe, Australia, and Antarctica —
that will be totally submerged. Everything that remains will be just a
fraction of what it used to be, floating in the middle of a great blue-
green sea. They won't have different names for different oceans. It will
just be one, The Sea, that takes up most of the planet, making land
seem more or less an afterthought.

But showing me the map wasn't the first thing Touch's father did
when he came to talk to me in my room. First, he asked me my name.

"You don't know it?"

"What do you think?" he asked.

"I think you know it." We sat there for a minute, staring at each other, and then I caved. Which probably was not a good sign.

"My name's Rogue," I said.

"The name Touch gave you."

"It's the only name I have."

"Well then, Rogue. You may call me King."

"*King?*"

He smiled, like my aversion to this was the funniest thing in the world. "It's the only name I have," he said, with just the teeniest trace of sternness. Then he showed me the map of what the world had become.

Staring at that image, I felt a huge sadness in my chest for everything that used to be. But I tried not to let King see. I hated the way he watched me, looking for reaction or emotion. Remembering what Alabaster had said, about how my face gave everything away, I tried real hard to just stare blankly. I reminded myself that, rising seawater or not, nothing lasts ten thousand years. Everything I ever knew would've been gone by now no matter what.

But to not even leave a trace of ourselves? I mean, think of everything our own anthropologists had found. Dinosaur bones, and the fossils of people who lived hundreds of thousands of years ago. The Anasazi villages like the one Touch and I'd walked through, those would remain. Whereas apparently, even under water, we'd manage to destroy all our tall cities, and all our little towns, so this new civilization, it didn't even know we ever existed. Not until Touch accidentally stumbled upon us. It was our greed, I felt sure, our greed and our blindness that had wiped us all out without leaving a trace. And now these people — Touch's family — wanted to wipe out Arcadia and head themselves in the same direction.

Anyway. I could certainly understand why Touch hadn't been able to read my Rand McNally atlas. The map King showed me was like the photo Alabaster had brought up of her and Touch's son.

Hovering in the middle of the room was a great big picture of the ocean, and he could zoom in to different spots. As he went east, away from what was left of North America and toward what used to be Europe, I tried to imagine Mississippi as nothing but the ocean floor. No bayous, no gators, no river. Did the loblolly pines and tupelo trees still sway down there in the water? It was a hopeful image, but of course trees need a whole lot more sunlight than ever makes its way down to the bottom of the ocean.

"So you see," King said to me, "everything you knew is long gone. What you have left is here and now, this world. Our world. Your future, our present. And we'd like to make it a place you want to stay."

We were sitting in my room — the guest room at Alabaster and Touch's house, the place where they'd been a family. I sat in the armchair and King sat on a little stool he'd brought in with him. I guess he was too polite to sit on the bed where I slept. I had propped the bathroom door wide open, so that through the far window I could see the building where they were holding Touch. Where they were holding Touch? Or where he was staying? I still couldn't say for sure. They still hadn't let me see him, or talk to him.

King sat there on his stool, all bundled up in a parka. There was a knock on the door, and King whistled in reply. A man in a thick white coat came in carrying a kind of table/tray and set it in front of me. Finally. I'd started to worry they weren't going to feed me at all. At this point I was so hungry I didn't care if they'd poisoned it.

The utensils were different than ours, these kind of chopsticks that connected at the ends. It took me a minute to figure them out. With my first bite, I could see why Touch had been less than impressed by our food. It was some kind of white fish and I'm not even sure it was cooked, but it just melted across my tongue, the most delicious and fresh-tasting bite of anything I'd ever had. Same with the salad, nothing cooked, just clean and crisp greens like I'd never seen before, a little sweet and a little spicy. Heaven.

"Let me ask you a question," I said to King, after several bites, when my hunger had started to subside.

"You can ask me anything you like."

"How come you don't put on one of these suits?" I pointed to the garment that I was still wearing, the green jumpsuit that would keep me comfortable if I went outside my special, cooled off room. "Instead of getting all bundled up, I mean."

"Ah," he said. "You're hitting upon one of the problems of this world, our time. The material for that suit you're wearing is a prototype. Like Touch's golden ring. He constructed it using resources that belong to Arcadia. But since it's still under development, distribution is regulated. He developed the material. Alabaster had enough to sew one for you."

"But why does anyone else need one?" I said. "If they're all comfortable with the climate? Seems like nobody who's not coming into this room would need a suit made out of this material."

"My point exactly," King said, throwing out his hands and smiling in way that was meant to make me think I had his approval. "All this nonsense, this red tape, this hyper concern with equality. It goes against common sense."

My head started to hurt a little. "I need to see Touch," I said.

"And so you shall."

"When?"

"When the time is right."

He got to his feet. Honest, he looked so much like Touch — and at the same time so not like him — it made my heart hurt, which I suppose was the point. To leave me lonesome in this room, trapped and unsure, and work on me with the promise of Touch as my reward.

"There's something I'd like you to see first," King said. "Before you see Touch."

"What's that?"

"The place where you'll be living. If you choose to stay here with us."

"Listen," I said. " 'Choose' seems like a real funny word to use, when you got me locked in one room and Touch in another."

"Touch isn't locked in any room."

"That's a lie."

"He can come and go as he pleases."

"If that were true," I said, "he'd be in here with me."

"You forget his wife."

Dang. He held out his hand. He wasn't wearing gloves, but I had the ones built into the suit Touch had made me, like he'd remembered those sweaters I'd had to leave behind along our travels.

"Come with me, Rogue," King said. "There's so much more to show you."

IT WAS DIFFERENT THAN TRAVELING THROUGH TIME. FASTER, with more of a dropping sensation in my stomach. I don't think I ever closed my eyes, but at the same time when we arrived, I had the distinct sensation of opening them.

King and I stood on a broad, grassy hill. Way far off in the distance was the ocean, with wide, rippling waves. But closer than that was the most amazing building I'd ever seen. It didn't settle into its surroundings the way Touch's house had, but reached way up toward the sky with spires and angles. Every aspect of it seemed to shimmer, and I got the feeling that the crystals catching the sun also fueled the power inside.

"This is one of the homes our ancestors built," King said. "Of course it's been improved on over the years. And I'm hoping one day soon it will be your home."

He looped his arm through mine and we started walking toward the castle. There wasn't a moat, or guards, or anything like that. Instead wildebears paced out front. At first it looked like they were just meandering, no particular method, but as we got closer I saw that they crisscrossed each other's path, snarling. It would take a mighty brave outsider to try and get through their pacing.

"Go ahead," King said. "See what happens when you step closer."

The healed place on my shoulder gave a little thrum, warning me not to listen. But I felt a weird sort of kinship with these animals, fearsome though they looked. Even if King hadn't told me to, I would've wanted to do what I did next, which was step forward and hold out my hand. The wildebears' snarls turned tame in an instant, and they fell back to let me pass.

"They recognize you as one of us," King said. "Come." He took my arm like he meant to lead me into the palace. Seeing those wildebears, though, had reminded me of something. Namely the strength inside me. I pulled my arm away.

"I don't care about the palace," I said. "If you think you can tempt me with things like castles, you're barking up the wrong tree."

"Listen," King said. The sun shone down so hard and bright, I had a tough time seeing him, like staring through heavy fog.

"I'm done listening. You got something you want from me? Well, I got something I want from you, and that's Touch. You take me to Touch, or bring him to me."

"Rogue," King said. "Did Touch ever tell you why he went to your world? Your time?"

"Of course he did," I said, though actually the question got me a little shaky. It had always bothered me, Touch's vagueness on that front. "He went there because of you," I said. "Because he had to escape and keep you from overthrowing Arcadia."

"Arcadia has already been overthrown."

"I don't believe you."

"But it's true." He held out a hand, indicating the castle. "That's why this belongs to us. Do you know what it is, this place? It's where people like you live. Where we teach them how to control their very special powers."

This stopped me cold. Here we stood, right on the threshold of the place I'd most wanted to go. If what King had said was true, all I had to do was turn and walk past those wildebears and past that wide, sparkling fountain. From where I stood, I couldn't see any doors, but no doubt a portion of the wall would disappear when I approached. When I got inside, I would not only meet them, people like me, I would learn how to control my affliction. I would learn how to touch people without harming them.

Touch.

I couldn't think. Not till I saw him. What had I been doing, standing here, negotiating with this man, talking to him like he was a reasonable person? Something came over me, a sort of rage, and I remembered all my power, my strength, and my speed. I stepped forward and pushed King to the ground.

"No more," I yelled. "You want to convince me of something? Send Touch."

Then I turned and started running. Obviously I didn't have much of a plan. But I figured if I lost myself somewhere in this world, Touch would find me. I knew King couldn't run fast enough to catch me. I just forgot those wildebears could.

King whistled. And all of a sudden thunderous footsteps sounded behind me, hundreds of claws carrying their furry owners across the ground. I tried to pick up speed, I had a head start, but I guess a couple of the ones chasing me were faster than the ones I'd absorbed. The first one landed right on my back and threw me to the ground, while the others gathered around in a circle, snarling. Through my suit, I could feel the huge paw on my back. A little sliver of drool hit the nape of my neck and I shuddered.

King whistled. The wildebear stepped off me. I turned over and sat up. King strode to me, his face contorted in fury. Then he reached down and grabbed my hand — a whole lot less courtly than the first time — and with a whoosh and a rush we were back in my room. My prison.

Soon as our feet hit the wood floors, King let go of me. "I've been trying to be gentle with you, Rogue," he said. "But I think it's time you heard the whole truth."

"I won't believe anything unless I hear it from Touch."

"Because he's always been so forthright with you?"

No. I wouldn't let him get into my head. I'd stay strong.

King took a minute to exhale the rage from his voice, so when he spoke he sounded eerily calm. "Here's the reason Touch came to your time, straight and simple. We lost one of our most important weapons. His name was Gordium, and he had the same powers as you. Touch figured out a way to search time and space for someone who had the same gene — the same rogue gene — as Gordium. Do you know that was our code name for you, before we even knew the one we found *would* be you? Rogue. And then he went to your world. To you. To bring you back here."

"That makes no sense at all," I shouted. "Touch works for Arcadia!"

"No," King said. "Touch works for me. He always has."

"Touch would never work for you," I said. "He believes in Arcadia. He wants everyone to be equal."

"There's no such thing as equal," King snarled, fierce as the wildebears. "Whatever lies Arcadia disseminated. Some people are born with more than others. Naturally. You of all people should know that."

It wasn't exactly a point I could argue, so I just sat there, real quiet. I wondered what had happened to Gordium.

"Let me ask you one more question," I said. "*King.*"

He tried to rearrange himself, get back to the diplomacy he'd been using earlier. "Ask me anything," he said.

"If Touch is really on your side. If he wants what all you want. How come he's not here convincing me instead of you?"

"Alabaster . . ."

"No," I said. "That won't work. Not this time. If Touch was like you — evil and lying, that is — he'd pretend anything he needed to pretend. And y'all must know he'd do a damn sight better job convincing me than your sorry ass."

Abruptly, King stood up. He gave me one long, narrow-eyed look and left the room, clicking the door shut and locked behind him. I got up from the chair and went into the bathroom. Through that window I looked out at the tunnel-like structure where Touch was held prisoner in a world where prisons hadn't existed at all for a long, long time. I wished he had a window, too, where he could look up at me. I closed my eyes against everything King had told me. When I opened them, I could see Alabaster, sitting out on the grass with a small, blond boy.

I put my hand to the window so it would go black. My brain was too full of too many contradicting thoughts. But just as suddenly I wanted to see them, Alabaster and Cotton. If Touch wasn't a prisoner, why wasn't he out there with them? I tapped the glass again and it went clear. This time I rapped it with my knuckles and the little amethyst ring I still wore — that had lasted through everything I'd been through, the one Cody had given me — made the barest little scratch in the glass.

I pressed the ring a little harder against it. The glass went black again, but still the ring made a deeper indentation. My room stood about three stories above the ground. But that was a problem I could work out later.

If the panes could be scratched, who's to say they couldn't be shattered?

• • •

I WANTED TO BREAK THROUGH THAT WINDOW RIGHT THEN AND there. But it made more sense to wait until dark. To calm myself down, I took a long and steamy shower. Then I changed back into the suit Touch had made for me and lay on the bed, watching the shadows from tree branches speckle the walls. It had been hours since I'd eaten, but the meal had been so filling and nutritious I didn't feel the slightest bit hungry.

And of course I couldn't help but think, *What if everything King had told me was true?*

I was a newcomer to this world. Everything I knew about Arcadia, I knew from Touch. What if Arcadia weren't so great, but filled with red tape and mediocrity, like King had said?

And what if Touch wasn't working for Arcadia but against it? Did it really matter, who was in charge of the government, so long as he and I could be together? And had Arcadia really fallen? Alabaster made it seem like the war was still going on. But if Arcadia was already over and done with, why shouldn't I move into that castle, and learn how to control my powers, and stay here with Touch? Especially if Touch and I were going to escape back to my world to raise our own family in Mexico, what did it matter?

No, I thought. It *did* matter. Whatever happened to me, and my power, or my affliction. I wanted to work for good. Not evil.

Time passed in twitching starts. The sunset took so long I couldn't admire its beauty. By the time it set, I already knew what I'd use to break the window, which was the stool King had been sitting on — simple and wooden and heavier than you might think. Soon as the world outside went properly dark, I picked it up and smashed it right through the glass.

I waited for sirens to go off, but the night stayed quiet. I guess you don't get around to inventing burglar alarms in a world without any burglars. So I picked pieces of shattered glass out of the pane until there was a clear enough space to haul myself through. Then I crouched on the ledge, gathering up my courage. At this point I knew from plenty of experience that a wildebear could run real fast. But could it leap out a three-story window and land on its feet?

There was only one way to find out.

It was one thing to know you had to be brave, and another thing to convince yourself to jump out of a window. You want to do it, you mean to do it, but your body just won't follow the order that your brain gives it.

"Jump," I whispered to myself. "Come on now. *Jump.*"

Nothing. I wouldn't budge. I may even have started into trembling a little.

I closed my eyes and thought of Touch. And I couldn't let my own fear of a broken foot stop me from doing what needed to be done, which was push off of the ledge and jump out into the hot night air.

That hot air whooshed against my face as I fell; it blew back my hair with a gust that could've come from a blast furnace. In fact the air was so hot it almost kind of lifted me up a bit, making me fall slower. So it might not have been just the wildebear inside me that let me land on the dust unhurt, but the thick quality of the air itself, acting almost like a cushion. Whatever the reason, I landed on my feet, my hands flat to the ground, crouched and ready to start running.

If only the track coach back at Caldecott County High could see me now! Back in my sophomore year I hadn't made the cut when I'd tried out for the team. Now I dared his fastest runner to even try catching up with me. I covered the distance in seconds. When I got to the building where they were holding Touch, I did what Alabaster had done, simply raised my hand to make an opening appear. And it worked.

The corridor was deserted, not a sound coming from behind any of the doors. I hoped I'd remember the symbol marking

Touch's — they all looked awful similar to me. I paced up and down a few times, and finally when I got to what I was sure was the right door, I waved my hand again, and stepped through.

The room was just as light as it had been during the day, bright as a laboratory lit by fluorescent bulbs. But this time there wasn't a glass partition. Just a huge, wide, open room, with a long wooden table in the center. And at the end of the table, sitting real close together, were Touch and Alabaster, playing some kind of card game. They both looked up like I'd interrupted them in the middle of deep concentration. Then Alabaster smiled, that slow and dimpled smile that everyone else on Earth must have found real charming.

"Oh, it's you," she said, like nobody in the world mattered less. "We wondered what was keeping you."

Don't ask me what I expected to find when I burst into that room. But it sure wasn't this. The cards weren't cards, exactly, they were made out of some thick, round material. Touch sat still, kind of shuffling them. He wasn't wearing gloves. Why would he? Playing cards on his home planet, which was just the right temperature, and sitting next to a woman he could touch without fear of harm. I stared straight at him, trying to read the expression in those blue eyes. Wrong as the situation felt, I couldn't stop the surge of happiness in my chest at the sight of him, the face I loved most in all the world. What I wanted to do was run to him, and take that face in my hands, and cover it with kisses, which of course I couldn't do.

But Alabaster could.

Mind readers, these people. Alabaster reached out her skinny, ivory arm and threw it around Touch's shoulders. It was a very casual gesture, slow and easy. She'd done it a million times before. It looked natural. Touch just sat there, holding those weird cards, and looking at me. I guess if I'd come from his time, I'd have known what he was thinking. But I didn't. Hell, I didn't even know how much time had passed for him since he last saw me in Arizona. From where I stood, he looked totally unreadable. He could've been a stranger, sitting there next to his beautiful wife.

Alabaster let the tips of her fingers kind of tickle his neck. Then she lifted her hand off his shoulder and ran it across the top of his head. She took the little elastic out of his hair and ran her hands right through it. All things I would die to do, that I never could. Touch just sat there, maybe the tiniest bit of a smile tugging at the edges of his lips. Then he — *he*, not her — leaned forward and kissed her. His lips right on her lips. Kissing her. No itchy balaclava between them. Just a lip-to-lip kiss. Like normal people in love can share.

Fast as a wildebear, I turned around and ran the hell out of there.

AND RAN. AND RAN. UP UNTIL NOW I'D BARELY BEEN ABLE TO use that wildebear's speed. The farthest I'd run was the mile between Joe Wheeler's house and the parked Chevy truck. Despite everything going on inside me, the thunderstorm of jealousy and sorrow and panic, it felt right good to run this way, even with the hot air against my face. My legs moved like strands of spaghetti, hurling through the air so fast I could barely feel them underneath me. It seemed I was covering miles and miles, without getting a bit tired, just running so fast I was very nearly flying.

The thing is: it really doesn't matter how fast you run, when the people you're running from can transport themselves right to you with a little whoosh and a zip.

I skidded to a halt, my heels kicking up dust. Standing on one side of me were two of those ponytailed henchmen from the Chevy lot, huge and fierce-looking. I whirled around, and there on the other side stood Alabaster, King, and Touch.

"Rogue," King said, taking a step forward. "You already know it's no use running. Just come back with us now."

Probably I should've found a way to play it cool, close to the vest, keep my emotions hidden. Instead, I turned to Touch and yelled at the top of my lungs, for all these enemies and the whole wide future world to hear. "You were kissing her!"

Finally Touch spoke. He said, "She's my wife."

He said it so calm. So matter-of-fact. The way you'd say, *I have blue eyes*, or *I'm from Mississippi*. A statement of fact that can't be got around and won't be changed. Just like all Wendy Lee's memories had tried to tell me.

Those thunderclouds in my chest broke open, raging, lightning along with them. I felt like I'd bust open, raining down on all of them. I *wanted* to rain down on all of them. What did I have to lose at this point? I'd already left my whole damn world behind. Everyone I ever knew in my life had been dead ten thousand years. Except for Touch. My married boyfriend. There was no way in hell I'd go back to that room — *their* house. The only thing that had felt any good was running. Suddenly I remembered that I didn't only have wildebear speed. I had wildebear strength.

So I spun around and kicked one of them henchmen-type guards. I kicked him hard as I could, right in the stomach. And when he hit the ground like he'd been shot by a bazooka, I went ahead and kicked the other one, too.

Then I ran.

From behind me I could hear a great commotion of whistles and long, low notes. I thought I could tell that Alabaster was saying something like "Shoot her, shoot her," and King was saying something like "No, we still need her." But someone back there must have agreed with Alabaster, because I heard a kind of whooshing, crackling noise, coming up behind me faster than I could run, and when I turned around I saw a red-orange ball rushing toward me, the same kind that had blown up that '65 Mustang back in Napoleon, Ohio.

Time seemed to click into slow motion. I ducked down, and the ball whizzed over my head, missing me, but then another one came, aimed at my new level, and I had to jump out of the way. And then another. And then Touch appeared beside me, out of nowhere, not flanked by his wife and father, but all by his lonesome.

"Trust me," he said.

And then he lifted both hands and kind of flicked his fingers out at me, like you would to splash water at someone if your hands were wet. But instead of water, rushing out from his fingertips came great, golden threads of light. Never mind what he'd just said. I thought to myself, *Touch is going to kill me. Right here. Right now. The only person in the world that I love is going to kill me dead.*

Except that's not what happened. Instead of striking me like a weapon, the threads took form all around me, crackling like electricity. And the next thing I knew everything — the night, the henchmen, King, Alabaster, and Touch — was gone.

FOR A WHILE THE WHOLE WORLD WENT VERY QUIET. THERE was no sensation of moving. No sound. I couldn't even see or feel a floor beneath me. Everything was just white, like traveling in a cloud. Or really more like sitting in a cloud. A very thick, still cloud on a day with no wind at all.

Trust me, he'd said. It wasn't like I had a whole lot of choice. Trust him or not, here I was, just floating, maybe in the air, maybe not. I couldn't even be sure of the time zone, or the planet. Had he blasted me back into the past? Or the future? Or had he sent me to another realm entirely, another world, another galaxy?

Finally the feeling of stillness shifted a bit. There was a little sort of drop in the center of my stomach. Then a rush, like an elevator going down. The falling grew faster and faster until finally I felt myself plunge underwater. When I opened my eyes, the white had gone, and I could see bubbles from my own breath rising up in front of me, and a whole lot of blue-gray water. I looked up, holding my breath, and saw the surface not too far above, the bright, bright sun shining through it. There was nothing to do but swim, upward. To where I found a raft waiting for me, a good-sized wooden raft, flat enough that it didn't take much to haul myself on top of it. For a while I just lay there, facedown, clinging to the boards in relief. When oxygen finally moved in and out of my body in a normal way, I sat up and took a look around me.

Water. Nothing but water for miles and miles. No birds in the sky, no land in sight. Just softly rolling waves, blue sky, and that huge, burning sun. I hoped Touch had thought to make the jumpsuit material UV-resistant. As it was, I sure wished I was wearing a hat. And sunglasses. The sun beat down mercilessly, and I squinted into the light, raising my hand to shield my eyes. For some reason the light out here seemed less foggy. I felt I could see much more clearly. This, I thought, is the real Earth. A vast ocean, no sight of land, hot sun, and waves. We humans were land animals in a world made out of water, just biding our time till the planet's real substance rose to cover us up for good.

And then, there on the edge of the horizon, I saw a boat. A beautiful white sailboat, headed straight toward me. A little flicker of fear rose up, along with a glimmer of hope.

I thought of everything Touch had done for me, like turning back time to come and get me out of Jackson. Even as a prisoner he had found a way to forge a suit for himself so he could travel back across the years to find me. Would a man who did all that for a woman leave her to go back to his wife?

You bet he would, said Wendy Lee's voice inside my head. I pushed that voice aside.

Trust me, I heard instead.

Sure enough, that boat came clearer and clearer into view. Only one person on board, steering straight in my direction. Wearing gloves, not on account of the cold but so, when he came up beside me, he could reach out to take my hand and help me on board.

I climbed aboard that boat and stood on the deck with Touch.

Then I threw my arms around his neck and buried my face in his chest, reveling in the feel of his breathing, the scent of him, and most especially his arms, hugging me back just as hard. Maybe even a little harder. It felt so damn good I forgot to worry or even think about anything else, until I remembered I couldn't kiss him, which was just about all in the world I wanted to do.

Instead we just held each other, pressing as tight as we could, till it was a wonder our bones didn't crack beneath the grip of it.

TOUCH STEERED THE BOAT, AND I STOOD BEHIND HIM, MY ARMS around his waist, my cheek resting on the spot just below the nape of his neck, safely covered by his shirt. Obviously I had a lot of questions, but what I wanted to know first didn't have anything to do with the politics in this new world.

"Hey, Earthling," I said. It felt so good just being with him again, all quiet and together, that I almost hated to start talking.

"Yes, Earthling?" he said. His hair kind of tickled against my face.

"How long has it been, since they took you out of Arizona?"

"Much longer for me than it has been for you," he said.

Of course he must have known I'd figured that much out. "Like how long?" I said.

"A year?" he said. "Maybe a little more."

A whole year. That's how long it must have taken King to find me without Touch's help, sifting through time and space. Meanwhile, for me, three days without him had been like an eternity.

"That's a long time," I said.

"It is," he agreed.

"Did you think about me?"

"Every day," he said. I couldn't see his face, but I could feel a smile, radiating from his skin through his shirt to my face. I smiled, too.

"Were you happy to see me when they brought me in to you?"

"Well," he said, "the truth is I'd been working hard for quite some time, to keep exactly that from happening. But the heart doesn't always know logic, does it? I couldn't help but be happy to see your face. Because I love you."

"Still?"

"Yes," he said. "Still."

"How come you didn't just come with me?" I said. "How come you sent me out here alone? That scared me to death."

"I had something to do," he said. "Before I came for you."

"Cotton?"

"Cotton."

He turned then and put his arm around me. At the same time he adjusted me a little bit so that we stood shoulder to shoulder. I leaned against him and put my other hand on the steering wheel. Without asking, I assumed we were heading toward land, so I let my gaze search the horizon. At the same time I didn't care if I ever saw land again. It was perfectly fine with me to stay out here, on the water, the sky melting around us and Touch's arm around me, holding me close.

JUST THE OTHER DAY AND ALSO TEN THOUSAND YEARS AGO: King found Touch in Arizona and whisked him on back home.

But before that, when Touch first came to my world, he hadn't been working for Arcadia at all. He'd been working against it, just like King said.

"Why didn't you tell me?" I said.

"What would you have thought? How would you ever have trusted me?"

"So is it true what else he said?" I asked very carefully. "That the whole reason you came was to bring me back and use me like a weapon?"

"Yes," Touch said. And I guess that should have terrified me. But I knew that we wouldn't be here, and that he wouldn't have answered that way, if it were still the truth.

"Listen," he went on. "I was raised on certain ideas. Of everything that had been taken from me, from us. Our families. My father has been planning this takeover his whole life. He's been grooming me my whole life. But when I got to your world . . ."

"You saw what it was like," I said, real quick. "You landed in Smith Park, and you saw what happens in a world where the wealth belongs to just one small group."

"Yes," he said. "And then I met you."

"And you fell in love."

"Yes," he said again.

"Alabaster said that you summoned her. And told her to bring the wildebears."

"I wanted to make you stronger. I wanted her to think I was still trying to bring you back, so they wouldn't come after me as much."

"And in the caves?"

"I couldn't think of any other way. To get us out of there." My silence at that must have worried him, because after a minute he added, "I love you."

Call me a simple girl. But for right at that moment, those three words were all I needed to hear. Above our heads, a little pink had started to paint itself across the sky, and the bright, bright sun seemed to move lower. Same old Earth. I could even tell which direction we were headed, watching the sun go down directly behind us. I wondered which part of the country lay underneath us, beneath all this water.

And at the same time, I didn't really care. I had everything I needed in the world, right on this old boat.

TOUCH AND I SLEPT BELOWDECKS, IN A COZY CABIN. HE TOLD ME
some more of the story. How it was kind of true that Arcadia had
fallen — King and his followers had reclaimed the castles and gotten
all their people off the fishing boats. But Arcadia wouldn't go down
without a fight; people were even now gathering on the sea and land
to take back their world.

"It's something we haven't seen in hundreds of years," Touch said.
"A war. It will go on for a long time, and it will be ugly. Dangerous. My
father's people are outnumbered, but they have powerful weapons. In
the end, I do believe Arcadia will win."

I asked Touch if he could escape, why he hadn't gone to help Arcadia in the first place.

"Because I knew they were still looking for you," he said. "I
couldn't risk them finding you without my knowing."

"But Touch," I said, "what was with that kiss?"

He smiled, looking a little chagrined. "I needed you to run," he
said. "It was the only way I could send you to safety. It wouldn't have
worked inside that cell."

"And now that you're free?"

"I go to war," he said.

"So Arcadia will have you," I said. "You can build weapons for them."

Touch nodded, real solemn, and I thought on who those weapons would be used against, his very own family. I guess I should've been scared, or at least freaked out. But truthfully what I felt was overjoyed. I didn't even want to fall asleep. After Touch drifted off, I lay awake, my head on his chest, my arms wrapped around him. I felt so glad to be in this time, with him. I felt so sorry for the girl I used to be, the one who'd run away, out of Jackson, without him. One thing I felt sure of: I didn't ever want to be without him again.

Finally sleep took hold of me, even through my happiness. I expect I slept the whole night with a giant smile plastered on my face. When I woke up, Touch was lying beside me, raised up on one elbow, watching me sleep.

"Hey there, Earthling," he said.

"Hey, Earthling." I reached out to touch his hair, and he lifted up the edges and tickled the edge of my nose with it, which made me smile.

We went up on deck and ate a little meal he'd prepared. Fish again, this time some kind of shellfish with a brown sauce, even more delicious than the meal King had brought me. But I couldn't concentrate much on the food.

"So, is Cotton with the Arcadia people now?" I asked.

Touch got a very sad look on his face. "It's a tough call," he said. "The truth is, for all Alabaster's flaws, she loves her son. But if I leave him with her, he'll grow up like I did, poisoned by all the wrong beliefs. And if I bring him over to Arcadia . . ."

"Either way," I said, "he grows up in the middle of a war."

"And he'll never be safe with either side. Even with Arcadia, his family's history will dog him."

"You have the same history."

"Did I say I'd be safe? I'll never be safe, Rogue, not in this world. Not until it's all over. But that doesn't mean I don't want to — don't *have to* — stay and fight."

"You've got to do what's right," I said, feeling proud of him.

Touch nodded. He looked real sad. "It's been a lot of hard decisions," he said. "Like the fact that the thing that's best for the two people I love most is to be far away from here. From me."

I nodded like I agreed with him. Then I said, "Wait a minute. What?"

"Rogue. You must know I have to get you out of here."

I told myself to calm down. I had to trust him. So I waited to hear the rest, figuring he was taking me to some rebel spot. Like, maybe an outpost in the middle of the ocean, or a piece of land on another continent.

"So where are we going?" I asked.

"You're going back."

"Back where?"

"Back to your own time," he said.

It wasn't on account of Touch's specially constructed suit that my whole body went cold. "No," I said. "No way. Not gonna do it."

"Rogue . . ."

"No!" I didn't care how delicious the food was. I picked up my plate and sailed it overboard like a Frisbee. The shrimp or whatever flew up into the air and then rained down into the water. It goes to show how far out to sea we were; there were no birds to swoop down and get it.

He stood up and took a few steps toward me. I didn't yell, but my voice came out so strong and fierce it might as well have been a yell. "I'm here," I said. "With you. Where I belong. Where I've always wanted to be."

A funny kind of expression crossed over his face. Smart man,

Touch, and I knew he was reacting to the world "always." After all, how long had I known Touch? Nowhere close to ten thousand years. Nowhere close even to one year. A matter of weeks, really. Still what I said was exactly true. Being with him was what I had *always* wanted, going way back to before I ever knew he existed. I'd wanted to be with him all those lonely years, living with Aunt Carrie. Even when I'd leaned in to kiss poor Cody, what I was really doing was yearning toward him — Touch — I just hadn't known it yet. Across all these millennia, again and again, we were meant to be together. Somewhere. Sometime. Together.

"I love you," I said, like it was an incantation. Like it would bring him to his senses and make him realize that I couldn't go anywhere, not ever, except for where he was.

"And I love you," he said. "But Rogue. Don't you want to know what happened to Gordium?"

"I don't care," I said. "Because it's not going to happen to me."

"He died," Touch said. "By his own hands. Because he could no longer bear all the memories of the people they made him . . ."

"Stop!"

"Don't you see how valuable you are?" Touch said. "Not only can you incapacitate people with a touch, you can absorb all their knowledge. No interrogation needed. Just one touch from you, and whole worlds of information can fall into the wrong hands."

"I won't let them."

"If they catch you again, you may not have a choice. I can't risk it. Not for you. Not for Arcadia."

"So, even if you send me back, what makes you think they won't just track me again?"

He stood up and went down belowdecks. When he came back, he held a little box in his hand. It buzzed and hummed louder as he came toward me. Before I had a chance to ask him what it was, he held it up in front of me, moving it all around, while it clicked and clicked.

"OK," I said, when he'd finally put it down. "What the hell was that?"

"Something I've been working on," he said. "It changed the structure of your DNA, the way it's read. Changed the design of your fingerprints, too. So you can't be traced."

"How do you know it works?"

"Because you're not the first person I've used it on."

Of course. Cotton. It wasn't just me that Touch had to keep safe. I hadn't even realized how fast my heart had been beating. Now it slowed down. I reached out my hand and took his, wishing that when he'd engineered this suit he'd thought of a way for me to feel the skin of his hand through it. To make up for it, I gripped him very tight. "I wanted to be here," I told him. "But if you want to come back with me, to my time, well then that's OK. I don't care where we are. Hell, take us all the way back to caveman days. Before that even." I almost loved this thought, me and Touch, like Adam and Eve before the dawn of time. "It doesn't matter to me," I said. "So long as we're together."

He put his hand on top of mine, and pressed down just as hard as I pressed his hand. "But Rogue," he said.

Dang. Dang and damn. My eyes filled with tears. Nothing I said would do any good. Because of course he didn't mean to come back to the past with me. Not my past, not any past. He meant to stay here, and fight for Arcadia, on account of a force way stronger than me. A force so strong, it kept a very evil woman from being completely evil.

"She showed me his picture," I said, through tears. "He's beautiful."

"Thank you," Touch said, real quiet. He had tears in his eyes, too.

"I'd fight for him," I said. "I'd fight for all of you, if you'd let me stay."

For one long, quiet minute, I had hope. In that minute I saw a whole world — the past, the present, the future, none of them having anything to do with any place in the galaxy or the space-time continuum other than my own heart. Here we sat, in the midst of the one great ocean. Never in my life had I seen the ocean, and now it was all I could see, on all sides of me. I sure did want to see what it looked like, lapping over a beach. I wanted to walk out into the waves and ride them back to shore.

Touch sat looking at me, his big blue eyes full of love and anguish. I barely even saw his handsomeness when I looked at him now. All I saw was what I felt. Love. And the rest of my life moving forward with him, exactly with him, because anything else felt exactly unbearable.

"I love you," I said, trying to make the force of my voice match the force of my desire.

"I love you, too," Touch whispered. And I can't tell you how much I hated it, the danger I posed, not only to the man I loved but to his whole entire way of life. The lethal skin, one thin layer away from the world, could bring the whole thing crashing down.

So you see, pretty much all my hope had melted away even before we were surrounded by great, bursting, flashing lights, and Alabaster and King appeared on the deck with us, along with what seemed like a hundred of their minions.

IF ONLY I'D BEEN BORN INTO THIS WORLD IN THE FIRST PLACE. Then I could've been something different. Not a freak or a monster, but a person with a place to go. But such was not my lot in life, and right now all hell was breaking loose. For one thing, that crazy language of theirs. I sure wish Touch had thought to give me one of those translators. Because no matter how many times it happened, I couldn't get used to these thugs that called themselves aristocrats appearing out of nowhere and whistling away.

In the blink of an eye, Touch turned and ran down belowdecks. I could hardly believe he would abandon me, and my first instinct was to run to the side of the boat and dive in. No orange balls whizzed through the air, just the sound of a powerful electric current. It seemed to slow me down somehow, as if the air were super-thick, too thick to move through, and too hot. I gave up on running and turned around. There stood Alabaster, her hands outstretched, silver light bursting from her fingers and coming toward me, but it wasn't meant to whisk me off to safety. Instead the light was trained on me real steady, melting away the suit Touch had made — the suit that protected me from the heat — thread by thread.

I looked down. Piece by piece the material was disappearing, leaving my skin exposed, leaving me naked. Didn't they know then, what my skin could do? Remembering all that Touch had told me, I guessed that was the point.

That sun bore down and the heat closed in. With every thread of the suit that was removed, the protective coolness left, and it became more and more like someone was pressing a fist against my larynx. I could hardly breathe. It felt like I would melt.

Where was Touch? If only I could step forward. The material now had melted from my hands. Alabaster stood before me, her perfect white skin somehow untouched by the sun, and oh-so exposed by her usual skimpy outfit. If only I could jerk out of these rays she pointed at me, I could land my hands on her and suck the life out of her.

But I couldn't. I mean, even if I could, I couldn't. Mother of Touch's child and all.

Anyways, at that moment my morality was a moot point. I couldn't move. The nameless men had formed a barrier, all standing in a ring against the railing of the boat. From downstairs, King emerged, holding Touch by both elbows. For the first time in this world, Touch was wearing that long leather coat, and my mind leaped to what magic items he might have in his inside pocket.

Alabaster lowered her hands. Her work was done, me sinking to my knees from the heat, hardly able to breathe, wearing nothing but my underwear. King kept coming toward me, holding Touch like a shield, and I saw the plan in an instant. To make Touch put his hands on me, long enough for me to absorb everything he knew, all his talents, all his knowledge. Leaving nothing but an empty shell in his place.

"There's no use in fighting," King said, and since I could understand him, I knew he was talking to me as well as Touch. "If only you hadn't fought against what was rightfully yours." His voice sounded quavery, like maybe he was actually having a moment of regret over killing his own son.

"Don't worry," Alabaster called to King. "Your grandson will inherit all that he was meant to have." The two of them, so greedy they even had to gobble up this moment, talking to each other. Congratulating themselves on their own future riches.

It was so hot. I was losing my ability to concentrate. All I could see was Touch. Coming closer and closer. When I looked up, it felt like looking at him from across that sauna, steamy and foggy, but about a million times hotter. Hotter. So damned hot. I choked on the very air. As King propelled him toward me I barely had a moment to wonder why Touch didn't fight, and overpower him, before I saw that same sort of silver thread, pouring out of King's fingertips, Touch's own magic stolen and perverted to do him in.

And me. I was the other piece of the puzzle, the second part of the weapon, meant not only to destroy the world he loved, but him. Petty human that I was, I had to admit, I cared about the second part more than the first. I could almost live with destroying a world that wasn't mine. But destroying Touch? Never.

From somewhere deep inside, I summoned something strong enough to let me look into Touch's eyes. Let me read his mind the way he always read mine. And I knew that I hadn't been alone since that day under the tupelo tree with Cody. Ever since I'd had him — Cody — inside of me. And then I'd had the kitten, and Wendy Lee, and the wildebears, and Tawa. And in a different way — the most important way of all — I'd had Touch. So it wasn't with my own strength, but the strength of all of us, that I hauled myself to my feet and stepped forward. I reached past Touch, my naked arm dangerously close to brushing his face, and placed my hand flat on his daddy's cheek.

King shuddered. He spat a little. As soon as he staggered back — letting go of Touch, losing the silver threads spraying out from his fingers — I pulled my hand away. For a moment I could feel it, the rush of another person coming in. The last thing I wanted on Earth was King's memories or feelings, but I barely had time to think on it. The heat came crashing in again. I could hear Alabaster's voice hollering something mournful and furious. And then Touch thrust something wonderfully familiar into my hand , and the two of us flew away into a nameless realm, the golden ring the only vehicle we needed.

IT WAS A GOOD THING THAT MY MIND WAS OPEN TO THE CRAZY things that occurred in nature. Like time travel, or human skin that morphed into a weapon or a curse, or a race of humans so advanced they'd learned to harness energy in their actual fingertips. Because what happened from the moment Touch handed me that golden ring — it was the oddest thing of all. Not what happened so much as the way it felt.

Honest to God, my first thought was that I'd died and gone to heaven. And I don't mean that in the way Wendy Lee might say it, biting into a fresh éclair. I mean that I had this strong sense of leaving my body behind somewhere, and floating off, away from it, on my own. To say that I felt lighter than air would be an understatement. I felt lighter than lightness, like weight could never apply. At the same time my body was very much with me. I could hear my heart beating in my ears. I could feel the buzz of my bare skin, and the air against it didn't feel hot anymore. It felt perfect.

And time. Time didn't matter. It was like I could actually hear it skidding to a halt. It didn't exist on either side of us — not in my past or Touch's future. All that existed was this moment, carved out of space — out of any continuum — for us.

Me and Touch. On a beach. Me still wearing what I'd had on when he whisked me away, which is to say practically nothing. We stood just at the tide line, facing each other. Waves lapped over our feet. The shoreline sloped upward, and I could see, about fifty yards up, a little thatched hut surrounded by palm and banana trees. That perfect breeze brushed across us.

"Your hair," Touch said.

I reached down and picked up a strand, examined it. Brown. I shook my head so that it fell like a curtain in front of my face. The streaks were gone. No white. Just brown, a color I hadn't seen, all by itself, in ages.

I pushed all that hair out of my face. "What about my eyes?" I said.

Touch peered into my face. "Brown," he said. "Dark and beautiful."

A smile came over my whole self. I closed the eyes, my own eyes, that Touch thought were beautiful. I let them look inward. Alone. Nothing else in there. No kitten or wildebears or Tawa. No Cody or Wendy Lee or — thank goodness — King. Just me. Anna Marie, plus everything she'd become. Rogue.

"Where are we?" I whispered. My eyes fluttered open. Touch looked just the same as ever, except his hair was loose, and he had a cleaner shave. He wore baggy white pants and nothing else.

"We," he said, "are out there, traveling through time. It takes longer than you realize, you know."

I nodded, remembering my trip with King. "Ten thousand years is a long way to go."

"It is," Touch agreed.

"So," I said, for once understanding right away, "our bodies are making the trip without us. They're out there, spinning the years away. While we . . ."

"We get to take a little time here. Together."

"And where is here?"

"A place out of time and space. A place of our own making. Yours and mine."

It didn't seem real, the possibility, and at the same time it seemed like the most real thing in any age, in any universe. Touch let a smile wash over him. I could see it form on his lips and move over his throat and shoulders to his elbows, flooding down his torso all the way to his toes.

He took a step toward me. I took a step toward him. My hands trembled at my side, knowing absolutely, and at the same time not daring.

By now it was pretty clear that between us, Touch was the braver of the two. He reached out both his hands. He placed them on either side of my naked waist. For a moment I feared that out here — in this place of our own invention, so far removed from either of our bodies — I wouldn't be able to feel him. But I could. His hands. Strong and gentle and just the slightest bit chapped, his ungloved hands, the half-moon fingernails pressing against my skin. Setting off the most joyful fireworks inside my mind and body.

"Oh my God," I said. "Touch."

And I threw myself into his arms, and he held me, our chests pressed together, his lips against my ears, his hands curved into the small of my back.

HERE'S WHAT WE DID. HELD EACH OTHER A LONG, LONG WHILE. There is nothing in the whole wide world like skin on skin. Then we took off what clothes we had on and swam out into the surf. We dove, and we splashed each other. He showed me how to ride the waves back to shore, and we did it again and again.

The simplest thing in the world. Two people in love, so much so that the whole universe stops existing. After a while we found ourselves on the sand. I lay back. Touch sat there, looking at me awhile. And then he started in to touching me, everywhere he'd never been able to. Starting at my feet. Moving over my whole body. When he got to the top of my head, he very gently rolled me over and went the opposite direction. I let my face rest on my crossed arms, just feeling him, his lips and his fingertips. No way would I let myself think about where we went from here.

After a while we stood up and walked together toward the little hut, holding hands. When we got closer we could see a little shower stall just next to the hut. It had a great big barrel on top of it, for catching rain. We went inside and Touch pulled a string; rainwater fell down on top of us, washing away the sand and grit. There was some shampoo that smelled like coconut. Touch lathered me up, including my hair, and then I did the same to him. Then we stood under the stream of water, somehow the right temperature for both of us, pressing against each other and kissing, kissing, until that rain barrel emptied itself and only sun poured down into the shower stall.

We went on into that little thatched hut. The two of us had waited so long. It didn't even work, really, to call it waiting, because it wasn't something we ever thought could happen. At least I didn't.

"Did you plan this?" I asked, as we lay down on top of the bed, white curtains blowing through the glassless window.

Touch hovered over me, his face so close, the sight of my hands against his shoulders the most wonderful thing in the world. "I spent more than a year," he said, "figuring out how to make a stop like this, if ever we had to travel through time again. I knew you could do it. Ever since you absorbed the Anasazi, you've been able to get onto an astral plane."

"Is that why you sent me into those ruins?"

Touch smiled. "That was mostly for the strength. But I thought this might come in handy, too. Do you remember meeting me on the beach?"

"That was real?"

He nodded. "The first time I succeeded. So I knew I'd be able to do it again, when I needed to."

A whole host of new questions burst into my head. But I didn't want to hear the answers to any of them. I just wanted to be here, and now. The only thing I wanted to look forward to was Touch's lips on mine. The only question I wanted answered was what it would feel like when Touch made love to me.

Luckily I didn't have to wait long at all to find out.

EVENING, WHEN IT FELL, TOOK ME BY SURPRISE. TOUCH AND I sat out by the water, wrapped in a blanket, staring at the sunset.

There was so much I wanted to ask him. Like *Please take me with you*, or *Please come with me*. I wanted to ask why we couldn't just stay here forever, but of course I already knew the answer to that.

And as far as the other questions, I knew something else. That when a person has given you the greatest, most enormous gift you are ever to receive in your whole life, what you don't do is open up your mouth and ask for something more.

So all I said was, "I love you, Touch, and I will my whole life."

He didn't have to say *I love you, too*. He just had to risk everything in the world to let that blanket fall away, and put his arms around me, and kiss me, kiss me, till both sets of skin faded away, and there was nothing in all the universe except the two of us, blessed and enveloped, together. Touching.

A little while later, back in the white bed, I said, "Will we still be here in the morning?"

"No," he said. "When we wake up, we'll both be home."

"Then I'm never going to sleep," I said.

It might as well have been never. That night lasted so long, and we made love so many times. Until finally my strength drained so completely that never didn't so much end, as it turned into never again. But I couldn't even mind that, at least not as long as I slept in Touch's arms, no clothes or blankets, no barriers at all coming between us, in this, our very own stretch of time and space.

HOPE SPRINGS ETERNAL

TOUCH AND I MUST HAVE HAD OUR LAST STANDOFF WITH Alabaster and King high above what used to be the Great Smoky Mountains. When I finally woke up — a few minutes or a few hundred years after I fell asleep in Touch's arms — I found myself on the very top of Clingmans Dome, all by my lonesome, wearing nothing but Touch's long leather coat. The bed of pine needles I'd used for a pillow had left indentations in my cheek so deep I could feel the grooves when I ran my fingers over my face. I shook more pine needles out of my hair, and when I did, I could see the same old white streaks, and I knew I was seeing them with my green cat's eyes. I could feel Cody inside me, and Wendy Lee, and the wildebears and Tawa. But search as I might, much to my relief I couldn't feel any trace of King. Maybe it was because Touch had whisked me away so fast. Maybe it was because it happened so many years in the future. Or maybe it was just some force of will inside me, refusing to take such evil into my own heart. Maybe like Gordium I'd learned — at least for that one moment — to control my power.

I looked around me from up on top of that peak in Tennessee. It felt like I could see the whole wide world — so much green and so much beauty. Way up high, fall had set to changing some leaves to red and gold. I felt a pang of wishing Touch had stayed around to see the autumn colors, and I knew it was only the first of many pangs I'd have, every day, for the rest of my life.

Even though it was a mite cold, I unbuttoned the front of that coat and reached into its inside pocket. The first thing I found I knew would be there, the golden ring. I didn't have to ask Touch in person to know what he'd want me to do with it. The second thing might as well have been a little love letter from Touch, for all it said, *I need you to be OK*: a plain and simple cabinet-tip screwdriver, looking for all the world like somebody had just bought it at Home Depot for nine dollars and ninety-nine cents.

Just then, there was a little break in the clouds overhead. I tensed, somehow knowing before the sounds arrived that a visitation would occur. My body braced for the usual sounds, the crackles and the bams, and before I even had a chance to worry that it would be Alabaster or King, or hope that it would be Touch, a little boy stood in front of me.

He was about seven years old, wearing clothes made from the same material as the jumpsuit I'd worn. He had blond hair and his father's kind blue eyes. He wasn't smiling, but I knew that when he did, I'd see dimples just like his mother's.

"Hello, Cotton," I said.

He nodded, too scared and sad to speak. But he also looked resigned. Like he trusted the person who sent him here absolutely.

Now, a person whose skin can send a grown person into a permanent coma has no business raising a child. But — especially if she's been given the means to provide, in the form of one very useful screwdriver — she can certainly deliver a child to a safe place. There wasn't any such place in my own past. I couldn't bring Cotton back to the commune, for instance, and I certainly wouldn't bring him to Aunt

Carrie. But there happened to be a set of parents who I knew to be very kind and loving. They'd already provided one good, solid childhood. And they happened, at the moment, to be very much in need of a child.

THE BLUE CHEVY TRUCK THAT I DROVE INTO CALDECOTT County wasn't the same one Touch and I had stolen in Colorado, but it looked real similar. I bought it fair and square at a dealership outside of Memphis. When that used car salesman saw the stack of bills I pulled out of my pocket, he didn't ask questions. He hardly even bothered counting. He just handed over the keys.

On my way back through Memphis, I planned on taking my time. I'd stand in line and take a tour of Graceland. I'd walk down Beale Street, and order up a plate of dry rub ribs.

But there was no time for that now. Because now, I had a delivery to make. In the dead of night I drove down the dusty road that led to the Robbins' farmhouse. Between Cotton and me sat a bag filled with the special material Touch had invented. Mrs. Robbins was real good at sewing. She could make clothing for Cotton until he managed to adjust to the climate.

Halfway up the road I stopped the car and cut off the engine. Cotton and I walked up the road to the house. I wore gloves, so he could slip his little hand right into mine as we walked. My heart rolled over, and I sure did wish I could keep him with me.

But I couldn't. So I knelt in front of him. "Cotton," I said. "These people are real nice, and they'll take good care of you."

Cotton nodded, real solemn. He had already told me how Touch had spent the last year teaching him to speak English. I took his other hand and said, "You're a good boy. And a brave boy. I know you won't get a chance to have your naming, so if it's OK with you I'd like to go ahead with that now."

He nodded again, with a little trace of those dimples. "Your name is Conrad," I said. "Because it means brave. Real brave. That's you, honey."

I didn't dare risk hugging him. I just stood there in the driveway, where I'd stood a thousand times before, and watched Touch's son trudge on up toward the farmhouse, and a real nice upbringing, with people I knew would always be kind, and grateful to have him.

OF COURSE I HAD TO GET OUT OF CALDECOTT COUNTY AS FAST as possible. Once I'd done that, I went ahead with my plan and took some time to enjoy Memphis. Afterward I drove west, toward Colorado, with the windows rolled down and whatever country music station I could find on the radio drowning out my thoughts as best they could. This time I was traveling solo, but my hands were covered. With the money the screwdriver got me at an ATM, I'd bought a good supply of leather jeans and sweaters with built-in gloves. And I had Touch's coat. You never could take a chance that someone just passing by would reach out and touch you. Luckily the air had already grown nice and cool. I even let myself speed a little. On account of my new DNA and fingerprints, I was now safe from the law. Anna Marie was officially gone forever. Only Rogue remained.

SOME THINGS IN THIS WORLD YOU NEVER FORGET. LIKE EVERY single step I'd traveled with Touch. I had no problem finding my way past the Sand Dunes to the place where we'd stolen the original blue truck. Just as I suspected, nothing had changed. I don't suppose anyone had yet noticed it was even missing. I parked it over the same patch of dead grass, and left the keys on the floor underneath the seat. Then I began the long, slow walk to Hooper, where I caught a bus to Salt Lake City. There I bought myself a used Camaro with a busted up bench seat. I drove it on to Lake Powell, and rented a boat from the same Navajo, and puttered it on out to a spot where the water was still and black.

That's where I left the other thing Touch had given me that he didn't mean for me to keep. The golden ring. I sailed it on out into the sky, where it hovered a moment, glimmering under the sun with all its impossible properties.

And then it fell, just like anything would, and cut through the water. Only in my mind could I see it slowly falling down to the very bottom, where no tide could ever bring it back to shore.

THAT LAST TASK COMPLETED, I HAD TO FIGURE OUT WHAT TO DO with the rest of my life. What does a freak like me do after experiencing all that I had in the past weeks?

What would any girl do? I ran away, hoping to forget, and at the same time knowing I'd always remember. I drove east and north, headed to Maine, so I could finally see a lighthouse, and eat a lobster. I rented an apartment and got myself a job icing cakes in a bakery. At first they weren't real impressed with the sight of me, you could tell, but when they saw Wendy Lee's handiwork they couldn't very well say no. I knew I couldn't use the screwdriver very often, and I also knew its powers likely wouldn't last forever. Nothing ever did.

Every day I woke up, went to work, came home. Sometimes I bundled up and walked along the cold, gray beach. It sounds like a lonely life, I know. Maybe it even sounds desperate. And honestly I did feel desperate, every now and again. But that time I'd had with Touch — that time out of time — it sure did last me awhile. The kind of happiness brought by loving someone who loves you back, it doesn't just float away, no matter the circumstances.

Not only that. When the man you love knows how to travel across space and time, you never can be absolutely sure that he doesn't mean to come back one day. Especially when he's parked his child here. So I knew I had to watch myself — make sure my choices landed toward good rather than evil — so if Touch ever did decide to come back, I'd still be worthy of him.

But that wasn't the only thing that kept me hopeful. Though I'd never got the chance to meet Gordium, I knew from Touch that he existed. Here, on this planet, ten thousand years from now. And if he existed ten thousand years away, and I existed now . . .

There always stood the chance that before too long, I'd run into someone else like me. Maybe that was just hope springing eternal. Or maybe, just maybe, it was what the future would hold.

CHRISTINE WOODWARD is the pseudonym of Nina de Gramont, author of *Gossip of the Starlings* and *Of Cats and Men,* and the novel for teens *Every Little Thing in the World.* She lives in coastal North Carolina with her husband and daughter.